Rainie Knights

Melody Muckenfuss

Acknowledgements:

I owe thanks to Ron, for all the time and computer expertise he has expended on my behalf.

Also, thank you Gerry, both for your editing skills and your nagging texts that kept me moving until it was done.

Chapter One

"Bob, I understand what you're telling me, but it is a little difficult to believe that someone is breaking into your house at night just to eat your TV dinners."

"And they drive my car. Don't forget that part!"

"Right, and they drive your car. But they always return it by morning, and they carry their trash out with them."

"They must. I never find any empty boxes, but my favorite dinners keep disappearing from the freezer. I've tried to stay awake and catch him, but I keep falling asleep. It's all this damned medication I'm on."

I hid a sigh. This discussion had been going on all morning.

Bob Davis was 92 years old, still amazingly spry, but getting somewhat forgetful. Until recently there'd been no sign of true dementia, but his obsession with this story sounded like the product of a very confused mind.

I know quite a bit about confused minds. My name is Rainie, and I do home care for the elderly. Oh, I also write poetry and I work part time as a private detective's assistant, but right this minute all that mattered was my job with Bob.

"Like I said, we should call your son..."

"No! I told you I don't want to call him. He's already thinking I belong in a home somewhere, and if he hears this story he'll damn sure put me in one."

"Daryl only wants the best for you, Bob. He only suggested the nursing home because he thought you might like the company. Besides, it was really just assisted living..."

"Assisted living, bah! A place where a bunch of old people sit around with piss in their pants watching Animal Planet or playing Bingo for a roll of toilet paper! Do I look like I'd enjoy a place like that?"

"Maybe not, but I know a lady who went to Brentwood a few months ago and she loves it."

"Good for her. Maybe she collects toilet paper. Now please, Rainie, you're always saying you're here to help me. Well, I really need help now. Help me figure this out."

I worked with Bob three days a week, Monday, Wednesday and Friday from 8 a.m. until noon. I stood by while he took his showers so he wouldn't fall, and made him a hot breakfast. I also fixed him lunch and left a home cooked meal for him to heat up for dinner. On the days I wasn't there he ate cold cereal for breakfast, sandwiches for lunch (if he bothered at all, which I suspected he didn't) and heated up frozen dinners in the evening. He always ate better when he had company, and yet he preferred living alone. His wife had died twenty-five years before, and he had gotten quite used to his own routine. I tried to respect that, and worked within his schedule as much as possible. That was my job, after all: to help him stay comfortably in his own home, hopefully until the day he died.

I did his laundry and kept his house clean and drove him to appointments and the grocery store. He still ranted about that, too. His son had determined six months ago that he should no longer drive, so he'd been forced to take a driving test. Sure enough, he failed and lost his license. Now his Buick sat in the driveway unless I or one of his family members drove him somewhere.

"How do you want me to help?"

"I don't know, you're the big shot detective getting written up in the paper and all. You tell *me* how to figure it out."

Ha. Big shot detective. As I said, I was only a P.I.'s assistant, relegated to running background checks and interviews. Most of my work was done by phone or on the internet. There were a couple incidents in the early spring though, and one, when I took a bullet in the arm, did make the paper.

"How often did you say this is happening?"

"A couple times a week."

"But so far never the night before I come?"

"What's that supposed to mean?"

"It doesn't mean anything. I'm just gathering information."

"Oh, you're detecting," Bob nodded sagely, but I saw the spark of humor in his eyes. Bob was a retired physics professor, and I had no doubt his mind was still sharp enough to teach a group of college kids a thing or two. That was, providing someone could drive him to class and he remembered what he was there to do.

I grinned at him. "That's right. They call me Sherlock down at the office."

"Good. So you can just perform a series of brilliant deductions and tell me what the hell is going on around here."

"You know you're forgetful. Isn't it just possible that you ate the lasagna and the macaroni and cheese meals and simply don't remember?"

"Rainie, I'm lucky if I can eat either one of those meals all at one sitting, let alone both of them. I just don't have that kind of appetite. Never did."

Rainie nodded, knowing that was true. Bob was tall, just over six feet, and thin as a rail. He still wore some of the same clothes he wore when he taught 30 years ago, and they fit fine except for a little bagginess in the butt. Funny thing, they really didn't look much out of style, yet another advantage for men I guess. Women who wanted to keep up with the latest fashion had to shop constantly: long skirts, short skirts, then no skirts; wide legged pants and peg legged pants, high-waisted and then low risers...the styles literally changed with the weather, and then again, it seemed, at every new moon. I had given up long ago. I still wore broom skirts and t shirts like I had for a decade, or jeans if the weather was particularly crummy. I didn't care if I was fashionable or not. Life was too short to wear uncomfortable clothes.

"Okay, I can believe that. Could it be you forgot to buy them the last time we were at the store?"

"You were with me, don't you remember?"

I gave it a moment's hard thought. I did remember him buying several of those red boxed dinners, and I was pretty sure he'd bought lasagna and mac and cheese, his two favorites. But hey, that had been two weeks ago, when they'd been on sale. How could I remember for sure?

"I just can't remember."

"Then explain to me why my car was unlocked. I went out to get my hat because I forgot it Monday when we came back from the doctor. I *always* lock that car, just can't leave it sitting in the driveway unlocked."

He had told me this four times already this morning, but he'd either forgotten or just wanted to be sure I hadn't.

"We all forget sometimes..."

"But you were with me. Are you saying you forgot?"

"I might have." The Buick had electronic locks. One switch on the passenger or driver's side door locked them all. Quite often Bob and I both hit the lock switch at the same time, it was such a habit. It had become somewhat of a running joke between us, to see who would hit it first. I couldn't specifically remember Monday morning, but actually it would be rather odd if we'd both forgotten.

"You don't believe that either." Bob looked triumphant.

"Okay, I admit it is a little strange. So what do you want me to do?"

"How about you stay here one night, help me stay awake? I'll pay your regular hourly wage, even a bonus since it'll be overnight."

"Gee Bob, I don't know…"

"What? Your lizard can't live without you for one night?"

He was talking about my only roommate, George, a two foot long iguana who had pride of place in my living room. George wouldn't care if I was there or not, as long as he had fresh food and water at some point. I was long divorced and didn't really have any one else waiting at home for me. I had broken up with Brad just before the whole shooting incident, and although he still called now and then, maybe wanting to rekindle something, I was pretty sure that was a dead horse not worth flogging.

I had met a new guy who seemed promising. His name was Dan Hastings, and he sang and played lead guitar for a pretty popular blues band. He was on the tall side with broad shoulders, maybe an extra layer of fat over his muscles but still pretty sexy in a good ol' boy kind of way. I always thought he looked more like the lead for a country band, but he insisted blues was his passion.

The problem was his band was popular in Chicago, where he spent most of his time. He had a place just outside of Niles, but he hadn't been home in more than a month. I wasn't sure the relationship would ever get any traction.

There I went again, following that little inner voice on an irrelevant journey. I often wondered what I looked like when I went off on those interior jaunts. Did I just stare off into space like I'd forgotten my name, or did my eyes cross with the effort of trying to look inside to talk to myself?

I got back to Bob.

"Before we do that, I can think of a couple of other things we can do." I dug around in my purse and found my notebook and pen. "Grab the car keys and follow me."

Bob did as I asked, and we went out to the Buick. I took the keys and started the engine; the odometer was digital. "I'm going to write down the mileage. When I come back on Friday I'll check it, see if it's been moved."

"That's an excellent idea. I can't believe it didn't occur to me."

"Now let's go take an inventory of the freezer." I was sure to lock the Buick before we went back inside. "I'll write down everything in there. When you eat something, write it down. We'll compare notes on Friday."

"That won't prove whether or not I ate them. I might just forget to write it down."

"True, but if there's too many missing we can weigh you. If you're really eating mac and cheese at that rate you're bound to gain some weight."

"Very funny. Okay, we can try this. I know I'm not crazy."

"I'm sure you're not. Now," I opened the freezer. "Call out what's in there while I write it down."

Chapter Two

I ate a grilled cheese sandwich and a tossed salad with Bob before I left at noon and headed for my other job as a private investigator's assistant. I work for a company in Niles, Michigan called B&E. They provide a wide variety of security, including investigations, personal and business security guards, and even on occasion act as bounty hunters.

A friend of mine, Eddie, works for them, doing lots of dangerous stuff that he usually can't talk about. Eddie's friend Jack, who like Eddie was ex-Special Forces and a very fine physical specimen of a man, had casually suggested I get a job with B&E, doing background checks and running computer searches. It sounded simple enough, and steadier than being a caregiver, so I decided to give it a try.

That's how I came to get blown out a fourth story window, and later shot in the arm. Few things are ever as simple as we expect them to be, are they? But that's another story.

Since then a lot of physical therapy has brought my arm back to its original working condition, and actually left me a bit stronger. I have always struggled with my weight, wrestling it down to 140 pounds through sheer strength of will and keeping it there-most of the time-with a combination of exercise and strict adherence to one food rule: don't keep much food in the house, and you won't be tempted to eat it. I must admit I went a little nuts after being shot, and it seemed I was eating everything in sight. I ballooned back up to 150 pounds. I'm like an alcoholic who can never have just one drink: I must be ever vigilant about what I eat.

My fridge usually held fruit and the makings of a salad, and on good days a half gallon of fat free milk. My freezer usually had some boneless, skinless chicken breasts and maybe a loaf of whole grain bread. My cupboards had peanut butter (for a fatty indulgence now and then as well as the protein) and several varieties of cereal, mostly healthy, but always one sugary type.

If I wanted to indulge in junk food it required a special trip, and I could talk myself out of that on all but my worst days. I had already lost five of those pounds I gained, and I was determined to lose the other five.

As usual, I digress.

I went to the B&E offices, planning on a day of dull data base searches, but hoping for an interview or two. Those were usually somewhat interesting. When doing a thorough background search on someone it helped to speak in person to the references they provided. It was amazing the stuff people would reveal if they were handled just right. It seemed even the apparent pillars of the community had some hidden dirt in their basements.

I breezed past the receptionist with a wave and a smile and stopped by Belinda's office door to say good morning.

Belinda was a tall, sexy woman who emphasized her height with big hair and an assortment of high heels that I could never wear. I'd tried, and it was like walking on ice skates. Guess I don't have the ankle strength or something.

Today Belinda was wearing an emerald green pant suit with a low cut white blouse and big earrings. Her blonde hair (the color changed with the seasons) was piled high as usual and held in place with an emerald green scarf. She was gorgeous and sensual and self-confident, the kind of woman you would expect to find selling high fashion or in charge of a huge corporation. Instead she was Harry Baker's personal assistant.

"How's it going Rainie?"

"Same old. How about you?"

"Nothing new, but I'm not using the word old. You should be careful how you bandy that word around. After the age of thirty it's best if you never get anyone to think "age" around you."

"Is that the secret to youth?"

"One of many. You'll never hear me asking a guy to go to an antique show or even a used car lot. You're a poet, you should realize how words bring images to mind."

I laughed. "I just never thought of it that way. I guess I don't want some guy thinking I'm 'used.' "

"Or, God forbid, an antique!" Belinda grinned.

Before I could reply we were interrupted by a new arrival. Rachel was a new hire at B&E, a college graduate and newly licensed P.I. She didn't have any ambiguous feelings about the job; she was all gung ho and for the cause. She was also attractive, if you liked the type who spent an hour and a half in front of their mirror every morning getting their hair and makeup just perfect, and who always fit into their size 6 jeans even if they did have pizza and beer for lunch.

"Belinda, Harry says you have some forms for me to fill out, something about my military service records?"

Oh yeah, that's another thing about Rachel. She had done two tours of duty in the desert with the Marines and come out of it a decorated hero, Purple Heart and all.

"Yeah, right here." Belinda grabbed a thin sheaf of papers from her outbox and handed them to Rachel. "I hear you're already making a name for yourself here. You tracked down George Blankenship?"

Rachel grinned, managing to look pleased and a bit humble at the same time. "Hey, it was mostly luck. I didn't even know he was a big deal!"

"Wait. Blankenship. Wasn't that the guy who jumped bail on an armed robbery attempt and then killed three people on his way out of town?"

"That's the one!" Rachel grinned, then lowered her voice and glanced around to be sure there was no one else in the hall. "Just between us girls, though, I didn't realize who he was at the time. I just saw a guy pointing a gun at me and did what came natural: I took him down!"

"Natural for you, maybe!" Belinda laughed, and I couldn't help but join her. I wanted to hate Rachel, but I just couldn't. She looked like a preppy little cheerleader on steroids, and a person might expect her to be rather full of herself, but she wasn't. She was sweet and funny as well as a competent, trained killer. On the spot I invented a new adjective for her: bad-ass perky.

"I admit it was a good take-down," Rachel nodded. "Textbook, even. I wish they all went that well." She raised the papers in a little wave. "Well, I'd better get these done and hit the streets. See you ladies later!"

Belinda motioned me into her office and went around behind her desk. "I have a couple new files for you." She picked up a small pile of manila folders and held them out to me.

"Anything interesting?"

"Not particularly."

"Then again, Rainie hasn't gotten into them yet."

I knew that voice. It affected me on a visceral level, and filled me with a stew of mixed emotions: lust, fear, excitement, amusement, fear...yeah, I know I mentioned fear twice.

"What's that supposed to mean?" I glanced over my shoulder at Jack Jones, who was standing in my personal space, so close that if I could rotate my head like an owl I could have kissed him. That thought caused a rush of heat somewhere low in my belly, and I'm afraid I might have blushed.

16

"It just means that seemingly simple cases tend to get interesting around you."

"Around me? I think you have that backwards. It's only when I'm around you that I get blown up and shot at."

"Really? So that incident at the mall was my fault?" Jack looked amused. "As I recall that was wholly related to one of your elderly clients, and my only involvement was to swoop in for the rescue."

"Yeah, just like Batman," Belinda grinned. "Except I don't remember Batman ever running the bad guys over with the Batmobile."

"I didn't run him over, I just tapped him with my bumper."

"Tapped him twenty feet into the air!" Belinda laughed.

"I don't believe in doing anything halfway." From the corner of my eye I could see Jack's grin. It looked good: kind of mischievous and sexy at the same time. Like maybe he wouldn't take himself too serious in bed...okay, I didn't want to go there.

"So what's up, Rainie? Need help with anything?"

"Don't think so." I held up the folders. "I'm just going to go over these, follow the usual routine."

"Aren't you getting bored with that desk work crap?"

"Not really," I lied. Actually, I *was* getting a bit tired of computer searches, and even the interviews were feeling a little stale.

"Maybe you should work with me for a while. I have a thing going next week, and I could use a little feminine assistance."

"Uh oh, watch it Rainie." Belinda's smile had faded a little. Everyone who knew Jack knew that his "things" usually got out of control. He was a well-trained, fine tuned machine, but he thought everyone could do what he did just as well if they'd only go for it. At least, he seemed to think that I could.

"Hey, it's nothing that bad. It'll be fun."

Fun did not have the same meaning for Jack that it had for most people, but I had to admit, it was a lot more interesting working with him. The problem was working with him was also dangerous. Never mind that a couple of times I had called him in on a project. It didn't change the fact that he expected me to play commando, performing deeds that were way out of the scope of my natural skill set.

"I think I'll pass." I held up the folders again. "I'd better get on these."

"Okay." I could hear the disappointment in Jack's voice, and I couldn't help a little thrill of pleasure. Hard to believe the hot, sexy, out of my league P.I./bodyguard extraordinaire wanted so badly to spend time with me. I wanted to spend time with him, too, but only in my dreams, where he wasn't scary and I didn't have any cellulite on my thighs.

I waved goodbye and turned to go. I had to brush up against Jack to escape the doorway, and he didn't give way. I felt myself blushing again at the body contact.

"Let me know if you need me." Jack murmured the words as I moved past, his tone nearly turning my knees to water. I just nodded, not trusting myself to answer in anything more than moronic monosyllables, a tendency I had when I was around Jack.

I slipped into the computer room and nodded in greeting to two other people already engaged in data base searches. I chose the computer in the back corner, my preference when it was available. None of the assistants had assigned desks. We just checked in and took whatever was available. Even so, it seemed we all had our favorite spots. I think it's just human nature to want the familiar. It's probably why most of us prefer to have a home, and don't all live like nomads. Of course, even they return to the same oasis season after season.

I sighed and turned to the computer screen. I was definitely getting bored with my routine when I spent so much time thinking about minutia. I could get on a track and run for miles, starting with a simple thought like wanting ice cream and ending up thinking about nuclear war.

While the computer was booting up I took the time to look through the new files. The first one was a deadbeat dad that needed to be found so he could pay his child support. I especially hated those. Not only did I despise a man who wouldn't assist in raising his own children, but the first one I chased almost got me killed. Twice.

I put that one aside. The next two were routine background checks. Some companies and individuals were content with a standard computer background check when they were looking to hire someone, but others wanted something more in depth. That's where the interviews came in, checking references in person rather than relying on letters of recommendation or simple phone calls.

The fourth file was just a list of phone numbers. I was to do a reverse lookup on them and report back to Tim Goldthwaite, the P.I. in charge. A reverse lookup would find the name and address of the person that belonged to the phone number. I wondered whose phone bill Goldthwaite had gotten access to, but that wasn't my business. I was just the data collector, not a private investigator.

Not that Harry Baker, one of the owners of B&E (and the only one I'd ever met) hadn't been encouraging me to become one. He had offered to pay for classes if I wanted to get a degree so I could qualify for a license, but I wasn't sure that was the career path I wanted to follow.

I liked being a caregiver. I liked knowing that the elders I took care of were living better lives outside of nursing homes because of the service I provided. Being a full time P.I. might be interesting, but it was also dangerous, and quite often required hurting people, emotionally if not physically. Sadly enough I had discovered I was capable of doing that, but I didn't like it, and it wasn't the side of me I wanted to embrace.

I logged onto the site B&E contracted with for address searches and started on the reverse look up list. I got it started on the first one and reopened the file on the deadbeat dad.

His name was James Bolin, age 46, last known address in South Bend, Indiana. That might sound like a long distance from Niles, Michigan, but in reality it was only ten or fifteen miles. Niles was the first city over the Southwestern state line of Michigan, and South Bend was just south of the Northwestern border of Indiana. Niles was small enough that there weren't a lot of shopping and entertainment opportunities, not to mention jobs, so it was common for people from Niles and Buchanan- the tiny town I lived in- to run down to South Bend on a regular basis. In fact, the whole area was called "Michiana," as if we couldn't quite decide where we lived.

James Bolin had two kids, ages 13 and 15, and he'd been paying support on a regular, timely basis for 11 years since he and his wife, Cindy, had divorced. Then suddenly, about three months ago, he just stopped.

In fact, he stopped all contact with the kids; not a visit or phone call in three months. His ex-wife figured he'd skipped town. She wanted us to find him and bring him back.

Fine. I'd do my best to find him. The bringing back part, though, was the actual P.I.'s job. I didn't get paid to do the physical stuff.

The first reverse lookup was done and I made a note of the name and address and typed in the next one. Dull stuff. A six year old could do it, maybe even faster than I could. What the heck, it was a paycheck.

I moved on to the next file. The McDonalds in Buchanan- that and a Subway were our only fast food choices- was looking to hire a woman named Joyce Heely as the store manager. Hmm, interesting. The restaurant franchise was owned and managed by the Gleasons, but word was (and the gossip mill in a city of five thousand souls grinds swiftly) that they were having marital difficulties. This was quite a juicy tidbit, but being a rather private person myself I wasn't really into gossip. Besides, it seemed unethical to pass on information gathered in the course of my job.

I guess Buchanan would find out about the management change when, or if, the Gleason's hired a new manager. That is, unless in the course of my job I needed a bargaining chip to get information out of someone else; then this bit of news was fair game.

Joyce Heely's file included six letters of reference. My job was to interview all six of them in person. It was pretty easy to sing someone's praises on paper, but a little tougher to be sincere in person if you were only writing to fulfill an obligation. For instance, some people might write a reference for a client's nephew, even though they'd never actually met them, or for the boss's daughter, even if they had. In person a trained professional like myself can read nuances of expression and language and determine the facts. Sort of. Actually, although I am pretty good at reading people, it's more that I hope they'd screw up and I'll catch them in a lie. Whatever. It usually works.

I glanced at the computer screen, made a note of the next address waiting for me, and punched in the next phone number. I went back to the file.

"Wow, you are amazing at that computer stuff."

I looked up at Jack, feigning a casual attitude.

"Hey, I'm a woman of many talents."

"I know." His grin was suggestive, and I flushed. Why couldn't I be all cool and clever when he flirted with me?

21

Belinda and Thelma always had a quick comeback. I usually just got flustered.

"Don't you have someone to kill or a body to guard somewhere?"

"Not until later."

Funny thing about Jack, he never actually denied having to kill someone. Then again, he didn't admit to it either, but sometimes his grin had a tinge of meanness to it, an "I season my mashed potatoes with ground up pet hamsters" kind of mean like you'd see on the school bully's face. Still, I'd never seen him be unkind to anyone who didn't deserve it. Like meth dealers and wealthy, bald-faced liars. So maybe I was just misreading him.

Anyway, his smile was friendly enough now.

"I just wondered if you'd had second thoughts yet about my offer."

"It's only been twenty minutes."

"Twenty minutes of reverse phone lookups and I'd take up someone's offer to shoot me. I guess you have a higher boredom threshold."

"No, more like a lower pain threshold. I told you Jack, I'm done with adventure. Getting shot once was enough for me. That really hurt!"

Jack laughed. "Yeah, it does. You should try it in the chest once."

"You were shot in the chest?"

"Sure." Jack said it like "hasn't everyone?" He pulled up his tight t-shirt all the way to his neck. I assumed he wanted to show me his scar, but I couldn't seem to tear my eyes away from his washboard abs. Damn, he was finely tuned. I really wanted to play him.

"See?" Jack pointed at a puckered, roughly circular scar about the size of a quarter on the right side of his chest, about two inches from the nipple. I forced my eyes up the length of his torso and gave it the attention it deserved, my mouth dry.

"Wow," I croaked. "Must have been bad."

"Lung collapsed." Jack shrugged, as if that was to be expected. "Worse than a bullet wound is shrapnel." He turned slightly and showed me a long thick scar running across his side, about level with his navel. He kept turning, and I followed the scar's progress all the way to his back.

His back was just as gorgeous as his front, but it was criss-crossed with thin, barely perceptible lines that showed white against his tan.

"What are those?"

"Nothing." He abruptly pulled his shirt down and turned to face me, and for a moment his face shut down. His eyes got that faraway, hurt look I'd seen so many times in Eddie's eyes. I wondered if it was a Special Forces thing. What the hell did the armed forces do to their elite soldiers, anyway?

"I've got some routine stuff to take care of over the next few days, but my big project starts next weekend. If you get tired of this crap, give me a call."

"Sure Jack. I'll call if I feel like getting shot or run over or..."

"Exactly." Jack grinned. "You know you miss that adrenaline rush." He leaned in close and lowered his voice so it was little more than a breath in my ear. "Remember the elevator? Going to the movies with Dan Hastings can't possibly compare."

I felt my breath quicken. Boy, did I remember the elevator. I was revved on adrenaline after being blown out a fourth floor window onto a collapsing fire escape, and Jack and I had shared a hot kiss that still made me wake up in a sweat now and then. Even now I felt a tingle on the back of my neck that was rapidly traveling downward...

I pulled my head away from Jack so I could turn to look at him, hoping he'd mistake my newly flushed face for annoyance.

"I don't consider risking my life appropriate foreplay."

"Who's talking appropriate?" Jack laughed and backed away. "Anyway, call me."

He strode out of the room, as sleek and confident as a jungle cat. I sighed and turned back to my work.

Chapter Three

I spent two hours on the reverse lookup list, emailed my results to Goldthwaite, and managed to schedule two interviews for late afternoon on the first reference check. I also scheduled an interview with the ex-wife of the deadbeat dad for Thursday evening, after I left Thelma's.

Thelma was technically a client. She paid me to spend time with her every Tuesday and Thursday from 8 am to 4 pm.

At 75, she was a bit younger than my average client. But then, very little about Thelma *was* average.

She needed a caregiver less than I did. She dressed like a teenager half the time and like an aging debutante the other half. She was spry and smart and had the most amazing sense of humor. In fact, she'd hired me because she thought it was funny, being able to pay for companionship; at least, that was her spoken reason. As I'd gotten to know her she'd admitted more than once that she had been really lonely. She was a long time widow, and the friends she had left that hadn't "up and died on her" couldn't begin to keep up with her energy level.

Now she was my best friend. I hated taking money from her, but she was wealthy and had no family that she wanted to leave anything to. As she said, if she wasn't paying me I would have to find a paying gig for Tuesdays and Thursdays, and I wouldn't be able to hang out with her. It was a weird arrangement, but it worked.

So every Tuesday and Thursday we hung out together. Sometimes I even did little things for her, like maybe we'd clean out a closet together or rake the leaves, but mostly we just did what friends with lots of leisure time do: talked, went to lunch, went for walks. One time we did a little P.I. work together, but that had been neither planned nor sanctioned by B&E, and I had resolved to avoid a repeat of that behavior.

I didn't get home until 6:30. I said hello to George and opened the top of his cage so he could climb out on his shelf. He did so eagerly, but there was no look of reproach for my day long absence, and no puddles by the door. I loved having an iguana as a pet, and I thought more single people should consider it.

He was sitting there, looking regal, by the time I returned with a bowl of fresh fruits and veggies for him. He dove into the food without even a glance at me. Okay, so maybe it wasn't the same as having a little dog leap on me with joy at my homecoming, or a cat who would rub against my legs in gratitude at the sound of the can opener, but did I mention the lack of little yellow puddles at the door? And the lack of pet hair scattered on the furniture?

I ate a bowl of raisin bran for dinner while I watched Jeopardy. I always ate Kellog's Raisin Bran. As a rule I don't go for brand names. I mean, I don't want to pay for the advertising that bombards us daily from the TV, the radio, even people's clothing. But in this case it wasn't brand recognition that drove my purchase, it was the taste. Oh, almost any company can get the bran flakes right, but raisins are different. If treated properly they are more than just little dried grapes, they are little bursts of sweet joy nestled in their bed of bran, and the Kellog family knew how to treat them right.

My phone rang seconds after the final winner was announced. I answered, assuming it was my mother. She knew my habit of watching Jeopardy, one of the few times I turned on my TV other than for the morning news, and she never wanted to disturb me while I watched.

"Hi Rainbow, it's mom."

"Hey mom."

"I was wondering if you could come over for a few minutes."

"Sure, I guess. What's up?"

"Well, I'm not sure, but I think there's something terribly wrong with your sister."

"What?" I stood up, ready to run out the door. I didn't have a whole lot in common with my sister, and I didn't hang out with her much, but she *was* my sister.

"She's packing up her clothes. And her shoes!"

"What? Why?"

"She says they all have to go!"

I was stunned into silence for a moment.

I was relieved to hear that Brenda wasn't having seizures or turning some dark shade of purple that portended imminent death, but I could understand why my mother thought there was something wrong with her.

My sister was four years older than me, bright, educated and hard-working. However, she had some obsessive/compulsive tendencies (all right, I suppose it was a full-out disorder) that included collecting clothes and shoes. Lots of them. She had converted an entire bedroom in our mom's house into a closet, and it was crammed wall to wall and floor to ceiling with clothes and shoes, many unworn, tags still attached. It was this obsession that kept her from having enough money to move out with her frighteningly intelligent daughter, Sierra.

"Are you there, Rainbow?"

"Uh, yeah mom, sorry. I was just absorbing the news. Has she said why everything's got to go?"

"Not really. Her aura is an odd mix of blue and green and some ugly purple that doesn't bode well at all. She's going around like a crazy person, throwing stuff in boxes, muttering and crying. I can't figure out what's wrong with her and I can't calm her down."

I didn't necessarily believe that mom could see auras, or that people even had auras to see, but I knew that she had an uncanny ability to read people, and far be it from me to question my mom.

"I'll be right over."

I grabbed my keys and dashed out to my little Escort- an old, beat up vehicle that seemed to keep running no matter how many miles I piled on it. It was well over 200,000, and although the paint was faded to an odd non-color where it wasn't rusted through, and there were a few dents (not to mention a couple of bullet holes), it was great on gas and very dependable. I admit I had to remind myself of that fact now and then, especially when someone made fun of the tacky old thing. The trunk was kind of stinky thanks to a burst gallon of milk a couple summers back, and the carpet was worn through to the metal in spots. I was also aware of the many stains on the upholstery and the fact that the door handle was broken on the back passenger side and the window handle broken on the back driver's side. It's not like I had to ride back there, so what did that matter?

Besides, it was paid for.

It only took a few minutes to drive across town to my mother's house. Actually, it only took a few minutes to drive anywhere in Buchanan; it is, as I mentioned, a small town.

I went in without knocking and headed for the stairs, where I could hear some kind of ruckus going on.

"Brenda, honey, please, slow down and talk to me." My mother was standing in the doorway to Brenda's "closet," pleading with her.

"Can't slow down. Gotta get this done." Brenda's reply was muffled, and when I reached the doorway I saw why:

she was half buried under an armload of clothes. She draped them across a chair and grabbed another armful off a rack.

"I could help you if you'd only tell me why you're doing this."

"I made the mess, I've got to clean it up."

"What mess?" My mom had put her hands on her hips and was looking stern, an unusual state for her to be in. Mom was naturally mellow, and her "herb garden" helped her stay that way.

Brenda didn't answer the question. She was pacing around with a thick stack of formal dresses, searching for a place to put them. "Let's see, these to the dress drive, and maybe some of the shoes..."

"What dress drive?" I was hoping that I could get her to talk about the specifics of what she was doing, since she obviously wouldn't - or couldn't -talk about the big picture.

She stopped and looked at me. "Don't you watch the news, Rainie? Mizer's Cleaners is collecting dresses for prom night. They clean them and let the girls come and choose one for free. Did you know that a lot of girls can't go because they can't afford a dress? How sad is that? One of the biggest nights of a young girl's life, maybe second only to her wedding day, and she can't go because she can't afford a dress. And here I am with all these clothes, so many I can never wear them..." Suddenly her eyes filled with tears. "Oh, I'm so selfish. How could I be so self-centered?"

"You aren't selfish." *Well, no more than the next person*, I thought but didn't say. "Besides, I didn't go to the prom, and I don't feel like I missed out."

"That's because you're different." Tears were running down her face, splashing on the green dress she held on top of the stack. "You never seemed to feel the need to participate in school stuff. You were always content with your own thing, whatever that was. But it's important for most girls."

"Okay, I agree with that. So you're donating the dresses. That's good. What about the other stuff?" I indicated the other piles scattered here and there.

"Well, there are a lot of people going without, Rainie!" Her tone indicated that this was obvious. "There are people in Haiti stumbling through earthquake rubble with no shoes, and parents walking their kids to school with no coats. There are homeless people, who have nothing!"

"All true. So you want to give them your stuff?"

"Yes!" Brenda abruptly sat down on the floor, nearly hidden by the piles of clothes all around her. "I shouldn't have all this when so many have nothing. But it's too much." She started sobbing. "There's too much stuff, I don't know how I can do this."

"We'll help." My mother had her normal sweet smile again, and she went in and sat down next to Brenda. "If we all pitch in, it won't be so hard."

"Yeah?" Brenda looked at me. "You'll help, too?"

"Sure. I think this is a great thing." I couldn't just let it go. "But Brenda, I have to ask, why are you doing this?"

I shouldn't have asked, because it brought on another storm of tears.

"Be- because S-S-Sierra asked...if-if her f-friend's sister..." she gave up and sobbed for a few minutes on my mom's shoulder. My mom shot me a look, but I just shrugged. I was a curious kind of person; I could rarely help but wonder "why."

Finally the sobbing subsided, and Brenda wiped her sleeve across her face. She took a couple of deep, shuddering breaths and tried again to explain. "Sierra asked if her friend's sister could borrow one of my jackets for a job interview, and I said no. I was afraid she wouldn't give it back." Brenda made a sound that was part derision, part laugh, and waved a hand at a pile of suits she'd thrown in a corner. "I must have two dozen jackets, and I hardly even wear them. Some of them still have tags on them! When did I get so possessive of *things*?"

Hmm, at about the age of two, I thought, but again I held my tongue. After all, it wasn't her fault, and I had a quirk or two of my own.

"Oh honey, don't be so hard on yourself..."

"But mom, I have to be! What's the matter with me that I have all this stuff? How did I get to be so selfish?"

Okay, I needed to say something here. I might think my sister is a little strange - heck, my whole family is a little short of enough track to run their trains - but one thing she wasn't was selfish.

"Brenda, don't you always adopt a family and spend way too much on them at Christmas? Aren't you always first in line at the food drives or the first to call a telethon? And how about when Jason got arrested for DUI? Weren't you the one who put up his bail and hired a lawyer for him? And Sierra. Doesn't she go to the best school in the area and participate in every activity her imagination can dream up? How can you think you're selfish?"

"But... all these things..."

"You're obsessive compulsive. You buy things, and you like to organize and keep them. I think it's a security thing. You've always been afraid some disaster is right around the corner, and having all this stuff makes you feel like you have a safety net, something that's yours that no one can take away."

My mom was looking at me with something I didn't get nearly often enough: respect. Brenda was staring at me, wide-eyed.

"Wow. Did you take some psychology courses when we weren't looking? Because I have to say, that explanation...*feels* right."

I shrugged again, suddenly embarrassed. No, I'm not a psychologist, and a trained professional would probably tell me I was full of crap. But I am a caregiver, and part of doing that well includes paying attention to how people behave and what is important to them. I suppose it does give me a little insight.

"If that's true, and this is your safety net, are you sure you want to give it up?" Mom was watching Brenda closely when she asked, I suppose getting a read on her aura. Much of my ability to read people obviously came from her.

Brenda thought about that, gazing around at the piles of clothes, gently rubbing her fingers over the soft material of the dress in her hands.

"Yeah, I think I do. It doesn't seem right to have all this when others have nothing. Maybe I can collect something else." She smiled suddenly. "Like money. Now there's a safety net..."

I couldn't help but laugh. It was good to see her sense of humor return.

I told Thelma about Brenda's meltdown the next day.

"So what's Brenda going to do with all her stuff?"

"Donate it, I guess."

"Hm. I can see some stuff going to the dress drive, and some of the business clothes to the homeless shelter- they do good work down there, getting people back into productive lives. But some of the stuff...I don't know, maybe she'd be better off having a big rummage sale and donating the proceeds. She could give some to the food pantry. Won't do any good to dress people in fine clothes if they're starving to death."

"True." I laughed. Thelma was nothing if not plain spoken. "I don't think my sister is quite organized enough to hold a rummage sale, though."

"Do you think she'd let me help? I used to run a clothing store, remember. I know how to sell clothes!"

"You could talk to her about it. I never know with her, and especially now. I can't quite figure out what's happening to her."

"I wouldn't worry too much. We all go through life crises at different times. Doesn't have to be middle age or whatever. I'll give her a call. So what's going on in the P.I. life?"

"Not much. I have a few reference checks I'm working on."

"Huh. It hasn't been any fun since you quit working with that Jack Jones. Such a *fine* man!"

"Fine looking you mean!" I laughed again. "But I told you I'm done with that stuff. He was likely to get me killed."

"Probably knows better than to ask you anymore."

"Thelma, you're not very subtle. Yes, he's asked me, but no, I'm not going to do it."

"What does he want you to do?" Thelma perked up just at the thought of me working with Jack. She'd had a pretty full and adventurous life, and I think she missed it. The next best thing to crashing a backstage party at a rock concert or hitching a ride across country with hippies was living vicariously through me. Thelma sure hadn't spent all her time running that dress shop.

"I don't even know what he has in mind. I told him I wasn't interested."

"Oh come on, at least you could find out what he's up to! I'll bet it's something juicy! Drugs, or prostitution..."

"I'm content looking for deadbeat dads and doing reference checks."

"Not much to look back on in your old age."

"Is that what life is all about? Gathering a lot of exciting memories?"

"Hell yes! When you get old and feeble and your eyesight's too bad to read and your hearing's too bad for conversation, what do you expect to do all day? Think of it like this: you know you're about to be locked in isolation

33

for two years, but you can take a collection of DVDs to keep you amused. Don't you want them to be exciting ones?"

"I never thought of it that way."

"Of course not, you're too young. But when I get to that point, I don't want to be stuck remembering how many dresses I sold to fat old rich women or how clean I kept my house. No ma'am, I'm going to remember my adventures, and I'll be the one sitting in the corner with a big smile on my face. If you want to be smiling when it's *you* sitting in the corner, you call Jack and see what he has in mind."

"And if I get killed helping him?"

"Oh, I doubt that. Jack will watch out for you. And besides, you're not helpless. Do me a favor, at least ask him, okay? It'll give us something to talk about."

"Uh-huh. Okay, Thelma. I'll ask him next time I see him."

I left Thelma's at 4:00 and drove to Niles to meet with Missy Hicksenbaugh, James Bolin's ex.

She lived in a two-story duplex with well-kept grass and a profusion wild flowers growing near the front steps. There was a bike chained to the wrought iron post that supported the porch roof, and an old but serviceable looking Chevy in the driveway.

I grabbed my file and my notebook and went up the walk. I saw a curtain twitch, and guessed someone knew I was coming.

Sure enough, the door opened as I walked up the steps. A young girl wearing low-rise jeans and a high riding T shirt stared at me from under bangs that hung to her cheekbones.

"You the private investigator?" She sounded reluctantly curious, as though she wanted to be sullen and nonchalant but couldn't help herself.

"I'm Rainie Lovingston. I have an appointment with Mrs. Hicksenbaugh. You must be Courtney?"

She grimaced, as if the name hurt, and nodded.

"Come on in. Mom's in the kitchen."

She turned and headed back into the house and I followed, closing the door behind me.

The front door led directly into the living room, which was neat enough, the furniture worn but comfortable looking. My kind of place. We passed through a dining room with a scarred oak dining room table before we went through an open arch into the kitchen, another worn but comfortable looking space.

The appliances were dated but serviceable, the counters and linoleum no more than ten years old. The space was large enough to accommodate a kitchen table with four chairs. A pitcher of iced tea waited on the table along with a plate of what looked like homemade chocolate chip cookies.

"Ma, the detective is here. Doesn't look like much."

"Courtney, really!" Mrs. Hicksenbaugh turned from the stove with an embarrassed flush, but did a double take when she saw me. Was it the long brush skirt or the thin sandals that made them doubt my abilities? I mean, what was I supposed to be wearing, a tweed jacket with leather patches on the elbow?

"Actually, I'm not a detective. I'm a P.I.'s assistant, and I'm just here to gather information."

"So you're not going to find my dad?"

"Well, I'll try to find him, but a licensed detective will be the one bringing him in."

"Bringing him in?" Courtney's eyes narrowed and her tone went decidedly hostile. "What, you think he's some kind of criminal? You think you need to chase him down guns blazing like Dog the Bounty Hunter?"

"No, I..."

"Courtney, calm down." Mrs. Hicksenbaugh looked a little hostile herself, but she *was* paying B&E. I figured she wanted to at least talk to me. "Give me a few minutes to talk to Miss Lovingston, will you?"

"Why, so you can trash talk him?"

"Courtney Bolin, that's enough!" This was a mother's tone that I was familiar with. My mom seldom used it, but when she did it always made me want to drop my head and stand in respectful silence. It didn't work quite that well on Courtney, but she shut up and slunk away.

"Have a seat." Mrs. Hicksenbaugh indicated the table, and pulled a chair out for herself. "Iced tea?"

"Sure." I laid my notebook out and pulled out my pen, trying to regain some sort of professional upper hand.

"So from what I've read in the file your ex just abruptly stopped paying support and calling the kids, with no explanation. And that was about three months ago?"

"Three months, two weeks." Mrs. Hicksenbaugh smiled wearily. "Or so Courtney tells me. She has it marked on a calendar."

"She's close to her dad?"

"Sure, and why not? He's a great guy."

"Really? That's not the sort of thing I usually hear people say about their ex-husbands, Mrs. Hicksenbaugh."

"Call me Marie. I'm not really "Mrs." anyone any more. As for Jim..." She sighed and took a long drink from her iced tea. She picked up a cookie, motioning for me to do the same, and took a little nibble from it. I followed suit, pleased to discover my detective skills had served me well once again: they *were* chocolate chip, and also freshly baked.

"Here's the thing about Jim. He really is a good guy. Almost too good for his own good, you know?"

"Not really."

"He's always trying to help somebody out, and he wants everyone to like him. Unfortunately, I didn't get that back when. I just saw that he was flirting with everything in skirts, and I figured for sure he was cheating on me. So I divorced him. But that wasn't it at all. Jim just likes people. He's outgoing and friendly and...well, he especially likes

36

women. He can't stand to have a woman mad at him. Courtney has him wrapped around her little finger. Or at least, she did."

"Until he quit coming around." I frowned. "Could he have gotten wrapped around some other finger?"

"Another woman?" Marie shrugged. "Could be. It's not hard for Jim to fall in love, that's for sure. But he's done that before, and that doesn't keep him from paying support, or more importantly, seeing the kids."

"Maybe he's spending all his money on the new woman and he's too embarrassed to call and admit he doesn't have the support."

"Not likely. You know, Jim's dad died maybe two months after we were divorced, and he left him a lot of money." Marie grimaced. "Just my luck, huh? But anyway, the first thing Jim did was set up trust funds to pay for the kids' college educations. Decent colleges, too, not just some junior college. After that he bought himself a nice house and invested the rest of his money. That's the Jim I know."

I thought about that. He sure didn't sound like a typical dead beat dad.

"So what do you think is going on?"

"I don't know, but I'm a little worried. I even called the South Bend cops and asked them to check it out, but they think I'm just a bitter ex-wife." She grimaced. "Maybe I am, but my bitterness is best reserved for myself for being so quick to ditch him, right?"

I chose not to answer that.

"I see from this that you've called him regularly, but he won't return your calls."

"Kevin - that's my son - and Courtney even talked me into driving them by his house a couple of times. He won't answer the door. We left notes, but no replies."

"But you're sure he's been there? I mean, no newspapers left on the porch, signs of neglect..."

"His cell phone is "unavailable," which could mean it's been cut off or that he has it shut off. He hasn't had a land line for years. But there's lights on in the house, and no mail piled up. The lawn is mowed. He's there all right."

"Okay, well maybe he'll answer the door for me." I started to gather my things.

"What makes you think he'll answer for you if he won't answer for his own kids?" Marie sounded way beyond skeptical.

"Well…" I stood there, my folder tucked neatly in my arm, trying to look professional. "I'm not without skills."

"Skills? What kind of skills?"

"It's my job to get people to answer doors, even when they don't want to."

"True. That still doesn't explain your 'skills.' I mean, I'm paying a lot of money to B&E, and it's money I can't afford with the support not coming in from Jim. Are you sure you know what you're doing?"

"Trust me, Marie."

She looked me over again, slowly, and nodded uncertainly. "I sure *want* to trust you."

"Great!" I took that as an acknowledgement of my hidden skills. I mean, I could take it any way I wanted, right? I said good bye and scooted out of there, wanting to grab a cookie for the road, but staunchly denying the urge. My taste buds were disappointed, but my waistline was relieved.

Chapter Four

When I got back to Bob's on Friday the first thing we did was check the mileage on his car.

"I'll be damned. 63 miles more than there were Wednesday."

"You see?" Bob nearly crowed with vindication. "I told you something funny was going on!"

"Still...you're absolutely sure you haven't been going anywhere?"

"Rainie, do I seem that far gone to you? I might forget whether or not I had breakfast, but I'm sure I'd remember getting in the car and driving. Where the hell would I go, anyway?"

I sighed. Truth was, dementia was a cruel and often inexplicable thing. Some would forget their own children's names but remember every child in a class they'd taught 40 years before. Others would be clear on everything one day, but not remember how to toilet themselves the next. There were certain behaviors that might be called typical, but there was so much variation from person to person that it was dangerous to make assumptions about what they did and did not comprehend or remember.

Nonetheless, I was reluctant to believe Bob was losing it that badly. I know my judgment was influenced by how much I liked and respected him, but there it was.

"Bob, there could be more than one explanation for this. Maybe there's a problem with your meds, or you're just sleepwalking. My brother used to..."

"Hold on there," Bob interrupted me. "Both of those explanations point to the same thing, that I'm doing it. I'm telling you, I'm not."

"I believe you, but just in case…"

"You don't believe me." Bob waved a hand at me, angry and offended. "You're just like my son. You think I'm a doddering, foolish old man." He went off in a huff to his bedroom and slammed the door.

I hung around until noon. I dusted and mopped and vacuumed, periodically going to his bedroom door to knock and call his name. Every time he answered with "Go on, get the hell out of here."

Great. Now he hated me.

I fixed lunch for him and set it on the table. I stopped at his bedroom door to tell him it was there and that I was leaving.

"Good."

I sighed. "I'll see you Monday, Bob."

"Don't bother."

I knew I should put in some hours at B&E, but I was in a deep funk. I didn't blame Bob for being angry, but what was I supposed to do?

I felt grimy after all the housework, so I decided to go home and take a shower before I went back to work.

By the time I'd toweled off and dressed in a calf-length gauze skirt and a tank top I felt pretty decent.

I sat down on the front porch to smoke a cigarette and consider the problem of Bob.

I knew I had to call Daryl. The question was, should I tell Bob before or after I made the call? Either way, he was going to be pissed. He might even want me fired. Technically, Daryl had hired me. Bob had allowed my presence with great reluctance in the beginning, and it had taken weeks to gain his trust.

Now I was going to kick him while he was down. At least, that's likely how he would see it.

I sighed and exhaled smoke into the air. It was a gorgeous day, one of the near perfect ones we experience in Southern Michigan in the late summer and early fall: seventy degrees, a light breeze. The sky was that particular shade of deep blue that you only saw in September and October. It must have something to do with the angle of the sun. It was so blue it seemed you could dive into it, if only you could overcome gravity for a few moments.

I didn't want to do anything to spoil such a perfect day. Maybe I could call Daryl on Monday. Surely Bob was okay for the weekend?

But what if he wasn't?

With another sigh I reached for the cordless phone I'd brought out with me, knowing all along I had to make the call. I dialed Daryl's number from memory.

As I feared, he overreacted.

He wanted to rush Bob to the hospital for tests, but I finally convinced him to wait until Monday. He agreed, but said he would go and stay with his dad until then.

I bit back a protest. Bob would hate having his son breathe down his neck for two days, but really, it wasn't such a bad idea. Who knew when he would slip into another fugue and take the car out for another soon-forgotten joyride?

I only hoped Bob would find it in his heart to forgive me.

I put the phone back, locked up the house and went to log some hours for B&E.

Saturday morning I woke up at 6:30 and stumbled to the kitchen for coffee. I'm a morning person as a rule, but I don't like to be messed with before I've gotten that first blast of caffeine.

I was still in a funk over Bob, and not much in the mood to do anything. Even remembering that it was poker night

41

didn't cheer me much. That was hours away, and the day seemed to stretch interminably before me.

I drank two cups of coffee while watching the morning news, maybe hoping someone else's troubles would distract me from mine.

Not much going on in the Michiana area. They were mostly talking about a food drive at the TV station. People could drive up and donate a bag of non-perishable items or money to the Food Pantry, to stock up for the coming winter. They suggested that people just go to their cupboards and fill a sack with canned veggies or toilet paper or whatever and drop it off.

I thought about my own cupboards. I had an open jar of peanut butter and a can of tuna. I didn't think I'd be much help. I would tell my mom about it. She always had a lot of stuff on hand, just in case society collapsed into anarchy at a moment's notice. While I also thought such a scenario was quite possible, I didn't make any preparations. It isn't that I was a fatalist and figured that whatever happened, happened. I just knew mom was stocking enough for me, too.

I turned off the TV, making a mental note to mention the food drive to my mom, and rinsed out my coffee cup.

It was still early, so I cleaned my house and George's cage, did a load of laundry and considered grocery shopping. I still had cereal and a couple of bananas and the milk hadn't soured yet, so I had some raisin bran for a late breakfast and decided to go to my mom's instead.

I found her in the yard, as usual. Brutus, the big clumsy dog I'd rescued from a meth-head last spring, greeted me with his usual exuberance. His tail wagging made his whole body squirm like a worm reluctantly going on a hook, and I was awarded several doggy kisses when I bent over to pet him. He no longer leaped up and knocked me over, since my mother had had a talk with him, and explained that he was too big for that. Yes, among other things my mom seemed to be a dog whisperer. I sometimes thought she could talk a grizzly bear out of attacking if the creature would just stop and listen for a minute.

"Hey mom."

"Hi sweety." She frowned. "Are you okay? Your aura looks kind of blue today."

"I am a little down. I've got a little bit of a problem with Bob Davis."

"One you can't tell me about because of privacy issues." My mom shrugged. "I understand, but if you need some advice..."

"I know, mom. You'll be the first one I ask. So what's going on with you today?"

"Not much. I'm harvesting a bit." She pointed at a bushel basket full of ripe, red, organically grown tomatoes. My mouth watered at the sight.

"Go ahead, have one."

I did, biting into the sun-warmed flesh with a sigh of pleasure. Mom didn't use any chemicals or pesticides; she planted basil and dill near the tomatoes to keep the big green tomato worms at bay, and rotated her crops with beans to enrich the soil. I could safely eat the tomato without needing to scrub it first.

"Absolute nirvana, Mom." The luxury of munching free food reminded me of the food drive, and I mentioned it to her.

"I'll have Jedediah load some stuff into the van and we'll run it down. We're taking some produce over to RAM today anyway."

That's my mom for you. She would never be content just donating a grocery bag full of food. The pantry would get a few cases of stuff, and mom would just restock her own supplies. RAM (Red Bud Area Ministries) was a cooperative of all the churches in the area that mom was heavily involved with. Mom didn't believe in organized religion, or even in God, at least in any traditional sense. She did, however, believe in the human race, and the need to support a person in need both spiritually and materially. Apparently that was enough for the people of RAM, because they treated mom like one of them.

"Well, Thelma seems to be making a lot of headway with Brenda."

"Thelma?"

"Well yes, didn't you tell her to call?"

"Not really. She said she might call and offer to help her get organized."

Mom laughed. "Well, I'm not sure help is the right word. Thelma came in yesterday like a miniature dynamo and simply took over. She's up there now, ordering Brenda and Sierra around like Napoleon without the violent streak. "

"Huh. Maybe I'll go up and see what's going on."

"Okay, but be prepared to work. Thelma had your brother stepping and fetching until ten o'clock last night, and he only stopped by to pick up some tomatoes."

"I can handle it."

I went upstairs and entered a scene that at first blush looked like chaos. The hallway was filled with clothes, leaving only a narrow path to walk down. Closer inspection showed that it wasn't chaotic at all. Each pile was carefully sorted, one for dressy blouses, one for casual tops, those further divided into long sleeve and short. It was hard to believe all this stuff came from one room.

"Thelma? Brenda? Are you here?"

"Here Rainie! Did you come to help?" Thelma emerged from Brenda's closet-room, her face flushed, her hair in disarray.

"Not really. I just wanted to see what was up."

"We're opening a store!" Brenda appeared at Thelma's shoulder, her own face bright, her eyes shining with excitement.

"A store?" I looked at Thelma for an explanation.

"Yep, we're going to look at a space downtown. You know, where the lawyer used to be? I think it's perfect; we're going to do a resale shop."

"Some consignment, some straight purchase, but only the highest quality stuff!" Brenda interjected, almost breathless with excitement.

"But I thought you were going to have a rummage sale and donate the proceeds to charity?"

"We were, but this is better." Thelma took over the explanation. "Twenty percent of the profit will go to charity, and this will be an ongoing source of income for them."

"We plan to give a lot of it to the food pantry here and in Niles."

"And, of course, we'll allow the unemployed to come and choose an outfit for free to help with their job search."

I was swiveling my head back and forth as each one of them spoke, their enthusiasm nearly bubbling over. I gave myself a mental head slap. What did I think would happen if Thelma got involved? She was impulsive and always full-bore. Why settle for a molehill if you can create a mountain?

"Wow. All this because you didn't lend a jacket to someone?"

"I know, it seems kind of crazy, but you always thought I was, anyway." Brenda laughed, and I couldn't help but smile. I'd never seen her look so happy.

"Who's going to run it?"

"I'll be doing the days at first," Thelma said. "Except Tuesdays and Thursdays, of course; we'll have to hire someone for that. Brenda will work evenings until it gets going, but then she plans to quit her job and do it full time."

I shook my head. I couldn't believe how far they'd gone with their planning in such a short time. I didn't bother to ask where the money backing was coming from. I knew

Thelma had plenty, and she was probably thrilled to have a place to spend it.

"Well, I guess I'll leave you to it."

"Wait! Can't you stay and help? There's an awful lot to do."

"Gee, I'd like to," I lied, "but I have something I have to check out for a case." I felt a twinge of guilt. It seemed everyone was involved in charity work but me.

"Really?" Thelma was immediately focused on me, and I feared Brenda was about to lose a partner. "Some P.I. work? You need back up?"

"Not this time. I'm just going to talk to a guy. Nothing dangerous, just routine leg work."

"Oh." Thelma looked disappointed. "Well then, we'd better get back to this. I'll see you Tuesday."

I might have lied about wanting to help, but I really did have something to do. I wanted to drive by Jim Bolin's house. I figured Saturday afternoon was a good time to catch a person at home.

I decided I needed a little energy boost, so I drove to McDonald's for an iced tea. The drive thru line was all the way around the building. Being the only drive thru fast food place in town, they often did a brisk business. I couldn't see the point of waiting in that line, since there were only three cars in the parking lot.

I ran in and got my tea and was back out the door before the drive thru line had moved two cars. I glanced to the right to be sure there was no one coming before I stepped off the curb, and there was Jack.

He was only a foot away from me. How the hell did he get so close without me knowing it?

I let out a little squeak of surprise and he grinned.

"Hey Rainie."

"Hey," I shot him an annoyed look. "You could have said that from a few feet away."

"Sorry. I just think it's cute when you squeak like that. So what's up?"

"What's up? I think I should ask you that question. What are you doing at McDonalds?" With his sleek body, there's no way a Big Mac had ever passed his lips.

"I'm looking for you."

"And you just assumed I'd be hanging out here?"

"This isn't a really big town. Besides, I followed you from your mom's."

Okay, this was a little weird.

"Why?" And why hadn't I noticed?

"I need a favor."

"Is your phone broken?"

"I wanted to ask you in person."

"Uh oh. This isn't a favor I'm going to want to do, is it?"

"It's not that bad. I just need you to talk to someone."

"Talk? Like interview?"

"That might be a good idea. Maybe a survey. Or better yet, just ask for directions."

"Ask for directions to where?"

"It doesn't matter. You're not going there anyway."

I was losing the thread of this conversation. Or maybe Jack had finally lost it. Or I had.

"I'm not going where?" I asked as patiently as I could.

"Look, I just need you to get this guy's attention and keep it for a few minutes. Ask for directions to wherever you can think of, but don't let him be too quick about answering. You know, act confused, so it takes a while."

"And why am I supposed to distract this guy? And who is he, anyway?"

"He's a security guard, and I want to get past him."

"And you can't do that on your own?"

"I'd rather do it without physical contact. In fact, I'd rather he didn't know I was there at all."

47

"Okay." I was beginning to understand. "So will I be aiding and abetting a crime?"

Jack grinned. "Just a tiny one. Trespassing; it's no more than a little fine if you get caught."

"If I get caught? I'm not going to be doing any trespassing, am I?"

"Nope, just aiding and abetting."

"Still wouldn't look good on my resume."

"Come on, Rainie, what else you got going on?"

Good point. All I had planned was a cruise down to South Bend to talk to a guy who may not even be home. I had a good six hours before the guys would show up for poker, and I didn't want to just hang around the house waiting for them.

So maybe a little Jack time might be okay. This didn't sound dangerous, and at least it might be interesting.

"Okay, where to?"

"That's my girl!" Jack slung an arm around my shoulders and led me back to his truck. It was awkward walking that way. I didn't know where to put my arm. Should I put it around his waist? That seemed a little too familiar. I put my tea in that hand to keep it busy and let him figure out how to walk smoothly that way. Halfway across the parking lot he let me go, but I could feel the warmth of his arm on my shoulder lingering like a sunburn. I could never figure out if I wanted him to touch me or not. Bad boys, no matter how good looking, had never been my thing.

"Can't I just follow you in my car?"

"Sure, but why waste gas? We're going to South Bend."

"I need to go there, anyway. I'll follow you."

"Just ride with me, then I'll take you where you need to go."

I didn't know why he was so adamant, but I shrugged and got into the truck.

I loved his truck. It was a Ford Ranger, and everything my car was not. It was black and shiny with big tires and always clean inside, with a slight spicy odor that I couldn't quite identify, but that always made me a little hungry. The engine had a pleasing deep rumble to it. I didn't understand all the car talk, but he'd told me he'd had some special work done to soup up the motor. He must have had every amenity available installed, and even a few he made up for himself, because the dashboard was as complicated as the cockpit of a jet airplane. I thought there might even be a few more lights and knobs than there had been the last time I rode in it.

He started it up and I heard an old blues tune playing; John Lee Hooker, I thought. Usually he had it blasting; I guess he'd turned it down while he was in stealth mode, following me.

"So where exactly are we going?"

"Brisby Financial."

"Isn't that a collection company?"

"Collections and loans, some real estate."

"Aren't they going to be closed today?"

"Sure. Why else do you think I need the security guard distracted?"

I felt my eyes wanting to cross. So much for this being a simple thing. I thought about leaping out of the truck, but he was already on the road, and even at the 25 mile an hour town speed limit I was fairly certain it would hurt to jump from a moving vehicle.

"That isn't trespassing! That's breaking and entering!"

"I won't break anything. I will, however, enter."

"Damn it, Jack, don't go playing the semantics game with me! I don't want to get busted as an accomplice..."

"You won't." He was smiling calmly. "You won't even be on the property, just on the sidewalk outside. Piece of cake."

"Cake isn't particularly good for you, you know."

He grinned. "Come on, where's your sense of adventure? Here I go out of my way to give you something fun to do, and you're going all girly on me."

"I am a girl!"

"I've noticed."

I let that comment go.

"Besides, when someone talks about fun, I think of amusement parks or going to the beach, not getting arrested."

"I'll take you to the zoo when we're done."

"Yuk!" I shuddered. "I hate seeing all those poor animals confined in cages. It makes me want to chew my own arm off!"

"I forgot, you hate confined spaces. Okay, maybe Paris then."

"Yeah, you did promise to take me someday." Of course, I knew he'd been kidding.

"Can you take some time off? We could leave tomorrow."

I rolled my eyes. "Sorry. I have clients depending on me. Maybe in the spring."

"Okay. Paris is beautiful in April."

"I'll bet it is. Now, back to Brisby Financial. Shouldn't you be breaking in at night?"

"No, that's when everyone expects you to break in. During the day, with this beautiful sunshine, the guard will be thinking about cold beers and bar-b-q."

"But even if I distract the guard so you can get in, how am I going to keep him busy until you get out again?"

"I'll go in through the front door, out through the back. Can't go in the back; it's a fire security door, no handle on the outside. It'll open fine from inside, though."

"Won't there be an alarm?"

"Won't matter. I'll be gone before anyone responds, and I don't plan to leave any evidence behind. They'll probably think it's a false alarm."

"So let me get this straight. I distract the guy while you break in, then I just casually wander back to the truck and wait for you to come out?"

"Sort of. Actually, I want you to drop me off a block away and then drive up to him. It would look odd if you were on foot asking for complicated directions. Then all you have to do is drive off, circle around and park out of sight until I come out."

"Sounds simple." My voice was dripping with sarcasm, but either he missed it or chose to ignore it.

"It is."

I sighed and didn't say anymore, just listened to the blues playing. It was appropriate music for someone about to go to jail.

Chapter Five

South Bend is a relatively large city, with a pretty extensive downtown area. Some years before most of the roads had been converted to one-way to ease the flow of traffic. I suppose it worked okay, but it could be a pain to get where you were going. It involved a lot of overshooting your target by a block so you could get turned onto the correct road heading in the right direction. I didn't come downtown too often, so I was glad I wasn't responsible for getting us there.

"There's more traffic than I expected." Jack frowned at the flow of cars on the four lane road into town.

"I think it's the food drive." I pointed ahead at the brick building that housed Channel 16's studios. "It's kind of a big deal."

Sure enough, the right lane was backing up with people trying to pull into the station lot. They were winding around the parking lot to an open semi, where volunteers were taking their contributions. There were reporters with cameras stopping some at random to interview, causing a further back up.

"If those people were really charitable they'd donate without the TV cameras."

"You're so cynical, Jack. They aren't all getting on camera."

"But they might. I doubt if the line would be so long if this was taking place anonymously at the back door of the food pantry."

I hated to agree with his cynicism, but he might well be right. I shrugged. "Well, whatever gets them to donate."

Jack shrugged, bored with the subject.

Brisby Financial was three blocks south on the same street, but because of the one way traffic there weren't any people driving by to the TV station, so the traffic was lighter.

Brisby occupied a two-story brick building with a recessed entryway and plenty of windows, all with decorative but solid looking wrought iron bars covering them. There was a beautifully landscaped lawn surrounding the building.

"How will I distract this guard? Won't he be inside?"

"There's been a lot of vandalism in the neighborhood for the last year or so; mostly kids tagging buildings with graffiti. The guard comes out and takes a turn around the outside at quarter past the hour, every hour."

"How do you know?"

"I used a tried and true secret weapon of the private eye: I watched him. Some call it surveillance."

"Very funny. Okay, so at quarter after I drive up and ask for directions..."

"You should get out of the truck."

"Get out? Why?"

"Harder for him to ignore you if you're face to face with him."

"Also easier for him to get a choke hold on me until the cops get here."

"That's not going to happen. If it does, you know what to do."

Sure, he'd taught me what to do. Aim for vulnerable areas: the knees, the eyes, the balls. I'd never really practiced that last part much; being in close contact with

Jack while he showed me self-defense moves was hard enough without getting close to his more private areas.

"You know, I'm not all that sure about my self-defense skills."

"Maybe we should practice some more." His grin made me blush.

"I think Eddie is planning to work with me."

"Oh." Jack looked disappointed. "Well, he can teach you well enough. Probably won't be nearly as fun though."

"It isn't supposed to be fun."

"Sweetheart, everything you do in this life should be fun. The years are limited."

"Yeah? So Special Forces was fun?"

His face closed down, and I was immediately sorry I'd said that. There were some things you shouldn't joke about.

He didn't say anything, just pulled to the curb around the corner from Brisby Financial.

"Okay, I'm getting out here." He looked at his watch. "The guard should be coming around in 8 minutes. Pull up to the corner so you can see him come out and then drive up to him."

"What should I ask directions to?"

"I don't know...how about the Seventh Day Adventist Church?"

"Where's that?"

"There's two of them near downtown, one on Chapin and one on LaSalle. Whichever one he gives you directions to, tell him it's the other one you're looking for."

"What if he doesn't know either one?"

Jack sighed. He pulled a clipboard from behind the seat and shuffled through a few papers on it. He pulled out a map of South Bend streets and put it on top.

"Show him the map. No guy can resist interpreting a map for a woman; they all think you're illiterate when it comes to reading one."

"All of them?"

Jack grinned again, and I was glad he'd forgiven me for trespassing on his past. "There are always exceptions, but I think it's a safe bet."

He slipped away between buildings, and I slid behind the wheel of his truck. I have to admit I sat for a moment in something like awe; I don't know if it was all the flashy gear, the fact that the vehicle was so clean, or just the leftover warmth from Jack's butt on the seat, but I felt a little shiver of pleasure low in my spine.

I ran my hands gently around the steering wheel; it was smooth and polished and warm. I put my hands at 10 and 2 and gently gripped it. I was going to like driving this truck.

I started it up, feeling the low rumble of the engine under me, and resisted the urge to rev it up. Instead I rolled slowly up to the corner until I had a view of Brisby Financial. I put the truck in park and let it idle while I watched for the security guard.

I tried to rehearse in my head. I would just drive up, jump out of the truck with the clipboard in my hand and ask for directions to the church. Simple.

I thought about it, chewing my lip. How much time did it take to give directions? Two minutes? How much time would Jack need? And would the security guard even acknowledge me, or just wave me off, intent on his own business?

I decided I needed something besides a map to get his attention, and I could only think of one good item. Or maybe it was two.

I pulled my tank top down as low as it would go. It stretched over my boobs and clung, showing plenty of cleavage. That was one advantage to not being stick thin; I had some chest to work with. Now don't get me wrong, I don't have Pamela Anderson's chest, but I do okay.

Besides, when it comes to men boobs are boobs. Unless they're wrinkled like last year's weathered apples or covered in an oozing rash, a man will look at any available pair, especially if they're thrust into his face.

I saw the security guard come out the front door and turn to lock it behind him. I put the truck in motion. I felt myself revving up at the same time I hit the gas; I was nervous, and I might have hit the pedal a bit too hard. The tires squealed when I made the turn, and the security guard looked in my direction.

Well, that was okay; I wanted his attention, right? But then I hit the curb, still going a little too fast, and his eyes widened when I slammed on the brakes, two tires on the sidewalk. Really feeling the adrenalin now, I shoved the lever into Park and leapt out with the clipboard in my hand. I nearly tripped over the hem of my skirt getting out, recovered and rushed across the sidewalk, calling out "Excuse me, can you help me?"

The security guard, a solid looking guy in his thirties with little hair, had stopped a few feet from the door, staring at me. I forced myself to stop, holding out the clipboard, so he would have to come to me; even in stealth mode I didn't think Jack could get past him when he was that close to the door.

"I need directions. To the Seventh Day Adventist Church."

The guard just stared at me, his mouth slightly open, not moving toward me. His hand had drifted to the butt of his gun.

It suddenly occurred to me how I must appear to him: a demented woman, or maybe a drunk, leaping out of a recklessly driven truck waving stuff at him and demanding directions to a church.

He probably thought I was either a religious nut on a crusade or a terrorist on my way with a car bomb.

I took a deep breath, trying to calm myself, and smiled. At least I hope I smiled; it might have looked more like I was baring my teeth at him. My breath was coming too hard, and I had a death grip on the clipboard, trying to control the shaking in my hands.

"Please, I'm late for a meeting." I tried to sound girly and lost, but I wasn't sure exactly what that sounded like. I must have gotten close, because I could see him relax, at least a little bit.

I held up the clipboard so he could see the map. "I know it has to be somewhere close, but I've been driving up and down, and all these streets are so confusing, they're all one-way, and I can't seem to get anywhere!" I widened my eyes, attempting an innocent and confused look; the shaking in my voice came naturally. The effect must have been reassuring. He dropped his hand from his gun and started towards me.

"What church you looking for?"

"The Seventh Day Adventist. I found St. John's and Immanuel Baptist and even a Kingdom Hall of Jehovah's Witnesses, but I can't find the one I want!"

He reached out for my clipboard, but I held on with one hand, forcing him to get close to me. At the same time I used my other hand to surreptitiously tug my tank top down a little farther. I leaned in close, letting one breast brush against his arm.

I felt a slight pressure returned, and his eyes flickered over to my chest.

Ha. My booby trap was working!

See, I have this theory. Women's brains are complex, constantly multi-tasking and examining every situation on a dozen different levels, many inaccessible to men. We need that ability, because since the beginning of human history we've been responsible not only for ourselves, but multiple children.

A man's brain, on the other hand, tends to see things in a more straight-forward - all right, let's just say it - more *simple* way. Most men approach things with single-minded purpose, whether it's designing a new lunar shuttle or taking out the trash. This was probably a handy skill to have back when men were hunting game with little more than sticks and rocks. This is also what makes it so easy to distract them, especially with sex. Get their thoughts concentrated on the little man between their legs and they become so self-absorbed that it would take a tanker truck exploding into a ball of fire twenty feet away to get their attention.

From the corner of my eye I saw Jack slip up to the door. I exerted just a tiny bit more pressure on the guard's arm and heard him take in a sharp breath. He blinked at the map, as if he couldn't quite focus on it.

"I thought it was on this street, but maybe I'm misreading it."

"You're close." He swallowed and put a finger on the map just a couple of blocks from where we were standing. "It's right here on Chapin, two blocks over, but you have to circle around on Main Street going south and go one block past. Then you turn right on Washington, go one block up to Chapin and turn right again. I think the church is right in the middle of the block."

He finally looked into my eyes and smiled. It was a rather nice smile, and I felt a little bad deceiving him. Not too bad though. I assumed an expression of dismay.

"Oh my, Chapin Street? That isn't the address I have. It says LaSalle. Maybe they told me the wrong place altogether!" I wished I could have produced a couple of tears, but that was beyond my scope. I had to settle for pouting out my lower lip a little and trying to look like I was *about* to cry.

"No no, that's okay." He started to look away, and I realized my mistake; guys hate it when women cry, especially strange ones. Most of them tend to want to make it all better, being big hero men who always keep their women safe, but at the same time few of them knew exactly how to comfort a tearful female.

I pressed against his arm again, pulling in my pouty lip. "It is? Do you know where I need to go?"

His eyes were back on my cleavage. He was visibly relieved that he had some specific task that would keep me from blubbering all over him.

"Well sure, I can show you." It seemed to take some effort on his part to drag his eyes back to the map. He made no move to shift away from the pressure I was putting on his bicep.

"There's another Seventh Day Adventist on LaSalle. I don't know why they have two; I guess for the same reason we have about a dozen Baptist churches in town, but I don't know why that is, either."

"Slight differences in interpretations of the Bible," I informed him. "A lot of churches base their whole religious philosophy on the strict adherence to just a few Bible passages. They just don't always agree on which ones deserve the most emphasis."

He met my eyes again, and I realized that I was breaking character. I was supposed to be little-ditzy-girl-lost, not an anthropologist or student of Western religion.

I blinked and smiled. "At least, that's what Reverend Bob told me."

"Huh." He looked at me a bit suspiciously. I wanted to look over and see if Jack was still working on the door, but I didn't dare. I met the guard's eyes with what I hoped was an innocent expression.

"Well." He finally looked back at the map. "So the place you want is about three miles from here. You really must have gotten turned around." He pointed at a spot at the top of the map and started explaining how to get there. I pretended to listen, surreptitiously glancing over his shoulder at the door. No sign of Jack; he must be inside.

Now I just wanted the guard to hurry up so I could get away from him and back to the truck. I shifted away from him, and his eyes flicked toward my chest again, this time with a faint hint of regret.

"Okay, I think I've got it!" I gave him my best relieved smile and stepped back a pace. "Thank you *soo* much!"

"Anytime."

He watched me walk back to the truck. I threw the clipboard in and scrambled into the seat. He was still watching me, and I wondered if he was still suspicious. I started the engine and put it into Drive. I took off with a lurch and dropped off the sidewalk. At the last minute I gave him a little wiggly-fingers wave.

I took off, too fast again, and took the first right. It was only then that I remembered his directions told me to go straight for half a mile. Oh well; maybe he would think I was just a hopeless directionally challenged mess.

I went down a couple of blocks and circled back to where I'd started to wait for Jack.

I sat with the engine running, still a little shaky, willing him to hurry.

It seemed like hours passed, but in reality it was probably no more than 10 minutes. I desperately wanted a smoke, but I was sure Jack wouldn't like the stench in his pristine vehicle, and I didn't want to be outside the truck. I had a feeling when he came back seconds were going to count. For all his assurance that he didn't expect anyone to know he'd been there, I preferred to expect the worst.

Time passed, and my active imagination was beginning to construct all manner of worst case scenarios: Jack being held at gunpoint by the guard. Jack at the bottom of a stairwell, bleeding and unconscious after being pushed down the steps. Jack being beamed up to an alien spaceship...okay, I was getting desperate. What the hell was keeping him?

I heard the familiar tones of my phone announcing I had a text message. I flipped it open; it was from Jack: "come to front door now."

Front door? I thought he was going to slip out the back?

My hands began to shake again, but this was no time for hesitation. Never mind that all my survival instincts were screaming at me to take off in a straight line for Michigan and home; Jack had come in response to my text a few months before and had literally saved my life. I could no more run away than I could leap to the moon.

I put the truck into gear and took off fast again, ripping around the corner on two wheels.

The guard was nowhere in sight, and I realized he would have finished his outside tour some time ago. There was also no sign of Jack, so what was I supposed to do? Pull up to the curb and honk?

That question was answered almost before I could think it; Jack came bursting out the front door at top speed, heading for the road. The guard was right behind him, gun drawn, but at the moment he had it pointed into the air, not at Jack's back.

I acted without realizing a decision had been made and turned sharply, up on the curb and over the lawn, straight at the guard, who stopped abruptly and stared at me in open-mouthed horror. I had an instant flashback of Jack hitting Bob Peck, his body folding over the hood of the truck before flying into the air. Uh uh, no way could I do *that*.

I turned the wheel sharply again, this time aiming between the two men. The guard recovered from his shock; just my luck, the man was competent. He leveled the gun at me. Jack changed direction and headed for the driver's side of the truck just as I hit the brakes, digging the tires deep into the grass.

A bullet punched through the windshield, making a neat hole and star-shaped pattern before lodging in the seat inches from my right shoulder. I swung the wheel hard to the left. Jack raced past the driver's side door and in one smooth leap vaulted over the wall of the truck bed and landed in a crouch, already shouting "Go! Go! Go!"

I didn't need to be told three times. I really didn't need to be told once. I had switched my foot back to the gas as soon as the bullet made its entrance.

I tromped on it hard, fishtailing wildly, the back end almost clipping the guard. He leapt out of the way, for the moment unable to take aim. I bounced off the curb and hit the street, already moving at thirty miles per hour, picking up speed as fast as the supercharged engine could turn the drive shaft.

I forgot about Jack, forgot about cops, forgot about everything but the road in front of me and moving forward. It was a good thing it was Saturday afternoon and not a weekday. There was very little traffic, and the few drivers I passed just gave me a startled look and kept going at their own pace.

Finally my panic was pierced by Jack's shout.

"Wrong way, Rainie! You're going the wrong way!"

Sure enough, I had gotten turned around and was traveling at top speed north on the southbound street. No wonder the passing drivers were giving me startled looks.

I wanted to slow down and turn around but it seemed my foot was glued to the gas pedal, my knee locked in the floored position.

"Rainie, damn it! SLOW DOWN!"

Jack's voice roared practically in my ear. He was leaning over the side of the truck bed and was clinging to the open window, and I suspected if I didn't do what he said he would simply climb into my lap and take over.

I've seen that maneuver in movies, but I suspected that in reality having someone climb into your lap while you were hurtling 60 miles an hour down a city street would likely cause you to lose control and ram a building or flip over or something. In any case, it wouldn't be good.

I gripped the steering wheel tighter and concentrated on my right foot. I pulled it off the gas pedal, using the same effort I would have needed to lift it if there were a thirty pound block tied to my ankle.

I had barely begun to slow when I saw a Chevy van in my lane, heading straight for me. The driver's face was frozen in an expression of horror, and behind her I saw what looked like a whole T-ball team strapped into the seats. She jerked her wheel to the left and I did the same. She sailed into the next lane but in my panic I had turned too far; I bumped up over the curb and found myself in the TV station parking lot, heading at a good forty miles an hour straight at the line of cars leading to the semi truck.

There was no time to think; I just reacted. I pulled left again, not slowing down, and raced over the grassy lawn surrounding the studios. I flew past the line of cars waiting to drop off their donations, vaguely aware of a few screams and honks and a lot of finger pointing. I bumped over the curb on the other side onto Michigan Street and turned left again.

"Pull over! Pull over now!"

I knew why Jack was still yelling at me. I had turned the wrong way; Michigan Street was northbound, and I was now heading south. Did I mention I hated one way streets?

This time I reacted a little better. I managed to slow down and take the first available turn without rolling the truck.

"Pull over or I'm coming up there!" Jack demanded.

I gasped, realizing I'd been holding my breath. Pull over? At first it didn't seem like I could make sense of that, but it slowly penetrated my fear-fogged brain. Pull over. Right. Good idea. Let Jack drive. I really wasn't in any condition to be behind the wheel.

I hit the brake harder than I should have and Jack lurched forward. If he hadn't had such a good grip on the window frame he would have been road kill. I jerked the wheel to the right and slammed the front wheels against the curb, jerked the lever into Park and stumbled out of the truck, sure I was about to throw up.

"Come on, let's get out of here."

Jack had already leaped over the side of the truck as smoothly as a gymnast dismounting a vaulting horse. He slid into the driver's seat, only then seeming to notice that I was bent over in the middle of the street, holding my stomach.

"Rainie, it's okay. Get in the truck."

Once again I heard him and wanted to comply, but I couldn't seem to take my eyes off the white line at my feet.

"Don't quit on me now, babe!" Jack jumped back out of the truck and grabbed me around the shoulders, leading me double time. I went with him, my feet moving without my orders, and he boosted me into the seat and pushed me over, climbing in after me. Seconds later he had the truck moving again, this time at a more sedate speed. He took several turns, one right after another, and before I knew it we were out of downtown and into a shabby but quiet neighborhood.

"Thanks Rainie. You were great!"

"Gr...gr..." I couldn't get the word out. My teeth were chattering, and I was staring at him like he'd grown a second head. No, wait, that was just a little double vision, probably caused by brain damage from the flood of fear and adrenalin.

"Didn't I tell you this would be good fun?" Jack was grinning like a maniac.

"F-fun?" I pointed at the hole in the windshield. "He sh-sh-shot at me! Inches...inches..."

"Yeah, I didn't expect that. Most of those guys won't shoot; they don't like the hassle of paperwork, and the legalities can tie them up, out of work, for weeks."

I guess I was responding to Jacks' matter of fact tone, because I was calming down a little, and the power of speech was returning.

"I thought you w-were coming out the back."

"The damned door was chained." Now Jack looked pissed. "I ought to turn them into the fire marshal. That's a definite violation of code."

"Violation of code? You were breaking and entering."

"Yeah yeah, I know. They still shouldn't bar the fire exit."

"Maybe they didn't want anyone sneaking out the back!"

Jack grinned. "That's my girl! See, your sense of humor is already coming back."

He turned down an alley and slowed behind a big three car garage. I noticed the neighborhood had gone a step past shabby and right into run-down. The backs of most of the houses I could see were in need of paint or new siding, the lawns mostly brown patches of grass and well-trampled dirt. Many of the garage doors were broken or missing altogether, and I saw several cars that looked like they'd been abandoned sometime in the seventies.

"Where are we going?"

"Guy I know runs a body shop out of his garage. Need to get that windshield replaced before the cops see us. There are plenty of black Ford Rangers around, but plenty of people probably saw the shattered windshield, and for all I know they got it on tape."

Oh yeah. The TV cameras. I felt a new wave of nausea wash over me; I was going to jail.

He parked at one of the big doors and jumped out. I stayed where I was, trying hard not to shake. What the hell, I was just going to come down and do an interview. Why did I always let Jack talk me into this crap?

"I'm going to jail. I can't be locked up. I'll die. I'm claustrophobic. I can't even watch people get locked up on TV! If the clanging door doesn't cause my heart to stop I'll have to kill myself. I can't..."

"Rainie, calm down." He came over and opened my door. "No one's going to jail." He gripped my shoulders and gave me a light shake. "You were moving too fast. I doubt if anyone got much of a description."

"The cameras..."

"Maybe they didn't react that fast. They were there for a fluff piece, not expecting any action. But I need to go talk to this guy, get things fixed in a hurry. Are you okay?"

I nodded, although I was a long way from okay. Satisfied I wasn't going to pass out or puke in his truck, Jack walked around the garage.

A few minutes later the garage door rolled up and Jack jumped back into the truck. He pulled into the garage and got out. "Come on, Rainie. I want you to meet Smitty."

Smitty was an immense black man. He was wearing a sports jersey that with a couple of poles to support it could house a family of four. There was definitely some fat lurking under there, but the bulk of him seemed to be muscle. Think tall African-American Sumo wrestler.

He grinned at me, showing bright square white teeth with one gold incisor, and held out a huge paw. I held mine out, tentatively, wondering if he'd give me a simple hand slap or one of those complicated grips that people "in the 'hood" seemed to pull off with such panache. Instead he gave me a traditional handshake, his hand warm and calloused and, thankfully, gentle.

"Hey there little girl. Pleased to meet you."

I tried to smile, but I was still shaking and afraid I might throw up on his shoes. Still, I liked that 'little girl' stuff. It wasn't very often I felt little, but this guy could cast a shadow over half a county, and I did feel pretty small standing next to him.

"Have a seat, I'll get right on this." He indicated a couple of plastic lawn chairs by the wall. There was a big cooler between them. "There's soda and beer. Help yourself."

I waited while Jack and Smitty went to work on the truck. They made short work of pulling the broken windshield out, then came and stood by me, drinking beers while they waited for someone to deliver a new one.

"What are you smiling about?"

Until Jack asked the question I didn't realize I had been, but sure enough, I was smiling and feeling pretty happy. Or maybe giddy was a better word.

"I was just thinking about driving through that lot. I mean, what a getaway route, right past the TV cameras."

"Pretty smooth," Jack laughed. "But since when do you think that's funny?"

"I don't know." I started to laugh. "But did you see that reporter? His mouth was wide open, his eyes all buggy," I demonstrated, and Jack and Smitty both laughed, and that got me laughing harder.

"I mean... he was like...like a cartoon..." I was gasping for breath now, holding my sides, my ribs aching from laughing so hard. Tears were running down my cheeks, and I was practically sliding to the garage floor.

"Hey Rainie...whoa, settle down..." Jack was still smiling, but he was holding my shoulder, looking a little concerned.

"She hysterical?" Smitty asked, looking simply curious, and that made me laugh even harder, if that was possible. Now I did slide to the floor. My sides were aching so bad it hurt, I was gasping for air, but I still couldn't stop laughing.

"I think so," Jack nodded clinically and knelt next to me.

"Take a breath Rainie."

"Hey little girl...you gonna make yourself sick. Best quit laughing now."

But I couldn't. I kept seeing that reporter's terrified face, but instead of feeling sympathetic, it just made me laugh more. What the hell was wrong with me? I wasn't the type to laugh at other people's discomfort. I didn't think those TV programs that showed "funny" videos of people falling and getting hit in the groin were amusing at all. I just wasn't wired that way. But here I was, laughing to bust a gut- and for the first time, I thought that expression might be literally true!

"Rainie, you need to stop. You're hysterical."

I already knew that, but I still couldn't stop. Jack was holding me by the shoulders, trying to get me to calm down. But I couldn't.

"Here, let me." Smitty shouldered Jack aside and grabbed me with his shovel-sized hands. I sucked in a hard breath, suddenly terrified.

He lifted me off the floor as if I were a toddler and tossed me over his shoulder in a fireman's carry, my head hanging down his broad back.

"Eep!" I gave one of those squeaks that Jack seemed to think was so cute and grabbed a handful of Smitty's shirt, wondering if he was just going to let me slide down onto my head. Fortunately he had a strong grip on my legs. Even more fortunate, the flash of fear had made me stop laughing.

Smitty put me down, and I stood there, still hiccupping a bit, wiping my eyes.

"What the hell was that all about?" I asked no one in particular, but Jack answered anyway.

"Good old fashioned hysterics. You need to find a better way to deal with the adrenaline let down."

"You got any ideas?"

"A few." Jack gave me his best suggestive grin, but then just handed me a beer. "Try this."

"Huh," Smitty shook his head and smiled cheerfully. "If it was me, I'd recommend sex, then the beer, but hey, you white folks do have your ways."

That almost set me off again, but instead I took a long swallow of the beer. I followed that with another, feeling myself calm with every swallow.

"Can I smoke in here?"

"Sure." Smitty pulled a fat home-rolled smoke out of his pocket and held it out to me.

"Um...actually, I've got these." I held up my pack of tobacco filled cigarettes and he shrugged.

"That shit'll kill you, but we all got our monkeys, right?"

I lit up, gratefully dragging the nicotine saturated smoke into my lungs. The three of us stood and chatted like old friends, which Jack and Smitty obviously were, and fifteen minutes later we heard a honk in the alley. Smitty ran up the garage door. There was a Chevy pickup outside, driven by skinny white guy with a poorly trimmed goatee.

"Got your window." He pronounced it "winda." They unloaded it, Smitty handed the guy some money, and he drove away again.

I had no idea how or where the guy had gotten a windshield on such short notice. Maybe it was all perfectly legit, but I didn't think this sort of repair usually got taken care of this fast.

Within a half hour we were on our way, Smitty tucking some cash into his pocket and waving at us before he dropped the garage door.

"So, where did you need to go?"

I stared at Jack, not having any idea what he was talking about.

"Remember, you said you needed to come to South Bend to take care of something?"

"Oh, yeah. James Bolin." I shook my head. "Never mind, I think I've had enough for one day."

"Hell, it's only 4:00. Might as well take care of business while we're down here."

I thought about it for a minute. I did want to go by Bolin's house, but did I really want Jack to go with me?

69

Things tended to get a little too exciting when he was along. Besides, I was exhausted from my fit of hysteria, and I really just wanted to go home.

"I'll go Monday. Right now I just want to go home."

"Okay." Jack shrugged.

"By the way, did you get what you needed from Brisby Financial?"

"Of course."

"I didn't see you carrying anything when you came out."

"It's all up here." He tapped his head. "Just needed some info."

"I hope it was worth all the trouble."

"It always is."

After a few minutes of silence I once again remembered poker. "You coming to play cards tonight?"

"Yeah, if you're still up for it."

I gave him a look. "Duh, it's poker! Of course I'm up for it!"

"Hey, you don't have a little gambling addiction going on, do you?" Jack grinned.

"Of course not! I don't go to the casinos; I don't even buy lottery tickets. I just like poker night."

"Maybe because you always win."

It was my turn to grin. "Well, not *always*."

Chapter Six

Jack dropped me off at McDonald's to pick up my car and I stopped by the grocery store to stock up on snacks for the evening. Chips, dip, some pre-cut veggies since I didn't have a lot of time left, some cheese and summer sausage. I noticed they had the little cocktail wienies on sale so I picked up a couple packages of those and some bar-b-q sauce. Yep, I'm a real gourmet when it comes to poker night.

Mason arrived first, as usual, with a contribution to the snacks, also as usual. His wife was a great cook, and she seemed to delight in coming up with new and exotic dishes. Tonight was a dip for veggies that included cream cheese, hummus, feta cheese, olives, and who knew what else. It was delicious, but way out of my diet league. I know that Pam tends to sneak in low-fat cheeses in her dishes, making them a little healthier than they look, but I still wasn't going to get carried away.

Jeff and Eddie showed up a few minutes later, so we sat down to play a couple rounds of five card draw. Jack came in, looking as relaxed as if he'd spent the day lying on a tropical beach rather than speeding around town in the back of a pick-up truck dodging bullets. He didn't mention our expedition, and neither did I.

It was nine o'clock before Riley ambled in, looking a bit disheveled.

"Hey Riley, what's up? Haven't seen you around much." Mason greeted him with just a hint of underlying annoyance.

"Been busy." Riley took a long pull on his beer and didn't elaborate.

"You missed Karen's wedding last week. She was pretty disappointed." Karen was Mason's sister-in-law, a close friend of their crowd. I say "theirs" because in spite of the fact that these guys seemed to find an excuse for a social gathering every other week I seldom attended. It wasn't that I didn't like them all; they were actually a fun, diverse group, and every party was guaranteed to be full of lively, well-informed conversation. That is, until the alcohol really got flowing. But I wasn't much of a drinker, and I only liked crowds in small doses, so I tended to be a bit of an outsider. I was really surprised to hear that Riley had missed the wedding, though. He was an integral part of their group, and usually attended every event.

Riley only shrugged. "I got hung up. I sent her a gift."

"I don't think the gift was as important as your presence." Mason was clearly irritated.

"Hey, what's the big deal? It was a big wedding, I'm surprised she even noticed I wasn't there."

"You missed Greg's birthday party last month, too." Jeff pointed out. "Just what is it you've got going on lately?"

"What the hell is this, the Inquisition?" Now Riley was getting pissed. "Can't a guy have a life outside your little circle?"

"Come on, guys, he's right." I spoke up, hoping to diffuse the tension before the whole night was ruined. "We all have things to do now and then. Leave him alone."

Riley flashed me a grateful look, and I felt a little twinge of guilt. The truth was I wanted to question him, too. He had been acting a little weird, and I was worried about him. I watched him chug the rest of his beer and get up to grab another. It seemed he'd been drinking a lot more since the middle of summer, and I thought maybe it was time for someone to pry. I cared a lot about Riley. Not to take away from by big brother Jason, but Riley was like the kid brother I'd always wished I'd had. He was only a couple of years younger than me, but he always seemed just a bit more immature than the rest of the guys. Like he was stuck in frat house mode, resisting the inevitable need to become a responsible adult.

I would talk to him about it, but not now. We were here to play poker.

I didn't get to bed until 1:00 a.m., but for some perverse reason I didn't sleep well so I got up at 7:00. I was a little thickheaded from six hours of sleep, but after a cup of coffee and a hot shower I felt pretty good. The sun was shining, and the temperature was somewhere in the fifties. I threw on a pair of sweat pants and a t-shirt and went for a bike ride.

When I got home Tommy was sitting on my porch, drinking a large cup of coffee from McDonald's. There was another one sitting on the little table next to him.

"Hey." He held out the extra coffee for me and I accepted it and collapsed in the other chair.

"Hey yourself."

Tommy was my ex-husband. We were compatible in a lot of ways, and our marriage might have worked out well if not for the fact that he was gay. I hadn't known that when I spoke my vows, but to be fair, neither did he.

After a couple of years apart we'd run into each other and found out that all the good stuff between us was still there. Now we were friends, and I was happy to have him back in my life.

"What's up?"

"Not much, just hadn't seen you in a while. How's the arm?"

I lifted my left arm and flexed it. "Good. Stronger than ever, in fact. Plus I have a cool scar to show off if anyone starts comparing gunshot wounds."

"So, you been hanging around with Jack lately?"

"Some," I answered him, suspicious of the question. "Why?"

"Just wondered. I saw this really weird clip on the news this morning. Some crazy blonde driving a black pickup truck that looked a lot like Jack's terrorized the food drive yesterday. Couldn't really get a good look at her face, but there was a guy hanging on for dear life in the bed of the truck, and if I didn't know better, I'd have sworn it was Jack. I just can't imagine him letting anyone drive his truck though, can you?"

I widened my eyes and assumed my best innocent expression.

"Gee, no I can't."

"Unless, of course, it was you. Jack seems to have a thing for you, and I think he might let you drive just about anything of his."

I blushed and looked away, unable to maintain the lie. I wasn't a natural born liar, although I had found it was a learned trait. I had been forced to practice at it for my job at B&E, but I didn't think I'd ever learn to lie to people I knew and cared about.

"That's ridiculous, I'm not Jack's type." I kept my eyes carefully averted. "Besides, why would I terrorize a food drive?"

"That's what I've been asking myself all morning." Tommy took a long drink of his coffee. "So now I'm asking you."

I was busted, no doubt about it. I felt a little thrill of fear. If Tommy recognized me, could the cops be far behind?

"I wasn't trying to terrorize them. I was just trying to get away from a security guard."

"Why?"

"Because he shot at me!" There, that should vindicate me.

"Why did he shoot at you?"

Oh. There was that whole breaking and entering thing. And the part where I almost ran him over. I didn't think I wanted to tell Tommy or anyone else about that.

"I was giving Jack a ride."

Tommy sighed. "You're not going to tell me about it, are you?"

"I'd rather not. It was scary and stupid and now I'm afraid I might go to jail." I took a drink of my own coffee, wishing I had brought my cigarettes out with me.

"Jail?" Tommy leaned toward me. "Rainie, just what the hell did he get you into this time?"

"Quit blaming Jack! It's not like he held a gun to my head and made me come along!"

"Maybe not, but he keeps talking you into things that are way over your head."

I abruptly stood, indignant at the lecture. "It obviously wasn't so far over my head, or I wouldn't be standing here right now. I'm not some silly love-struck girl who can't say no to a pretty face." *Or was I?* I kept that doubt to myself.

"I happen to like Jack, and hanging around with him is a helluva lot more exciting than sitting around watching TV or drinking tea with the girls. When I'm with Jack I feel like I'm really *living*, not just getting through the day. If you're really my friend you'll support my decisions, not just come around to lecture me all the time!"

With that I stormed into the house and slammed the door.

Okay, so I know I had just been complaining about Jack getting me into trouble. And part of me felt that was true, and that maybe I shouldn't answer his calls anymore.

But another part of me felt strongly about the "really living" thing, and I don't think I fully realized that until I said it to Tommy.

It wasn't that my life before Jack was bad. On the contrary, it was pretty decent. I had a good routine going, doing pretty much what I liked when I liked. It was safe. It was comforting.

It was boring.

There, I said it. I loved caregiving and writing poetry and my family and friends, but I'd always been restless. I'd always known I couldn't work the same job for forty hours a week; I'd go bonkers with the endless repetition. Jack pulled me out of my safety zone, and I must admit I was learning to like the adrenalin rush.

Of course, there was the part about being shot at, and occasionally humiliated, and being threatened with jail time.

I found my cigarettes and went out the back door to have a smoke. Tommy was waiting for me on the back porch. Sometimes it was uncanny how well he knew me.

"I'm sorry, Rainie, you're right, and I'm the last person who should be lecturing you about an alternative lifestyle." Tommy smiled that boyish smile of his, and I felt my anger melting away. "If hanging around Jack makes you happy, then I'm all for it. Just watch your ass, okay? There are a lot of people who care about you."

"Thanks Tommy." He hugged me, and I felt tears prick the backs of my eyeballs. I blinked them away.

"I've got to go, but give me a call, we'll go out." Tommy turned to go. "By the way," he said over his shoulder. "If you do get arrested, call me. I'll get Thelma and we'll come bail you out."

There didn't seem to be much to say to that, so I just sat and smoked in silence.

A short while later my mother called.

"Hi mom."

"Hi." She didn't say anything else.

"Are you okay, mom?"

"Of course. I just thought there was something you wanted to tell me, and I didn't want to interrupt."

"But Mom, you called me."

"I called so you can tell me."

"Tell you what?" Boy, did everyone I know talk in circles, or was it me that couldn't follow a straight line?

"Jedediah and I took a few cases of food down to the TV station yesterday for the food drive."

"Oh." What I meant was, *uh oh.* I hadn't expected this. My mother and her boyfriend had a definite aversion to cameras in general, and public cameras in particular. They were worried about getting into the national facial recognition data base, which they said was just one more giant step toward Big Brother's total control.

"I thought you were just going to take the food straight to the pantry. You never go near televised events."

"We were on our way somewhere else so we dropped the food off at the curb, and some nice young men agreed to carry it up to the donation site."

"Oh."

"So?"

I sighed. No matter how much practice I got, I would never be able to lie to my mom, even by omission. I sucked in some air and got it out quick.

"So I was running from a guy who was shooting at me and I got turned around on the one-way streets and accidently ran through the TV station lawn but I'm fine and no one got hurt and it's all over now." I braced myself, but Mom sounded more alarmed than angry.

"Honey, there were TV cameras there! What if they filmed you and got you in their database?"

"Mom, it doesn't matter. I have a driver's license, remember?"

"Oh yeah." It was her turn to sigh. "I wish you'd let us take care of that for you."

See, Mom and Jedediah had driver's licenses, too, but through some complicated finagling by a computer hacker friend their official pictures in the data base had been replaced with pictures of people who had died.

"So is that it? You're just worried I had my picture taken?"

"Is there something else I should be concerned about?"

"No, not really."

Hm. How about the fact that I was shot at, or the fact that I was careening around the city streets at top speed going the wrong way on one-way streets? How about what was I doing to get myself shot at in the first place?

For all her peace-loving ways, my mom had some radical ideas, and a lot of radical friends. She saw nothing wrong with breaking laws, which had been written by The Man to keep The People under control. The only laws she was worried about were humanitarian laws - the ones where people just tried to do the right thing by each other. And even those, of course, didn't need to be written by a government. She believed they were already imprinted on our souls, if we would only choose to embrace them.

"Good. Well, be a little more careful next time. And really, if you're going to drive that fast you should have your passengers up front, not riding in the bed of the truck."

"That was Jack, and he kind of does his own thing."

"Doing your own thing is good, but he should think about his safety. I mean, I'm sure his mother worries about him, too. How would she feel if something happened to him?"

"I'm sure you're right. I'll mention it to him." Huh, Jack's mother. Funny, it never occurred to me to ask if he had any family.

"All right then. Are you coming over today? Thelma is already here working with Brenda, and I think Jason is coming over for dinner."

I didn't particularly want to get roped in to helping Thelma and Brenda, but I hadn't seen my brother Jason in a while. Seemed like a fair trade-off.

"Sure, I'll come for dinner. What time?"

"Oh, whenever everyone gets here, sweety. See you then."

"Whenever" was one of mom's favorite times. At least I never had to worry about being late getting to her house.

Geez, I loved my mom.

Chapter Seven

Monday morning I arrived at Bob's to find Daryl already there and in the midst of a shouting match with his father.

I stood aside, hoping that if I maintained silence I wouldn't be brought into it, but of course that's not how these things worked. No doubt medical decisions were ultimately those of the client or the family, but more often than not a good caregiver was consulted for an opinion.

I was considered a good caregiver. I was proud of that, but sometimes the responsibility weighed heavy. Maybe that was why I was enjoying my jaunts with Jack. Those decisions tended to be spur of the moment, with no deep thinking required, and if I made the wrong one it was likely only me that would suffer.

"This is your fault, Rainie!" Bob was shaking with anger and pointing a finger at me. "I told you something in confidence and you had to blab it around!"

"Bob, I'm sorry, but it's my job."

"He says he won't go to the doctor," Daryl growled. "Tell him, Rainie. Tell him he needs to go."

"I'm not crazy, damn it! But if you take me to the doctor he'll have me locked up for sure. No one is going to believe me!"

"Bob, I don't think you're crazy." I was using my most reasonable, calm tone. "I've never seen any sign of advanced dementia in you, either. But the fact is there could be a medical cause..."

"See? You don't believe me. You think I'm driving the car at night."

"It's the most logical conclusion. Daryl has the only other set of keys, and we know he isn't doing it."

"How do we know?" Bob glared at his son. "He's wanted me in a home for a long time. Maybe he's Gaslighting me!"

"Gaslighting?" Daryl looked at me, confused.

"It's an old movie. Some people were trying to convince a guy he was crazy so they messed with him, making him think he was doing oddball things when he wasn't."

"Exactly!" Bob nodded firmly, as if my explanation of the movie proved his point.

"Look Bob, all Daryl wants you to do is talk to the doctor. Let him run some blood work, make sure your meds are okay. I once took care of a lady who thought she was in a debtor's prison in Europe, and it turned out her hallucinations were just a bad reaction to her heart meds. You say yourself you take way too many medications. Maybe the doc will take you off some of them."

"Or maybe he'll just call the guys in white coats."

"It doesn't work that way anymore. They can't lock you up unless you're a proven danger to yourself or others..."

"Which is exactly what Daryl is saying I am!"

"No Pop, really," Daryl had finally calmed his tone. "I'm just worried. Please, just let the doctor check you out."

"I won't let them just lock you up," I promised. "Not without a fight." I glanced at Daryl, who grimaced. Bob caught the exchange and looked rather pleased.

"You hear that, Daryl? Someone's sticking up for me."

I wanted to reassure Bob that his son was sticking up for him too, but at this point it sounded like he was giving in. I didn't care which one of us Bob trusted, as long as he agreed to see the doctor.

"All right." Bob's shoulders slumped. "What time do we go?"

"Doctor Helms agreed to fit you in right away, so we're supposed to get there as early as possible."

Bob looked at me. "You're coming, right?"

"Of course."

"And you'll make sure I get back home today?"

"Yes." I wasn't too worried about that promise; it would take time to get test results back.

"Let me wash up and get a clean shirt." Bob shuffled off to the bathroom, suddenly looking all 92 of his years.

"You'll really fight me on this?" Daryl asked as soon as Bob was out of hearing.

"I needed him to trust me."

"So you lied?"

"Not really. If the doctor doesn't convince me he needs to be in a locked facility, then I will argue Bob's case."

"Fair enough." Daryl sighed and ran a hand over his face. He'd shaved, but not very well, and his eyes were rimmed with red. "It's been an exhausting weekend."

"You've been here since Friday?"

"Yeah. I'm thinking I'll go back to work tomorrow; he seems fine during the day. I'll have to stay overnight until we get the test results back."

"What if the tests don't answer the question?"

Daryl slumped, looking so much like his father it made my heart hurt.

"Then we'll have to put him in a nursing home." He looked at me, and I saw the anguish in his eyes. "I don't want to do it, Rainie. You understand that, right? I mean, I've asked him to move in with us, but he refuses. What am I supposed to do?"

"You could go to 24 hour care here, but that's expensive."

"Tell me about it. The agencies want $18.00 an hour or more. That's over 3000 bucks a week! His savings would be gone in six months, and then what? Some Medicare nursing home with overworked, underpaid caregivers? At least if we do it now he can afford some place a little better."

"We'll just have to wait and see how it goes."

Bob came out of his room and we let the conversation go for another time.

I didn't leave for B&E until 1:00. The doctor had ordered an immediate CAT scan, and Bob refused to go over to the hospital unless I came along. He was counting on me to break him out if anyone tried to keep him. I'm not sure what he expected to do if it came to that. Would we go on the lam? I could just see us driving across the country in my beat up old Escort, shoplifting dinner from the grocery store and robbing convenience stores for gas money. The papers would nickname us Bonnie and grandfather Clyde and eventually we'd probably have to drive off a cliff.

Okay, I was getting my movies mixed up. Probably none of that would happen anyway.

Doctor Helms had gone over Bob's med list carefully and determined that nothing he was taking would cause his recent behavior. He mentioned "sundowners," a relatively common condition in the elderly where they seemed fine during the day but once the sun went down they got confused or worse.

I was saddened and more than a little concerned by this possibility, but I had to put it aside and go to work at B&E. The hours I logged there were imperative if I wanted to make my mortgage payment.

I ran a few computer checks and filled out the forms for last week's hours. There was no time clock. I kept track of my hours in a small spiral notebook and recorded them once a week. B&E made periodic checks for accuracy, but for the most part assistants were trusted to log honest hours.

I was staring out the window, waiting for a search to complete, when Belinda stepped up to my desk.

"See any suspects out there?"

I grinned up at her. "Nope. Just a lot of clouds. I'm thinking it might rain."

Belinda gave an exaggerated shiver. "I hate rain in October. It's too damned cold."

"October?" My eyes automatically flicked to the wall calendar. Sure enough, the second of October. Where had summer gone?

"I know, it's hard to believe. It's been so warm the leaves have hardly started to change."

"Huh. Guess I've been too busy to pay attention to the date."

"So I've heard." Belinda smirked. "Jack talked you into helping him again, didn't he?"

"What makes you say that?"

"Well, I admit I didn't get a good look at the blonde driving, but I know for a fact that tricked out Ford Ranger was Jack's, and I couldn't miss his tight little butt sticking up from the bed."

"You saw the news."

"Of course! Everyone saw the news! They must have run that film 50 times Sunday morning, and almost as many times this morning. The cops are disappointed that they can't make an ID on the driver or the passenger, and it seems the plates were obscured by mud. Kind of strange, since the rest of the truck was so clean."

I blew out a sigh of relief. "I wondered about that."

"Jack is no amateur. It must have been something good he got you involved with."

"Nothing special." I grinned. "Just a little B&E work."

Belinda laughed at the play on words.

"Whatever it was, Harry had Jack in his office first thing this morning."

"Is he in trouble?"

"I don't know, but Harry probably just lectured him on keeping a low profile. Jack usually gets what he goes after, and that makes him pretty valuable."

"You don't think he'll call me in, do you?"

"Actually, that's why I'm here. He wants to see you at 2:00."

I swallowed hard. "Damn it, that's just great. I need this job!"

"Hey, I don't think he'll fire you."

"You don't think?"

Belinda shrugged. "Harry's funny about things. You never know what he considers crossing the line."

"But I was doing it for Jack!"

"Hey, don't tell me, tell Harry." Belinda looked at her watch, a slim gold thing with a tiny face surrounded by little rhinestones. "It's 1:30. Don't be late."

She patted my shoulder in what I thought was supposed to be a comforting gesture and walked - no make that *sashayed* from the room. I wondered how long it took to learn to walk with those swaying hips, and more importantly, how you learned to make it look subtly sexy instead of silly.

I knew my mind was wandering to minutia again, but I couldn't help it. When I got nervous my mind starting grasping for stupid things to think about instead of the problem at hand.

I tried to go back to the computer, but more often than not over the next half hour I caught myself staring out the window. I didn't want to see Harry Baker. He'd always been nice to me, but then I had never screwed up this bad before. How could I have been so stupid? I knew about that food drive, I knew there'd be cameras...but the thing was, at the time I actually did it I hadn't known anything much at all. Except that a guy was shooting at me, and I had to get away. I'd been operating on blind panic. That was

85

certainly no way for a PI, even an assistant, to behave. Maybe Harry was right to fire me.

By the time 2:00 rolled around I was feeling totally defeated. I couldn't help Bob, and now I couldn't help myself. I was a total loser and couldn't get either one of my jobs right.

On the verge of tears I shut down the computer and headed for Harry's office.

Harry Baker looked harassed and harried. Ha ha. No, really, he did. His suit coat was hung over the back of his chair, the sleeves of his slightly rumpled dress shirt rolled to the elbows. His tie was slightly askew, his hair mussed as if he'd run his hands through it frequently since his last shower. Great, he was probably in a lousy mood. I was going to be fired for sure.

When Belinda admitted me to his office Harry glanced up briefly from something he was writing and used his pen to point me to a guest chair. The chair was well cushioned and upholstered in fine leather. I perched on the edge of it, not wanting to sink down. I already felt small enough.

I was glad he didn't expect me to speak right away or shake his hand. My throat was dry and my palms were sweating, as if all the moisture from my mouth had leached to my hands.

I surreptitiously wiped my palms on my skirt and waited for him. I had never been fired before, but just the thought was humiliating. I hoped I didn't cry.

"Well, Miss Lovingston." He suddenly dropped his pen and looked across the expanse of his very expensive-looking desk. "Rumor has it you've been driving Jack's truck."

I nodded and managed to answer "yes," pleased that the word came out clearly.

"TV cameras? I would think your mother would have taught you better." Was I mistaken, or was there the tiniest hint of a smile on his face? Maybe he enjoyed humiliating and browbeating people before he fired them.

"My mother? Do you know her?"

"Background checks. I know everyone you know, at least on paper."

"There isn't much paper on my mom." Huh, maybe I wasn't totally defeated. Even I could recognize the defiance in my tone.

"Which is why my guys had to dig harder than usual to find out about her. And frankly, the lack of paper is suspicious in itself, isn't it? I especially liked the driver's license photo trick. I'd like to know how they managed that."

I swallowed and didn't say anything. He had to have known about the fake photos for months - since he hired me. I assumed he would have reported it by now if he was going to.

"Jack Jones is one of my best men. I can't afford to lose him."

Again I just nodded.

"For some reason, he's taken quite a liking to you. He thinks you have what it takes to be a full-fledged P.I., and after your performance last spring, I thought so too. But this...what the hell were you thinking?"

"I wasn't." There, I'd admitted it. "That security guard was shooting and Jack was screaming at me and I just wanted the hell out of there. So I went."

Harry leaned back in his chair and tapped his fingers lightly on the padded arms. His lips were quirked in a half-smile.

"You're saying you panicked."

"Yeah, I guess so."

Harry nodded and swiveled his chair toward the big window to the left of his desk. After a long moment of silence he turned back to me, his expression stern.

"P.I.'s can't panic. Panic gets you killed."

I nodded.

"Of course, if a P.I. does panic, she should never admit it. You should play it off as an adrenaline rush, a spur of the moment action kind of thing." Now he smiled full out. "That being said, you did manage to get yourself and Jack out of a sticky situation, and apparently no one can actually identify you; at least, no one in authority. It seems everyone in Buchanan knows it was you, but no one is telling the cops. I think they're having too much fun telling the story to each other and laughing about the crazy hippie chick."

Hippie chick? Funny, I always thought that was my mom. I mean, yeah, I ran around barefooted and wore long skirts and I suppose I tended to march to my own beat, but I paid taxes (most of the time) and even had a cell phone. How hippie was that? But Harry was still smiling, so I didn't argue.

"I suggested to Jack that he pick another partner for these jaunts, but I somehow doubt he's going to listen to me. If he wasn't so damned good at his job I'd fire him for insubordination at least once a week. The problem is I'm afraid you're going to get him killed."

"Me?" I leaned forward, outraged. "*He's* the one always dragging *me* into this stuff!"

"I have no doubt that's true. Like I said, he seems to have taken a liking to working with you. I know you haven't made a firm decision about becoming a full time PI, but I think you need to develop some skills. Jack says he's been working on some self-defense with you, and Eddie has taken you to the shooting range a couple of times."

"Which is pointless, because I don't carry a gun."

"I want you to consider getting a permit." My eyes widened. I might not be a hippie chick, but I sure wasn't okay with running around with a loaded weapon. I could hurt people!

Harry was still talking.

"I want you to get a little more serious about the training. At least two sessions a week with self-defense and the gun range. I also want you to take some driving courses."

"I know how to drive!" I felt myself flush. Did he think I was a total incompetent?

"Of course you do, but we teach special courses in evasion and offensive driving."

"Offensive?"

Harry grinned. "It's not your high school driver's ed. You'll learn how to evade pursuit, or if necessary to use your car as a weapon. Only against the bad guys, of course." There was a little tinge of meanness to his grin, kind of like Jack got now and then. It must be a macho thing.

"I'm not sure I want to learn to be that aggressive."

Harry leaned forward and clasped his hands on his desk, all signs of humor gone. "This is for your sake, as well as Jack's and the reputation of my company. If not...well, I understand you're a good caregiver. Maybe you should stick to that full time."

I swallowed hard. Okay, so he wasn't firing me, but he was definitely giving me an ultimatum. I stared at him for a long moment. I hated being told what to do, and I especially hated ultimatums. They made me instantly defiant. Maybe it was because of the way my mother raised us, rarely giving us orders, but instead making strong suggestions as to how we should behave and letting us decide what to do. Oddly, we almost always chose to do things her way; her approval meant a lot. Harry, on the other hand, was just my boss. I'd practically made a career of defying bosses.

I considered just getting up and flouncing out the door in a huff, but I didn't think I was any good at flouncing. My sister could have done it, and I'd bet Belinda was a good flouncer, but I'd probably just look like a spoiled, clumsy child stomping out the door.

Besides, maybe Harry was right. Maybe I should be better trained to help Jack. Better yet, maybe I should just stick to the reference checks I was hired to do.

But that would require me saying no to Jack, and I'd already proven that I couldn't be counted on to do that.

"Is the gun permit a deal breaker?"

He smiled again and sat back in his chair. "Not necessarily, as long as you learn to use a gun properly in case one comes to hand. But the driving and self-defense are a must."

Okay, so I didn't mind the self-defense stuff; it was good exercise, and besides, I liked thinking I could take care of myself. As for the driving, hey, that just sounded like good fun!

I nodded. "All right. I'll do more training."

"Excellent." Harry gave me a full-wattage smile. "You can do it on the clock, since it's company training. I'll set up a time at the driving school, and you can work the other out with Jack."

"Um…could I have Eddie train me instead?"

Harry shrugged. "Sure, Eddie is at least as good as Jack, maybe better. But why not Jack?"

Because I'm afraid too much physical contact with him will cause me to heat up until I spontaneously combust, I thought but didn't say. Instead I returned his shrug.

"Eddie's a good friend and I like working with him."

"Okay then, work it out with him."

Harry pulled his papers back in front of him and picked up his pen. I was clearly dismissed.

Chapter Eight

Since I was still employed I figured I'd better get on with finding James Bolin. I gassed up the Escort, ran into McDonalds for an iced tea, and headed for the bypass.

The bypass, as its name implied, took drivers around the traffic generated by all the businesses on the main routes between Niles and South Bend. Bad for the businesses of course, but convenient if you were in a hurry to get somewhere without a lot of traffic lights. Along the way the rain finally started, more an intermittent drizzle than anything else, just enough that I had to flick my wipers on now and then, not enough to keep them on. Oh well, it gave me something to do. Driving on the bypass was dull, with not much more than corn fields to either side.

Jim lived in Twykenham Hills, an old but still pretty well-to-do neighborhood. It was designed and built long before the cookie cutter sub-divisions started popping up everywhere, and there was an attractive mix of homes from small to extravagant.

I found the address and parked in front, taking a moment to get a feel for the place.

Jim's was a long, low ranch-style brick house. It looked to be in good repair, although it didn't seem like anyone cared a lot about the landscaping. The grass was neatly mowed but that was about it. The flower beds were raked but empty, the bushes more or less trimmed but not really shaped.

As his ex-wife had reported there were no newspapers piling up, no overflowing mailbox, no long grass. Nothing to indicate a long absence from home. The windows all had curtains drawn over them. There was no car in the driveway, but there was an attached garage that looked closed up tight.

The street was quiet, but I suspected that would change soon. Most people were probably at work, but it was almost 3:30. Kids would be coming home from school, parents arriving shortly before or right after, depending on how old the kids were. I suspected that between now and 6:00 there would be a lot of coming and going.

That didn't matter, of course, because I wasn't doing anything wrong.

I finally got out into the drizzly rain, walked up to the front door and knocked. I waited a long moment and knocked again. Nothing.

I looked around. There was no one on the street close by, but I could see a group of kids just turning the corner on the far end of the block. They were laughing and shoving each other, totally involved with each other, not paying any attention to me.

Good enough. I stepped off the little front porch and peered through a space in the curtains.

The house was dim, but I could see what looked like a living room. There wasn't much there; bare wood floors, no rugs. A new looking sofa, a coffee table and a nice wide screen TV that was the centerpiece of a wall-sized entertainment center. A newspaper had been tossed aside on the couch and a coffee cup was leaving a ring on the table. There was a pair of shoes under the coffee table and an empty bowl on top amid a scattered pile of magazines.

No people. Better yet, no dogs.

Now, why had I thought that? It wasn't like I was planning to break in and snoop around.

I shook my head. Of course not; that wasn't how I worked, that was Jack's gig. Besides, it was way too early in the investigation to go that far.

I stepped back on to the porch and knocked one more time. Still no answer, so I walked back to my car, slowly, thinking about that living room.

It looked lived in, yet there was something off about it. Something...unfinished.

Yeah, that was it. There are so little furniture, and nothing hanging on the walls. No rugs, no knickknacks, no family photographs. It just didn't look like a home a man had lived in for several years.

A car pulled in across the street. The occupant pulled straight into an attached garage and the door started closing behind him. The group of kids was down to two; the others must have reached home already. The last two shouted goodbyes and split up, each going toward a house on the opposite side of the street.

No one paid any attention to me. Apparently this neighborhood wasn't overly cautious about strangers. Good to know.

I got in my car and considered my options. Jim used to work in an insurance office, doing the traditional 9 to 5. He'd left that job three months ago, right about the time he quit calling his kids. Was he still working? If so, he might well still have a day job, and might be home in an hour or so.

I decided to kill a little time and try again. I drove out to Grape Road.

Grape Road was at one time, maybe thirty years ago, a country road leading to more country roads. Then someone had the bright idea to build a mall. It seemed like overnight every retailer in the country had to have a store in the area, and now there wasn't a corn field to be seen for miles. You could find anything from copiers to cars to comic books among the hundreds of shops crammed into a relatively small area. At Christmas time the road was barely navigable, but in early October, at least during the day, the traffic was tolerable.

I drove out to Borders, my favorite bookstore. Not only did I like the atmosphere, it was a mile down the road from the mall and the worst of the traffic. I bought a cup of coffee and browsed the books for a while. As usual I found about a dozen books I absolutely had to have, but my budget wouldn't allow it. I splurged and bought two. One was the first book in a fantasy series by one of my favorite authors, the other a clearance shelf tome about ancient civilizations. I know that might sound odd, but I loved reading that kind of stuff. My head was full of useless trivia, and I delighted in stuffing more in.

By the time I left the book store at 5:30 traffic was really picking up. I ducked out the back exit and made a beeline for less populated areas.

At 6:00 it wasn't yet dark, but the sun was far enough down in the western sky that most people had lights burning in their houses. It was clear that more than half the residents of Jim's block were home; one couple was out raking leaves, there was a man mowing his lawn, and there were a couple of little girls playing hopscotch. Huh. I didn't know girls still played that.

I pulled up in front of Jim's house and sure enough, there was a light burning in the living room. This was going to be simple for a change.

I went up the walk, smoothing my skirt and my hair a bit. I knocked on the door and was rewarded a moment later by an answer. I put on my best smile, relieved that this would be an easy matter; I would identify myself, find out why Jim had quit calling his kids and ditched out on the support, and then I'd go home and have a bowl of cereal. Maybe some Fruit Loops; I was in the mood for some sugar.

But the guy who answered the door was not Jim Bolin.

I had a picture of Jim in his file, and while I realize some people don't look quite like their pictures, there was no way Jim could have changed this much in a few months. Jim was a good-looking fifty-something with dark, lightly gray-shot hair that fell over one large brown eye.

The guy that answered the door was three hundred pounds of sloppy, balding manhood, his eyes little marbles squeezed between chubby cheeks and an overhanging brow.

They did share one thing in common: they both had a big, white-toothed grin.

"Well hello there, little lady. What can I do for you? Not Avon, I hope; I'm not married, got no girlfriend, my mom's long dead and I can't stand smelly man soap."

"Uh..." As usual, I was wonderfully eloquent when taken by surprise. "No, no Avon...I'm an investigator."

"An investigator?" The man raised bushy eyebrows that looked like they might crawl off his face and climb the wall under their own steam.

"Yes." I was recovering my surprise and regaining a professional attitude. I thrust out my hand. "Rainie Lovingston, B&E Security and Investigations."

He shook my hand, a firm dry grip. "So Rainie Lovingston of B&E Security and Investigations, I'm John, Big John Gosa they call me, and what can I do for you on this fine evening?"

Wow, this guy was a study in contradictions. His speech didn't match his look any more than his smile matched his overall slovenly appearance.

"I'm looking for James Bolin. Is he home?"

Now the brows drew together as he frowned, and I couldn't help imagining a nature program showing a close-up shot of two wooly caterpillars in a deadly struggle against each other. Or maybe a mating dance? With creepy-crawly things both actions often looked the same. I had to bite my lip to keep from giggling, and I focused on his mouth instead, which had drawn into a small frown.

"Don't know anyone by that name. Sure you got the right house?"

"226 East Calhound." I pointed at the house letters beside his door, as if he wouldn't know what house he was in, and nodded. "I'm sure."

"Well honey, then I'm afraid your information is a tad out of date. I bought this house a month ago, but I never heard of James Bolin."

"You bought it?" Aha, so I was right about the living room looking unfinished. I felt a small warm glow at acknowledgement of my growing detecting skills. I'd be smoking a pipe and wearing a hound's-tooth jacket it no time.

"Sure did, got a good deal on it, too, what with the housing market being so soft and all."

"But if you bought it, you had to have met Mr. Bolin, at least at the closing." I was adamant about this; the file showed that James owned this house outright. He'd bought it right after his divorce, paid in full with what I now knew was his inheritance.

"Sorry Miss, but there was no Jim. There was a Julian and a Steve, both representatives of the company that sold the house."

"A company sold the house?"

"Yeah, I figured maybe it was a foreclosure or some such. Like I said, I got a good deal."

"What was the name of the company?"

For the first time the gregarious guy hesitated. "Is there some sort of problem with the sale? I mean, I got my signed papers, and my bank approved it all legit..."

"No, no, there's no problem," I hurried to reassure him before the flow of information shut off. "I told you, I'm just looking for Jim. My records show he owned this house, but clearly, like you said, they're out of date. I just thought I might backtrack through the company that owned it, maybe find out where Jim has gone."

"Why are you looking for him?" Now he was suspicious, and I was sure he wouldn't tell me anything more. I considered the confidentiality of the matter. It wasn't this man's business what Jim had done. Then again, what did I care who knew he was a deadbeat?

"He's way behind on his child support, and I'm trying to locate him so he'll pay up."

Now the big man's face crumpled into full out anger, and I backed up a step, realizing I'd made a terrible error. Here was this guy, apparently living alone in a barely furnished house...odds were he was a recent divorcee on the hook for support, and not about to help me find a fellow sufferer who was getting away with it.

"Damn that makes me mad! My father was the same way. He skipped out when I was seven, left my mom to raise me and my brothers however she could. Poor woman worked herself to an early grave." He looked off into the distance, and I thought I saw his eyes tearing up.

I stayed where I was, surprised for the second time since I'd gotten out of my car. So much for judging people by first impressions. For that matter, my second and third impressions of him probably weren't quite right, either.

John blinked and looked back at me. "I'll help as much as I can. You run that man down and you make him pay, you hear me?"

I gulped at his fierceness and nodded.

"Good girl. Okay, so the company was Brisby Financial, over on Michigan Street."

"Brisby?" It was my turn to blink. What were the odds of that?

"Yeah, that's what I said. Julian and Steve, the reps, didn't seem like owners, more like lackeys. Maybe they re-poed the house from this James Bolin. If he doesn't pay for his kids, he probably doesn't pay his other bills either, you know?"

"Probably so," I nodded agreeably. "Well then, I guess my next step is to check with Brisby, see what they can tell me."

"Good idea. Look, there's anything else I can do to help, you tell me." Suddenly Big John Gosa smacked one meaty fist into the other meaty palm, producing a sound not unlike a fifty pound bag of wet sand striking a concrete floor. Apparently not all of that 300 pounds was fat. "Should you find him and need help *persuading* him to pay, you call me, huh?"

I smiled and backed away another step.

"You bet Big John. Thanks for the information."

I waved from a safe distance away and hurried to my car.

I called Jack on the way home and he answered on the second ring.

"Hey, what's up?"

"I just ran into a weird coincidence and I wanted to run it by you." I quickly filled him in on my search for James and my subsequent discussion with Big John about Brisby Financial.

"That is a coincidence."

"So?"

"So what?"

"So, are you going to tell me what info you got from Brisby?"

There was a moment of silence, followed by Jack letting out a little self-deprecating laugh.

"Actually, I didn't get anything from Brisby."

"What? But you said it was all stored in your head! Why did you lie?"

"I didn't really lie; if there had been anything, I would have memorized it. I just didn't want to let you down after the fun and adrenaline and all."

"Oh yeah, the fun!" I said it with exaggerated sarcasm, but my heart wasn't in it. It had been kind of fun. In a scared for my life, moments from death kind of way, but kind of fun nonetheless.

"Can you at least tell me why you were investigating them in the first place?"

"Sure, where are you?"

"On the bypass, heading home."

"Great. I'll see you at your place."

The call disconnected. I don't know why I was surprised. Jack wasn't usually much for chatting on the phone. But was it really necessary to discuss this in person? I know people could pick up cell calls, but I didn't think this was really that sensitive.

Maybe Brisby was into something bigger than I was imagining.

Maybe Jack just wanted an excuse to see me.

Ridiculous of course, but a girl needed her dreams.

He was there by the time I pulled into my driveway, leaning back in a lawn chair on my porch, his long legs propped on the railing.

"Hey."

"Hey."

"I've got to let George out and feed him. Come on in."

He followed me, silent as I opened the top of my iguana's cage, grabbed his food dish and went into the kitchen.

I rinsed out George's bowl and grabbed a handful of cut-up fruits and veggies from the fridge. Iguanas in captivity could survive on the specially formulated pellets you bought in the pet store, but there was no substitute for fresh foods.

"Did you have dinner yet?"

"Nope. I thought I'd have a peanut butter sandwich. Want one?"

Jack shook his head. "No. I ordered a pizza from Mirano's. Should be here any minute."

"Oh." I thought about that. It was pretty presumptuous of him to order food delivered to my house without asking, but then again I kind of liked it that Jack felt that comfortable with me. Hey, I didn't have much going for me in the man department right now. Dan had called to say he'd taken a gig in Detroit and wouldn't be back to town for at least three weeks.

I knew Jack was way out of my league. I'd admitted months ago that men as good looking and talented as he was simply didn't go for size twelve (okay, for the moment size 14) women with little rolls of fat above their waists. His flirting was a fun distraction, but he seemed to practice it on nearly every woman he met. I wasn't about to embarrass myself by taking it seriously. Nonetheless, I enjoyed his company and attention, so I let the subject of pizza go.

He followed me back to the living room and watched me put George's food up on the shelf. George lived in a 5x8 foot wood, glass and screen enclosure that took up one whole wall of my living room. There were special lights and small fans for ventilation, a filtered pool for him to soak in, lots of plants, and above it all a shelf bolted to the wall where he could bask under a sun lamp when I let him out.

"You sure love that lizard, don't you?"

"What's not to love? He's quiet and doesn't mess up the house."

"He also doesn't look very grateful for all the time and attention you give him. Couldn't you at least teach him to wag his tail?"

I grinned at that thought. An iguana's tail is long and leathery and spiny, a natural whip. They used it for balance when climbing, and it also made a great weapon.

Jack, who had obviously spent a lot of time in hot countries where iguanas actually lived in the trees, was grinning back at me.

"Yeah, maybe not."

"So tell me about Brisby."

"Damn, all business, huh? Can't even wait for the pizza?"

"Jack…"

"All right, all right. I was investigating on behalf of a guy who thinks Brisby stole his sister's life savings."

"Stole it?"

"Yeah. Everything, including her house."

"Her house? That is interesting! What makes this guy think Brisby stole it?"

"Because Brisby had control of it when she went missing."

"What? Well come on, Jack! It's obviously some kind of scam! They did the same thing to James Bolin!"

"Hold on, Rainie, we don't know that yet. Brisby Financial does buy houses; it's part of their regular gig. They also make mortgages and loan money on cars, usually to people who otherwise couldn't get the credit."

"At exorbitant rates, I suppose."

"They're pretty high, but hey, if not for Brisby they wouldn't be able to get a loan at all."

"Are you defending the place?"

"Not the place, just capitalism." Jack grinned that sly little grin of his. "Anyway, sometimes Brisby buys houses and resells them. It's a sideline they've just gotten into over the last couple of years. In this case they were working as a broker. They sold the house and kept 20% of the profit."

"And the other eighty per cent went to her?"

"No, she gave it away to charity."

"All of it?"

"Yeah, to the Newly Unified Church of Renewal. She donated everything she owned to the church just before she took off."

"And you don't find that strange?"

"Sure," Jack shrugged. "But people do that kind of stuff all the time. Look, she was in her fifties, never married, didn't even have an iguana to go home to. Her brother lives in North Carolina, hadn't seen her in 10 years, just phone calls and e-mails. That was her only family, and I couldn't find any real friends, just co-workers and neighbors that knew her to say hello to. What else did she have? So no, I don't think it's that strange she'd give all her money to the church. What I do find strange is that she just disappeared. She e-mailed her brother that she had found God, good luck and have a nice life, and that was the last he heard from her."

"I still say that sounds an awful lot like James Bolin."

"I have to agree. So what's next?"

"I'd sure like to know why his house was sold by Brisby Financial."

"Yeah? You want to have another run at that security guard?" Jack's grin made it clear he'd be happy to oblige. I shook my head.

"I'll pass. I think my next step is to talk to his old neighbors and co-workers, just like you did with the other lady. I don't think James was a loner though. From his wife's description he was just the opposite."

"That'd be good to know. You want some help with the interviews?"

"I'm just going to talk to them. I don't think anything needs to be shot or blown up."

"Hey, I can talk," Jack held his arms out and smiled almost boyishly. "Look how charming I can be." It didn't quite work on him. It was like a tiger trying to look kittenish.

The doorbell rang and Jack collected the pizza. I was pleased to see that half of the pizza was just veggie. I was touched that Jack remembered I wasn't all that fond of meat. I wasn't a vegetarian, mind you; I mean, who could say no to a crisp slice of bacon or a burger fresh off the grill? Well, real vegetarians I suppose, which as I've already stated, I am not.

"So, when are you going to do the interviews?"

"Well, I can't do them tomorrow because I'm with Thelma until four, and then I have to meet Eddie at B&E."

"Oh yeah, the self-defense training. You know, I would have been happy to keep working with you."

"I know, but Eddie's a good friend, and he sort of wanted to do it." At least, after I asked him to he did. I wasn't about to tell Jack that I couldn't stand to be in such close contact with him. The fact was, out of my league or not, the guy made me hot, and I was afraid he'd figure that out. My biggest fear was that he'd realize I had a huge crush on him and he'd laugh his ass off at the fat girl. Okay, so I wasn't as big as the fat girl I'd been back in junior high, but the memories still burned.

"I'll go Wednesday evening, after my driving lesson."

"Great, so what time should I pick you up?"

I took a bite of pizza so I wouldn't have to answer right away. Really, how much trouble could Jack get me into just running some simple interviews in broad daylight?

I looked over at him. He looked so calm and cool, as if butter wouldn't melt in his mouth. But I knew what lay beneath the surface, the daredevil that seemed to delight in risking life and limb for whatever cause he had at the moment. I finally swallowed and answered.

"I'll probably just go straight from the B&E facility. How about I let you know if I think I need help?

"Okay." Jack shrugged, but I thought he looked disappointed. Maybe Harry wasn't keeping him busy enough; this kind of interview was way below his pay grade. He changed the subject.

"Are you going to Mason's party on Saturday?"

"Oh yeah, I forgot." I sighed. The party was a faux Halloween party. Mason used to have a party every year on Halloween, complete with costumes and fake blood and the whole works, but since nearly everyone now had kids who trick-or-treated or had parties of their own, the adult party had been moved to mid October. It would be fun, I supposed, but not the same. No one would even be in costume.

"I'll be there. Are you going?"

"I'm thinking about it. Your new boyfriend going to be there?"

"Dan? I'm not sure he's really my boyfriend yet, but no, he's not coming. He's going to be out of town."

"Huh. Too bad." I thought I detected the slightest hint of a smile when he said it. What was that about? Did he think it was funny that I was dating a guy I hardly ever got to see? It wasn't that he didn't like Dan, because he'd never met him.

We munched more pizza, talking about nothing in particular. We touched on local events and a bit of politics and how the war in the Middle East was going. We didn't seem to agree on much of anything, but no fights broke out.

It seemed strange to chat with Jack; usually we were working, and he was focused on whatever task was before us, or playing poker, and he concentrated on his cards. This was another side of him, and I decided I liked it. Even if he was on the wrong side of the war issue.

Finally we closed the lid on the pizza; half of it was still in there.

"I'll stick this in the fridge for you."

"I'd rather you took it with you. I've had enough junk food for awhile."

"Yeah? Like what?"

I stared at him. I wasn't expecting to be asked. I thought about what I'd been eating lately. Hm, other than dreaming about ribs, I guess I'd eaten...cereal. Okay, even I knew that wasn't such a great diet.

"Just junk, you know how it is," I lied.

"Actually, I do. I have a sister, you know, and she's always obsessing about her weight, too." No, actually, I didn't know he had a sister, anymore than I knew about his mom or any other family members. "I think I'll leave the leftovers." He put them in the fridge and came back.

"See ya around."

I said goodbye to his retreating back.

Strange man.

Chapter Nine

Thelma called me at seven o'clock the next morning.

"Meet me downtown, the store next to the art gallery."

"The empty storefront?"

"It won't be empty for long! It's the site of the new 'Next to You' resale shop."

"Oh? That was fast."

"I've got people coming to do some work today, so I'll have to hang around here. Meet you at 8?"

"I'll be there."

But I almost wasn't. My good old Escort didn't want to start. At first there was no more than a click, then a click and a low groan, which I echoed. It was bad enough to pay for service, but I was just too busy to be without my car this week!

I tried the key again and it started right up. Relieved, I drove off. I'd worry about it next time.

The store Thelma had rented was narrow and long, as most of the places were in downtowns all across America. I assumed that was because in a town's heyday they wanted to cram as many storefronts into a block as possible. Many of the buildings shared a wall with their neighbor, and I guessed that was because they had put the building where an alley or empty lot used to be. This particular store had nice hardwood floors and a wonderful old metal ceiling complete with whirls and embellishments. Thelma was already arguing with the landlord when I arrived.

"I can't run a clothing store in the dark!"

"You'll have to think of something else! Those are the original light fixtures, and they stay where they are."

"I'm not asking to get rid of them forever! The electrician says he can remove them without damage and put modern lights in without changing anything else. You can put the originals in storage until I move out. I'll even pay to have them put back in!"

"I can't do it. The whole downtown is under scrutiny to be registered as historic; the lights stay where they are."

"Um, excuse me," I interrupted. "Why not mount some track lights on the walls? They don't look so special."

Thelma and the landlord glared at me for a moment and then both of them shifted their eyes to the walls and up to where they met the high ceiling.

"That's not a bad idea."

"I could live with that," the landlord nodded. "Of course, these are good plaster walls, not the wallboard you find in modern buildings. But a good contractor can hang stuff without wrecking them."

"I've got a good contractor."

The landlord nodded. "I know; Willy McCarthy is the best around. Okay, go ahead with that if you want."

"Thank you, Mr. Gentry." Thelma held out a hand, and the landlord shook it and grinned. "Make it Lou. I have a feeling we're going to be getting to know each other pretty good."

"Well, we'll get to know each other sure enough, but whether it's good..." Thelma shrugged and laughed. Lou Gentry laughed with her, nodded to me and left.

I mostly stood around all morning while Thelma dealt with contractors. It was kind of fun listening to her. She knew what she wanted, and she didn't take no for an answer.

Willy McCarthy came and went, picking up supplies for the new track lighting. Thelma didn't want to wait for special orders; she sent him to Lowes with a wad of cash and told him what to get. In the meantime Willy's men were carefully digging at the walls, getting to the electric lines, while a tech from the phone company installed a new three line phone.

"How many calls do you expect to get about used clothing?" I asked Thelma curiously.

"I expect plenty. I'm telling you Rainie, this is going to be one hell of a store. We'll have people from all over shopping here."

Hm, for used clothes? I didn't see it, but hey, I wasn't much of a fashion maven myself.

It was nearly one 'o clock before Willy finally called his crew off to break for lunch.

"Hey, I don't have a lot of time here," Thelma protested. "We want to be open by the first of next week!"

"Yeah, I know, but there *are* labor laws, you know. My guys need a lunch break."

Thelma threw up her hands. "Fine. Just make sure it's no more than a half hour."

"Sorry, they get an hour. You're lucky they agreed to skip the morning break. Quit worrying so much. We'll get it done in plenty of time."

"I need to eat, too," I told Thelma. "Let's go down to the Tavern and grab some lunch." The Tavern was actually Ye Olde Tavern, but only out-of-towners called it that. It did a decent tourist trade in the summer when people were heading out to Lake Michigan, but in the off season it was just a cozy spot to grab lunch during the day. I'd never been there at night, but I'd heard it could really get rocking with the occasional local band performing or maybe some karaoke.

"All right," she agreed reluctantly. "Let me get my purse." She headed for the back room.

"We'll be back at two sharp," Willy promised as he left.

Just as we opened the front door to leave there was a loud backfire from down the street, and we jumped. Two more followed. Thelma looked at me, her eyes wide.

"I think those were gunshots!"

"What? They couldn't be. Someone just needs a tune up." But I wasn't so sure; the reports had sounded sharper than a backfire, crisper somehow.

Thelma was already out the door. "Thelma, wait, if that was a gun..."

"Then I want to see what's going on!" She shook my hand off her arm and stepped farther out onto the sidewalk. I stayed a little closer to the door, ready to grab her and pull her back into the building if necessary. Yeah, like I could move faster than a speeding bullet!

"Hey, what's with that guy?" Thelma pointed up the street. A bearded man wearing a hooded sweatshirt had come out of The Tavern, running at top speed right toward us. He was stuffing something in his pocket while he ran.

"Thelma, get back in here, we need to call the cops..."

"Hey, is that Missy?"

Sure enough, I saw Missy, the bartender, emerge from the bar. She took two wobbling steps and collapsed on the sidewalk. Even from this distance I could see the blood covering the front of her blouse.

My knees went weak, and I saw those familiar little sparkles at the edge of my vision; I took a deep breath. This was no time to pass out.

"Thelma, please..." I plucked at her blouse, but to no avail. She'd moved to the middle of the sidewalk, looking like a linebacker setting up to meet the runner. Except of course, Thelma only weighed about 100 pounds and her shoulder pads were merely outdated fashion accessories, not protection.

I stepped over, planning to grab her and pull her out of harm's way, but by then the bearded man had reached us.

He swerved to go around Thelma, and she stuck out one small sneakered foot and tripped him.

He went flying face first with a startled cry. Thelma lost her own balance and instinctively grabbed the first thing her hand came in contact with, which was the pocket of his sweatshirt. At the same time I grabbed her and pulled her back toward the store.

The pocket gave way and a gun slammed to the pavement. It went off with a deafening roar and chips of concrete sprayed out from the building's façade. Thelma and I fell backward, but fortunately for her she landed on me, breaking her fall.

I was vaguely aware of sirens approaching. Oh happy day, the cavalry was arriving!

The bearded man pushed himself to his feet and turned glaring, murder-filled eyes on us. The rest of his face was obscured by the blood gushing out of his nose.

"You bitch!" He took a step toward us, focusing on Thelma, who was still struggling to get off me. The guy cast his gaze around, searching for his gun. I shoved Thelma off of me and scrambled toward the weapon on my hands and knees.

He saw where I was heading and easily got there first. He snatched up the gun and pointed it at me from two feet away.

I stared at the barrel of the gun, the black hole from which death would come, and realized it was the last thing I was ever going to see. I was afraid I was about to wet my pants, and my heart was pounding so hard I could hardly breathe.

He fired.

There was a click, but nothing else.

He snarled and looked at the gun with disgust and I realized it had jammed, maybe damaged when it fell. He was doing something to it, and he looked pretty competent; I didn't think I would be so lucky that it would jam a second time. I started scrambling away from him, but then Thelma was there, swinging her oversized purse.

"Thelma, no!"

But of course she wasn't listening to me. The woman had the balls of a Brahma bull and the sense of a milkweed plant. She hit the guy in the hands and the gun went flying again.

"God damn you!" He took a backhand swing at Thelma and connected with her face. She went down and the guy went after his gun.

A police car pulled in down the street, its siren whooping. A block in the other direction another siren started up; the police station was there, so I assumed it had taken this long for someone to run to their car. It seemed like it was taking them forever, but later I would realize that their response time had been phenomenal.

The guy picked up his gun, flashed one heated look back at us and took off running.

I started jumping up and down, pointing frantically at the man's retreating back. He raced through a narrow opening between two buildings; there was a path there leading to a scenic walk along McCoy Creek. The second police car screeched to a halt in the middle of the road and the cop jumped out, glanced once at me and then took off after the gun man.

I turned to Thelma, who was sitting up, cradling her left arm.

"Are you all right?"

"Yeah, just help me up."

I got behind her and squatted down. I put my arms around her waist; I didn't want to grab anywhere near the arm she was holding so gingerly. She might be stoic enough not to be crying out, but I recognized the effort that was costing her; I was sure the arm was broken.

I lifted and she got her feet under herself, as always more spry than I thought it possible for a 75 year old to be.

111

I had recently watched a news story about a 113 year old woman participating in a ping pong tournament. I thought they might be doing a similar story on Thelma in another thirty years.

"I think we should call an ambulance."

"I think the ambulance is going to be busy." Thelma turned to look back toward the Tavern, where a crowd of people had gathered around Missy. The cop was kneeling next to her, apparently applying pressure to a wound. At least that meant she wasn't dead.

I thought of the gun barrel again, and how certain I'd been that I was about to die, and I swallowed, hard.

"Hey, what the hell happened?"

I jumped, but of course it was only Jack, who'd managed to sneak up on me again.

"What the hell are you doing here?" I don't think I was as mad at him as my tone implied, but I was scared and shaking and wasn't in the mood for any of his shenanigans.

"I was on my way to see you and saw all the cops." He looked at Thelma. A bruise was forming on one eye, and her arm was already swelling and turning color.

"Hey lady, your arm is broken."

She grinned at him. "Thanks for the diagnosis, doc. Geez, you're good looking *and* smart. Wanna get married?"

Jack laughed. "Are you kidding? I know your type. You'd use me and abuse me and toss me aside like a used tissue!"

"What the hell is the matter with you two?" I was shaking with fury, or maybe adrenalin, or maybe terror...whatever, I couldn't believe these two were carrying on this silly flirtation at a time like this. "There's a woman *dying* over there, and by the way, I almost died, too!"

"Hey, I'm sorry," Jack put an arm around me, and Thelma patted me with her good hand.

"So am I sweetie, I didn't realize how upset you were..."

"Up...set!" I choked out the word. "You...and that guy...the gun..."

That was when we heard more gun shots, their sound muffled by the buildings.

"The cop..."

"Damn, I hope that was his gun."

An ambulance wailed to a stop in front of the Tavern.

"There's nothing else we can do here," Jack looked at Thelma. "Come on, I'll drive you to the hospital."

"They might want me as a witness!"

"They can find you at the ER. You can't ignore that arm. And don't tell me it doesn't hurt."

"Well, to tell you the truth..." Thelma's eyes rolled up in her head and she fainted.

Lucky for Thelma my reflexes were finely honed when it came to people falling in my vicinity; I was after all, a caregiver. I caught her before she hit the pavement again and broke something else. We called a second ambulance, which arrived on the heels of the first. Shootings were rare in Buchanan, so they'd sent everyone. Even a fire truck showed up at one point, although I'm not sure why.

While Thelma was getting patched up in the ER I called the cops to report our involvement, since we had, after all, eye-witnessed the guy up close and personal. A Buchanan cop was there to interview us while they were fixing Thelma's cast.

"Let me get this straight," the patrolman frowned over his notepad. He pointed his pen at Thelma, who was looking rather frail at the moment, pale and woozy from pain and the drugs they'd given her to ease it. "You tackled the guy."

"No, I tripped him," Thelma answered impatiently. "Weren't you listening? I tripped him, and accidently grabbed his jacket, and then I don't know for sure what happened but I fell on Rainie and his gun went off."

"Uh huh. And then you," he pointed at me, "wrestled with the guy for the gun..."

See, this is how stories get distorted and falsified. The little details get twisted in the telling, even if the guy listening is supposedly trained to get details right.

"I didn't wrestle with him, we both went after it at the same time. He got it first."

"So you hit him with your purse before he could shoot her." He pointed at Thelma.

"Not really." I gulped at the fresh memory. "The gun misfired the first time."

The cop looked at me, and a fresh sympathy showed in his eyes. For some reason that sympathy did what none of the rest of the insane incidents had done: it made me want to cry. No way was I going to cry in front of Thelma, Senior Wonder Woman.

"You can thank god for miracles, lady," the cop told me. "That gun didn't misfire when he shot Dick Nemith."

"What? Who's that?"

"Officer Nemith, the cop that chased after him. He was shot; they're airlifting him to Memorial Hospital down in South Bend."

"I'm sorry to hear that." And I was. I might not be a big fan of the Buchanan cops, but I'd seen Nemith take off after that armed suspect with no hesitation. He deserved some respect for that.

"If there's nothing else for you to report, I'm going to head down to Memorial myself."

"I think we covered everything."

"Okay. Someone else will probably be in touch. We'll want you both to talk to a sketch artist."

"Wait," I stopped him before he could leave. "What about the shooter? Did Nemith get him?"

He shook his head, slowly. "No. The bastard got away."

"Do you think Thelma and I are in any danger? I mean, we got a really good look at the guy."

"Naw, I doubt it. He's probably long gone and still running."

The cop left, confident in our safety. I only wished I felt the same.

Jack hung around the ER, waiting to give us a ride home. He alternated between being solicitous and raunchy with Thelma. I wished I could have such a casual relationship with him.

On the way back to the store I thought to ask him why he'd been looking for me.

"I had a little job I wanted you to help with, but I think you've had enough fun for one day. I'll ask Rachel to help me tomorrow."

"Oh." I was disappointed - okay, maybe even a little jealous. I had a feeling that once he'd worked with Rachel a few times he wouldn't be calling me anymore. I mean, she was trained and competent and beautiful, just like him. I swallowed against a sigh and put a happy grin on my face.

We got the whole story by the end of the day, or at least the rumor mill's version of it. Right after the lunch hour, when the place was nearly empty but the cash registers full, Ye Olde Tavern had been robbed at gunpoint. Missy had given up the money, but the robber had shot her on the way out. She had staggered to the street, although no one knew why; shock I suppose. In the meantime the cook had called 911 from the relative safety of the walk in cooler, hiding behind the heavy steel door until it was all over.

Officer Nemith had almost caught up to the guy, who stopped running and started shooting. Dick dove behind a dumpster, but not before the guy hit him with a round right in the center of his chest. By the time backup had arrived the guy was gone, probably into the woods that bordered the trail to the east of town.

A manhunt was launched, assisted by the county police who arrived on scene within fifteen minutes, but there was no sign of the robber.

Both Missy Taylor and Dick Nemith were rushed to the trauma unit in Memorial Hospital, all the way down in South Bend. Their wounds were serious enough that no one thought the closer but much smaller hospital, Lakeside in Niles, could handle them. First reports were that they would probably both survive.

By 4:00 I'd had enough of rehashing the news. The contractors were working slowly around retellings of the story, and Thelma wasn't arguing about their reduced pace; she was just as bad as they were, speculating, sometimes wildly, about the origin of the robber. I didn't know how she was staying on her feet; they'd filled her with happy juice at the hospital before sending her on her way with a script for Vicoden. Elderly people were often quite sensitive to such meds and had to be careful about taking them, but I had a feeling Thelma had developed quite a tolerance for such things in her past. Probably while following the Grateful Dead across country in a psychedelic microbus.

"That's enough excitement for me," I told her. "I have to meet Eddie at 4:30."

"I still don't know why you're letting Eddie work with you. I mean, he's like a brother or something. If I were you I'd much rather be buttin' up to Jack!"

I felt my face flush, but I smiled at her candor. "I need to learn how to defend myself. I don't need to be distracted."

"I don't know, a man like Jack could distract me any day!" Thelma laughed and slapped me on the shoulder. "You could use a little distracting! You've been wound up tighter than an e string ever since you broke up with Brad, and you can't hardly call that Dan a boyfriend, seeing as how he's never here."

"I've got plenty of distractions, Thelma. The truth is, I don't have time for a man right now. In fact, I've got to run; Eddie hates it when people are late. Do you need a ride home?"

"Nope, Brenda's coming by at 5:00, she'll take me when we're done."

"Just don't overdo." I don't even know why I said that; Thelma always over did everything. Maybe that was her secret to longevity.

"I'll see you Thursday."

I drove to the B&E offices and went straight to the basement gym.

Eddie was already there, dressed in gray sweats and a T-shirt, pounding on a heavy bag. I watched him for a few minutes, intrigued.

Eddie was usually so reserved, but he was punching that bag like he meant it. He hit it high and low, left, right, left, left, a rapid flurry of blows that seemed to be propelled by a deep-rooted fury. He caught a glimpse of me and abruptly stepped back and let his hands fall to his sides.

"Five thirty already?" His expression was bland, but his eyes still held a hint of rage.

"Yep. You still have time for me?"

"Sure, go get changed, I'll get my gloves off."

I went into the locker room and changed into sweatpants and T-shirt, then met Eddie in the side room where we trained. It was a 20x20 room, the floor covered in padding and the walls padded about four feet up. That sort of thing came in handy when people were throwing each other around. So far Eddie hadn't thrown me much; I think he was afraid of hurting me.

"I thought we'd work on taking someone down today."

"Taking them down? I thought I was just going to learn how to defend myself."

117

"What's the first rule of defending yourself against someone bigger than you?"

"Run like hell."

"Right." Eddie grinned. He had laid out his first three rules our first session: One: Run like hell. Two: If you can't run then it's balls, eyes, knees, in that order. Three: After balls, eyes, knees, refer to rule one.

"So in some cases it might make it easier to run if you slow the guy down, first."

"I assume a kick in the balls will do that."

"Most likely," he smiled. "That isn't always your best choice, though. If you're confronting the guy head on and he's ready for you he might grab your foot, and then it's you that's down. We're going to work on a few moves that won't make you so vulnerable."

"All right, let's have at it."

Chapter Ten

Wednesday morning the Escort didn't want to start again. It groaned once, twice, three times, then reluctantly started on the fourth attempt. I sighed and pulled out of my driveway. I was going to have to take it in to be fixed.

When I arrived at Bob's he was still in bed. Daryl was in the kitchen drinking coffee, looking harassed and tired. Apparently he hadn't seen the news, or at least wasn't aware of my involvement in yesterday's excitement, because he didn't mention it. Kind of a relief, really. My phone had rung all evening with family and friends and even a few annoying acquaintances calling for details. I had finally shut off both my home and cell phone and went to bed.

"Dad won't get up, Rainie. Says there's no reason to."

"Did you get the reports back from the doctor?"

"I'm afraid so. Everything looked pretty normal, except some spots showed up on the CAT scan. They might be blockages, maybe signs of a minor stroke or two."

"Might be? Maybe?"

"The doc just says the brain is a complex organ, and they don't know everything they need to know. But given the circumstances, what with Dad's paranoia and his night time rambles, they assume it's dementia. Dad's going to have to go into a home."

"Oh god, poor Bob! No wonder he won't get out of bed!" I could hardly believe it. Bob seemed so with it during the day. Then again, I was familiar enough with the inconsistencies of dementia to know that the best expectation of behavior was no expectation at all.

"I'm trying to get him into Brentwood, but there's a list, so it could be a couple of weeks. In the meantime I'm going to stay at night."

"I'm sorry, Daryl. I know this is hard."

"Yeah, on everyone. I was wondering if maybe you could cover Friday night for me? It's my wedding anniversary, and I'd like to take my wife out to dinner."

I hesitated only a moment; I had planned to have dinner with my mom, but she'd understand. "Sure, I can do that."

"I can relieve you around midnight."

"I can stay all night if you want. I mean, you haven't been home with Maryanne for a week now."

"Hey, that would be great!" Daryl looked immensely relieved. "I didn't want to ask. I mean, it's okay to sleep, but it's best to be on the couch, just in case he heads for the front door."

"Has he been up since you've been staying here?"

"No, not once." Daryl shrugged. "Maybe there's something about having someone in the house that comforts him and he sleeps better."

I doubted that. Having someone in the house mostly just pissed Bob off, but I wasn't going to argue.

"In the meantime I have a lady coming from an agency when you leave. I know he's been okay during the day, but he's so damned depressed I'm afraid to leave him alone. She was here all day yesterday."

"You don't really think he'd hurt himself?"

Daryl gave me a tired smile. "More likely he'd pack his clothes and run away."

I smiled back, remembering the image of Bob and me on the run from the hospital. "You're probably right. Well, have fun on Friday. Try to take it easy."

"That's kind of tough when I feel like I'm about to send my Dad to prison." Daryl rinsed out his coffee cup. "Hey, since you're staying all night Friday, I'll have the lady from the agency come Friday morning. She'll stay until about 5, so if you can get here by then…"

"Sure. I'll be here."

"Call me if there are any problems."

I said I would, but I didn't think there would be. I had a feeling Bob was going to be laying low for the next couple of days.

After Daryl left I went in to check on Bob. He was lying on his bed, staring at the ceiling.

"Good morning."

He grunted in reply but wouldn't look at me.

"Bob, I'm really sorry about all this. It's a tough break."

"Yeah, it's going to take a chunk out of your paycheck, isn't it?"

I blinked, stunned by the sheer viciousness in his tone.

"Do you really think I'm only sorry about the loss of income?"

"Maybe not even that. I'm sure you'll find some other old man to take care of as soon as I'm out of here. Get lost, Miss Lovingston. If I want to pay for sympathy I'll hire a whore."

Stung, I backed out of the room. Truth is, Bob wasn't the first client to talk to me that way. Many very sweet natured people could turn mean when dementia set in, and I had taken care of my share. But Bob seemed to be perfectly coherent right now, and that made his words hurt a lot more.

I set about cleaning the house, needing to stay busy. I stopped at his door to check on him a couple of times and found him reading, but I didn't disturb him again until 11:30, when I offered him lunch. He refused to leave his room so I brought him a grilled cheese sandwich, a salad and a baked apple and left the plate on his bedside table.

At noon a woman from the Caring Hands agency showed up and introduced herself as Myrna Green.

"I'm afraid Bob isn't in the best of moods," I warned her.

"Is he ever?" She rolled her eyes. "He just sat in his room all day yesterday, hardly said a word."

"Yeah, well he's under a lot of stress." I wanted to defend Bob. This woman, who hardly knew him, was obviously mistaking him for a grouchy old curmudgeon.

"Aren't we all?" She shrugged, and I wanted to smack her. Where was her compassion? Didn't she even care why Bob was so unhappy?

I took a deep breath to calm myself. This was the problem with hiring through some of the agencies: you got minimum wage workers who would be better suited to slinging burgers than tending to live human beings. One of these days I should open an agency of my own where I could pay a fair wage and hire quality caregivers.

But right now all Daryl needed was someone to watch so Bob didn't take off. I thought even Myrna could handle that.

She assured me she knew where the emergency numbers were and promised to encourage Bob to eat his lunch.

I left with some reluctance, glad that Bob could mostly watch out for himself.

Once again the Escort required numerous cranks to start it, so I buzzed over to Alf's Garage. Alf had a rep for being able to fix anything, although I knew from experience he didn't always fix things according to spec. He had a way of rigging cheap repairs that got a car back on the road for a while with the promise that you'd have to come back. The thing was, he never did those temporary repairs without asking; he did them because a lot of his customers lived paycheck to paycheck, and they often just needed to get to work.

He wandered out of the back of the garage when I pulled up, wiping his hands on a filthy rag. I turned off the

Escort and started it for him again. It cranked on the second try.

"Need a new starter." He diagnosed. "I can do it Friday afternoon."

"Friday afternoon? Can't you get it in any sooner?"

"Nope, sorry." He waved a hand back at the garage. All three bays were filled, and I could see several more cars parked out back. "Been a busy week."

I sighed. "All right. I'll drop it off Friday morning."

"Good enough." Alf went back to his garage and I pulled away. I could ask my mother to give me a ride to Bob's on Friday and pick me up Saturday morning.

I grabbed a salad at McDonald's and headed into the B&E offices to run a few computer checks before my first "offensive" driving lesson. It seemed like every minute of my life was scheduled lately; had I really been thinking a few weeks ago that I was bored?

I was surprised by a call from Dan.

"Hey sweetheart, you missing me yet?" He had a great voice, low and a little gravelly, as if he'd just woken up.

"To tell the truth I've been too busy to miss anyone!" I laughed to take the sting out, but the thing was it was way too early in the relationship for him to be expecting me to miss him. Maybe Brad had been right, maybe I did have commitment issues. I know I have a lot of trouble giving up control in any situation, and since my failed marriage I guess that includes dating.

"I hope you're not so busy you'll miss Mason's party Saturday night."

"I'm planning to be there."

"Great! So am I."

"But I thought that Detroit gig went for three weeks?"

"Would have, but Gus came down with some wicked virus, and now Dave's got it. Can't have much of a blues band with no drummer and no bass player."

"So what if you're next?"

"Aw, not me Rainbow. I've got the constitution of a plow horse, haven't been sick in years. So I'll see you Saturday night?"

"Sure. Are you bringing your guitar?"

"Nope, just my own big cuddly self. Can't wait to see you."

"See you then."

I clicked off, pleased for the first time that day. Dan was just a likeable, happy kind of guy, another irony for a blues player, but he almost always managed to make me smile.

Suddenly I was looking forward to Saturday.

The driving lesson was immense fun. B&E owned a piece of property north of Niles that housed a second shooting range, a couple of buildings for classrooms, and a huge open field for people who wanted to drive like a crazy person.

Okay, it wasn't just an open field. There was a network of paved roads on it, and toward the back there was a long stretch lined with building facades and old wrecked cars parked on either side to simulate in-town driving. My instructor was Sam Mallard, an aging ex-Marine with a buzz cut and a slight paunch that testified to a few years behind a desk. I asked him if the wrecked cars were leftover from people who had failed the course, and he smiled.

"Nope. Those are left over from the people who passed."

I laughed, but later, after running through some beginning drills, I began to think he hadn't been kidding. I was glad they were providing the car; I think my little Escort would have shaken apart after the first ten minutes.

"By the time you graduate this course you'll know how to use this vehicle like the two thousand pound weapon it is," Sam assured me in a tone fit for a drill sergeant. "You'll quit worrying about things like insurance rates and traffic laws and remember that when you're driving for your life nothing matters but survival."

"Wow, I just thought I was going to learn how to shake a tail or evade capture."

"You'll learn that, too, don't you worry. Although from what I hear you've already got some of those tactics down. Going the wrong way on one-way streets, crashing through food drives..." Sam was smiling broadly.

"Oh, so you've heard."

"Girl, everyone at B&E has heard, all the way to the Chicago offices."

"What? That's ridiculous!"

"Are you kidding me? An untrained PI's assistant, a *caregiver* no less, hauls Jack Jones around in the back of his own damned truck through the city streets, gets caught on camera but doesn't actually get caught? Hell, you're practically a legend. What I can't figure is how you got to driving in the first place; Jack doesn't let many people behind the wheel of his favorite toy."

"It was sort of a necessity at the time."

"I'm sure it was. Besides, rumor has it Jack has a thing for you. Anything you want to confirm for the B&E rumor mill?"

"Why do people keep saying that? I'm not Jack's type. Besides, you're a Marine! Aren't you trained not to gossip?"

"Only about state secrets, sugar. Jack's private business is free game."

I laughed. "Anyway, there's nothing to confirm. I think Jack just thinks it's funny to get me into situations that are way over my head."

"Maybe so, but you swim pretty good! All right, enough gossip." He pointed up the wide asphalt road. "Hit the gas, girl, make this thing fly!"

After my lesson I drove down to Jim Bolin's old house to talk to his neighbors. It was hard to drive at a normal pace after two hours of speeding around corners and dodging oncoming automobiles. I kept wanting to "Juke left! Downshift! Brake!"

I managed to get to South Bend without a speeding ticket and parked in front of Jim's - no, make that Big John Gosa's - house. I started with the place immediately to the left.

A middle-aged woman with gray-streaked brown hair and tired eyes answered the door with the chain still in place.

"What do you want?" She asked the question as if she suspected I might be a process server, or worse, a Jehovah's Witness.

"Hello, my name is Rainie Lovingston and I work for B&E Security..."

"I don't need an alarm system." She started to shut the door so I spoke up quickly.

"I'm not selling anything! I just want to ask a question."

She stopped with the door barely open and glared at me. "What?"

"I'm looking for your neighbor, Jim Bolin."

"Haven't seen him. Don't know him."

"But he's been living next door for the last decade..."

"But he lives over *there*, and I live over *here*. You see the difference?"

With that smart comment she slammed the door in my face.

I knocked on the next door and found an older lady who was happy to talk about him. She introduced herself as Mrs. Bailey and invited me in. "Come on into the kitchen. You want some lemonade, or maybe a beer?"

"I have to drive home, but lemonade would be great."

Her kitchen was cheerful and homey. The refrigerator was covered with crayoned pictures of vaguely human figures and houses, and several snapshots of little kids. I assumed they were her grandkids, and the art work was from them, little gifts for grandma.

Mrs. Bailey poured two glasses of lemonade with lots of ice and set one in front of me. She sat on the other side of the table and gave me a bright smile.

"So, you're looking for Jimmy. You think something bad happened to him?"

"Bad? Like what?"

"I don't know, foul play of some kind. I mean, you are a detective, right? Why else would a detective be looking for him?"

"Um, well, actually I'm from a private detective agency, not affiliated with the police, and um…well, I'm just an assistant."

"An assistant?" Mrs. Bailey smiled. "Is that like an assistant manager in retail? You do all the work and someone else gets all the money and credit?"

I smiled back. "Something like that."

"Yeah, my Hank was in retail management for most of our marriage. I put up with his long hours and crappy pay while he worked his way up, and then when he finally got the store manager position with decent hours and benefits he up and left me for his new assistant manager!"

I winced. That had to hurt.

"Wow, I'm sorry to hear that."

"Oh, don't be. Turns out the only reason we stayed married so long was because he was always working. Once he started spending more time at home I figured out I didn't much like him, anyway." She laughed. "Funny how life can be sometimes. Anyway, Jimmy was such a nice man. I hope nothing terrible has happened to him."

"I don't think so. It's just that he's gone missing. He sold his house and took off, not even a word to his kids. We're trying to find him."

"Sold his house?" Mrs. Bailey looked off across the back yards, toward Bolin's old house. "And didn't say good bye to his kids? Then I'm sorry to tell you Miss Lovingston, but something bad has definitely happened to him. He loved that house, spent every moment he could spare working on something or other, and he spent every other minute with his kids. He wouldn't just up and go."

"But it seems that's what he did. Are you sure he never said or did anything that might have hinted he was planning to move?"

"Not that I recall, but we weren't best friends or anything. We would talk when we passed in the street, sit on each other's porches now and then on a nice summer evening." Mrs. Bailey's eyes suddenly narrowed. "But you know, he did have a new girlfriend."

"You didn't like her?"

Mrs. Bailey waved a hand to dismiss that thought. "I didn't really know her. Seemed like whenever I stopped to chat she wandered inside. Not exactly a snub, you understand, more like she just wasn't interested, you know?"

"Do you think Jim might have taken off with this girlfriend?"

"Why would he?" Mrs. Bailey frowned. "I mean, he had his house and all...unless maybe the girl was really rich or something. Or maybe she got him involved in something, maybe a crime ring?" Mrs. Bailey was really getting into the speculation now. "Maybe they killed someone!" Her eyes were wide and she actually looked a little worried. I smiled and shook my head.

"I doubt that, Mrs. Bailey. Maybe they just relocated to be closer to her family."

"Oh, maybe," Mrs. Bailey shrugged. "Anyway, I didn't know him all that well. Maybe you should talk to Angela Perez. She was *real* friendly with Jim."

Finally, I was getting somewhere!

"Where does Angela live?"

"Right over there, across the alley from Jim." Mrs. Bailey pointed out the kitchen window at the back of another house. "They talked across the back fence, and had a few dinners together when Juan was out of town."

"Juan?"

"Angela's husband. He's a salesman of some kind, travels a lot, maybe one week out of the month." Mrs. Bailey's smile was sly. "Angela's a young woman, and I suppose she gets lonely. And Jimmy was a real charmer."

"Huh." I considered that. "Is Mr. Perez the jealous type?"

Mrs. Bailey blinked, and then laughed. "Oh, you mean maybe he offed Jimmy for sleeping with Angela? I don't think so. Juan is the pocket protector type, you know? I can't see him getting physical about that sort of thing." She smiled again, a little meanly, I thought. "Maybe that's why Angela was looking over the back fence, you know?"

I nodded, but really, I didn't know. I mean, if you married a pocket protector kind of guy you knew what you were getting, right? Didn't seem fair to turn around and cheat on him just because he turned out to be what he'd been all along, did it?

"I appreciate your help, Mrs. Bailey." Although I wasn't sure how much of what she'd given me was information and how much was mean-spirited gossip. "I'll try talking to Mrs. Perez."

"Oh, you won't catch her at home right now, she works nights."

"Okay, I'll come back another time. Thanks again, Mrs. Bailey." I stood up, suddenly eager to be away from her. At first she'd seemed so genuinely friendly, but I was beginning to see that was just a façade to cover up her real motive: digging up and sharing dirt on her neighbors. I guess gossip wasn't a hobby confined to little towns like Buchanan.

It was getting late so I decided to pack it in. I was busy tomorrow and wouldn't have my car on Friday, so I figured

I'd come down to talk to Angela Perez on Saturday. I hoped Jim Bolin wasn't in any real trouble, because finding him seemed to be taking awhile.

Chapter Eleven

It was 10:00 and I was thinking I'd better get to bed when my cell phone rang. Uh oh; my brother.

"Jason?" I picked up right away, suspecting trouble. I was right.

"Rainie, can you come pick us up?" His words were a little slurred, a sure sign he'd been drinking, but he didn't sound as bad off as he usually was when he called me for help.

"Us?"

"Yeah, me and my buddy, Terry. Can you come kind of quick?"

"Are you in trouble?"

"Uh...no, not yet...I mean...really, could you just come get us?"

I sighed. No sense digging for information. He was my brother and I would probably go no matter what the situation was.

"All right, where are you?"

"We're in the alley behind the old library."

"The alley?"

"I'll explain when you get here..." I heard someone in the background, and my brother said, "She's coming, just hang on." Then he put the phone back to his mouth. "How quick can you get here?"

"Ten minutes."

"Oh, okay. Hurry, okay?"

Crap. I probably wasn't going to like this.

On the way over I heard sirens, and for a moment it felt like my heart was in my throat. Sirens were not a common sound in a little town like Buchanan, and I was sure it was no coincidence. Just what kind of trouble was my brother in?

The wail of the siren went off to the south and I breathed a sigh of relief. They weren't heading toward the old library.

I pulled into the alley and drove down it slowly, looking for my brother. He abruptly appeared from behind a dumpster, a little wiry guy in tow. When they crossed in front of my headlights I saw that the little guy's nose was bleeding.

"Come on, get in!" Jason urged his friend into the back seat and hurriedly jumped into the front. "Let's go!"

His urgency was contagious, so I took off, wondering what - or more likely, who - we were running from.

I hit the main road and turned toward Jason's apartment.

"All right, now tell me what the hell is going on."

"We had a little altercation. Well, actually Terry did." Jason pointed over his shoulder at the guy in back. "By the way, Rainie, this is my good buddy, Terry. Terry, my sister Rainie."

"Pleased to meetcha," Terry said in an oddly formal tone. Someone had taught him manners at some point in his life, even if they were a little rough around the edges.

"Yeah, same here I guess. So tell me about this altercation. Are there going to be people with guns?"

"Naw, no guns. That pussy wouldn't know which end of a gun to point at me, probably blow his own foot off."

"And what pussy would that be?" I asked calmly.

Terry snorted a little laugh. "Hey, your sister's all right."

"Told ya."

"Right, I'm wonderful. Are you going to tell me what's going on or not?"

"It could be a few guys are looking for us. You know, to kind of beat us up."

"Kind of? Is that like being kind of pregnant?"

"Who's pregnant?"

"Never mind." Never try to be clever with a couple of drunks. It just makes an already difficult conversation take that much longer. "Just tell me why the guys want to beat you up."

"Oh, not me," Jason corrected. "I didn't do nothin'. You know me, sis, I'm a lover, not a fighter."

I rolled my eyes. Yeah, a lover who hadn't had a steady girlfriend in five or six years. It was true that he wasn't much of a fighter, though. It seemed the more he drank the mellower he got.

"Yeah, they're really just lookin' for me, but if they catch us they'll beat up Jason just 'cause he's with me."

"So why are they trying to beat *you* up?" I prodded.

"'Cause I beat the hell out of Toad."

As if to emphasize his statement I heard the sirens start up again, a couple of blocks south.

"Sounds like they loaded him up." My brother said to Terry.

"Yeah, he must be in a world of hurt!" Terry laughed, more like a nervous giggle. "I think maybe I tore him up!"

"That's it!" I pulled over to the side of the road and shut the car off. I twisted in my seat so I could glare back at Terry. "I don't think beating someone up is funny at all, and if that's what you're all about I think you should get out and take your own chances."

"Wait, sis! This whole thing wasn't Terry's fault. We were just havin' a coupla beers, mindin' our own business."

"Yeah, and then I was talkin' to my girl's brother and BAM!" Terry emphasized the word with a fist in his palm, making me jump. "Old Toad came up behind me and sucker punched me in the ear!"

"Why?"

"'Cause he thinks I owe him money, but I don't!" Now Terry started talking faster. "See, about a month ago he loaned me a hundred bucks to get my car out of impound, and as soon as I got paid I went down to the bar to pay him back. But he was really drunk, and I guess I shoulda waited, but you know money always seems to burn a hole right through my pocket and I was afraid I'd spend it myself so I gave it to him only he was so drunk he musta spent it all at the bar and don't remember me givin' it back so he keeps tryin to collect, but I don't owe it, you see?"

I blinked, letting his rapid words sink in. I'm not quite sure how he got all that out in one sentence; I never heard him take a breath.

"Weren't there any witnesses? Didn't anyone else see you pay him back?"

"Hell, I don't know! The bar was crowded and everyone was drunk."

"So he sucker punched you, and you beat him up."

"Well, not right away." Terry was grinning, and he went back into his rapid fire explanation. "He's been asking for it for a month. He came to my job twice this last month, first with a 2x4, but my boss run him off. Then he comes back with two other guys, and the whole crew chased him away.

"So tonight I was leanin' in the car, talkin' to Crystal's brother - Crystal, that's my girlfriend - and along comes Toad and BAM!" He slammed his palm into his fist again and I found myself trying not to smile. There was something very animated and likable about Terry, although it was hard at this moment to define it. "So I turned to him and I held up my finger, like this," Terry demonstrated, holding up his forefinger. "So I says, 'all right Toad, that's one. That's all you get. Now wait while I finish talking to this guy and then I'll talk to you.' So I turn

134

back to Crystal's brother and BAM!" again, the fist in the palm, "He hits me again! Well, that was it. I mean, one sucker punch I might overlook, but two? Uh uh. So I jumped on him and took him down."

"Just how bad did you take him down?" I asked, remembering the sirens.

Terry grinned. "Well, his old lady called a few minutes ago and asked who all gave him the beat down. When I told him it was just me, she didn't believe it. She said he's messed up!"

"And you think this is funny?" Likeable or not, I didn't care much for people who enjoyed hurting other people.

"Only because Toad is about twice his size," Jason spoke up. "Toad looks like what his name implies; he's big and round, but he works construction so he's no weakling. He goes a good 260 pounds, so he thought he could just scare Terry."

I was looking at Terry, who weighed maybe 140 pounds fully dressed and fully soaked. "You beat up a 260 pound guy?"

"Yeah. I'm slow to anger, but once my temper's up I'm fire!"

Now I was smiling; I couldn't help it. The picture in my head was just too funny, and it did sound like the big guy deserved what he got.

"So if Toad is on his way to the hospital, who are you hiding from?"

"His three big brothers!" Terry laughed and slapped his thigh. "Toad's old lady says they're on the warpath, looking for me."

"What are you going to do when they find you?"

"I figure I just won't let them find me 'til everyone sobers up. They know how Toad is, and besides, Crystal's brother will tell the whole story. They'll leave me alone then."

"Yeah, so we just need to get to my place and lie low until morning," Jason explained. "So can we get going?"

Reluctantly I turned around and started the car. "Are you sure about this Jason? I mean, are you sure the brothers won't show up at your place and cause trouble yet tonight?"

"They don't know where I live, and besides, I don't think they even knew I was with Terry. We'll be fine."

I didn't say anything more until I pulled up in front of Jason's place.

"Jason, this sort of thing has got to stop."

"Hey sis, I didn't do anything! I wasn't even drinking all that much." It was true, he was far from as drunk as he usually got. "It's not our fault; Toad started it."

"I know, but..."

"Yeah, I know." Jason rolled his eyes. "I should stay out of the bars in the first place." Jason and Terry both got out of the car. Terry leaned back in.

"Thanks for the rescue, Rainie. It was nice meetin' you. We'll have to grab a beer together some time."

"Sure." Not.

Jason leaned back in, too. "Thanks Rainie. And uh, by the way...don't mention this to Mom, okay?"

I shrugged. "You're a big boy now, Jason. I'm way past the age where I feel a need to tattle on you. Just be careful, okay?"

"No problem." He shut the door and headed up the walk, but I knew that wasn't true at all. Jason's life was one big problem.

Chapter Twelve

Thursday morning I headed downtown to the new storefront. Nearly every business in town had some sort of sign posted regarding the two shooting victims. I saw "WE LOVE YOU MISSY!" and "THANK YOU OFFICER NEMITH." That sort of stuff always irritated me: when someone was killed or wounded in some spectacular or tragic way, suddenly everyone knows and loves them. Doesn't matter if you wouldn't have even stopped to hold a door for them the day before; now that the spotlight is on them, you were their best friend, and of course you'd do anything to help.

I didn't post any signs or hang any ribbons on my car. I'd never met Dick Nemith, and I only knew Missy as the woman behind the bar when I stopped into the Tavern for lunch. I had no idea if she was a wonderful, warm-hearted person or a cold-hearted bitch, so although if asked I could honestly say I hoped she recovered, the truth was if she didn't I would only experience a passing sadness. Of course, if she died the funeral service would be packed with people sobbing out their grief, many of them who had probably only known her to wave in passing. I thought it was an insult to the ones who really loved her.

I couldn't believe the progress Thelma had made in just two days. The store was now brightly lit, one wall was lined with shelving, and empty clothing racks were staggered all the way to the back of the store. In spite of the black eye and broken arm she looked happier than I'd ever seen her. She greeted me with a big grin, standing

137

behind her new glass-topped counter, a gleaming new cash register the focal point. She waved expansively with her good arm.

"What do you think?"

"What can I say but 'wow!' Maybe you will be ready to open next week."

"No doubt about it. Brenda is supervising the loading of the truck right now, bringing all her stuff over from the house. She took a couple of days off work so we can get everything hung and priced."

"This is really amazing, Thelma. You're putting an awful lot of money into this; I hope it works out."

"It'll be great. Oh, and I have a guy coming out from B&E to install an alarm system today."

"An alarm? Do you think that's necessary?" I couldn't imagine anyone breaking in to steal a used skirt. Besides, downtown Buchanan wasn't known for its criminal element, in spite of the incident two days ago.

"Of course it's necessary! There'll be motion sensors for at night, and a panic button under the counter, in case we get robbed. I just push the button and it calls the cops for me!"

"I don't think that's likely to happen."

"I doubt if Missy thought so, either, but she's lying in a hospital bed right now with tubes in every orifice probably wishing she'd thought about it!" Thelma opened a drawer under the cash register.

"Of course, I won't necessarily have to wait for the cops. I also have this!" She held up a gun and I backed away.

"Whoa! What the hell! Is that thing loaded?"

"Sure! What's the point if it's not?" She went into a classic shooting stance right out of the movies and pointed the gun at the front window. "Some guy comes in here, demands my money, and 'blam!' he's dead!"

"Thelma, for god's sake, give me that!"

She held the gun out and I took it gingerly. I'd never seen anything quite like it: it was thin, with a long barrel, and obviously old. I could see flecks of rust here and there, and I wondered when it had last been cleaned.

"Where did you get this?"

"Oh, I've had it for years. My husband brought it home from the war as a souvenir, bullets and all. I've always kept it in the nightstand, but I think it'll do more good here."

"Any good cop will tell you it's better to just give up the cash than to confront an armed robber."

"Yeah? Tell that to Missy. She gave up the cash and the guy shot her anyway. Nope, this old lady plans to defend herself!"

I was still looking at the gun, applying my limited knowledge to determine just how dangerous it was. I couldn't find a safety on it, and that rust didn't bode well for its inner workings; I had a feeling if push came to shove and she fired it, it was likely to either jam or blow up in her hand.

"Thelma, I think maybe this gun would do better service in a museum somewhere. I don't think it's safe."

"That's just because you don't like guns." Thelma reached out and grabbed the gun back from me - too casually for my liking - looked at it with appreciation and stuck it back in the drawer. I sighed, knowing that once Thelma was set on a course not high water or the fires of hell would turn her aside.

"Okay, but if you insist on having a gun why don't you at least go get a new one? You can afford it, and it would make me feel better."

"A new gun?" Thelma perked up at that. "Hey, that's a great idea! Maybe a shotgun..."

"How about if I ask Eddie to go shopping with you? Then he could even give you a couple of lessons, make sure you're proficient with it."

"How about Jack, instead? Think he'd have some time for an old lady?" Thelma grinned mischievously. "Unlike you, I can appreciate a hard body, even if I can't do much with one anymore."

I laughed. "I don't know, I can ask him."

"Okay, if you can get Jack, I'll do it." She looked at me expectantly. "Well? What are you waiting for? Call him."

I sighed and dialed Jack's number.

"What's up?" he answered immediately, and I explained the situation to him. When he finished laughing he agreed to take her out shopping that very evening on the condition that he first got to examine her antique.

"Are you going with us?" he asked.

"I'd like to, but I have an appointment at the B&E gym."

"Ah, with Eddie?"

"Yeah, I'm trying to get this all done as quickly as possible so I don't have Harry Baker on my back."

"Yeah, okay. I'll see you around, then." He disconnected, no more abruptly than usual, but there had been something in his tone...I sighed. There was no point trying to analyze what Jack was thinking. He was totally alien to all my previous experience with people, an enigma that I was never going to puzzle out.

Just then a big white panel truck with "RENT ME!" in bold red letters painted on the side pulled in front of the store and Jack was forgotten while I helped Brenda and Thelma unload their first shipment of goods.

Chapter Thirteen

I dropped my car off at Alf's Friday with the promise that it would be waiting for me in the morning, the starter brand new and properly rigged since I had a little money in my savings account. The lady from the agency was going to be with Bob until five, so I spent the day running around with my mother.

She picked me up in her cargo van. It had once been a basic white utility vehicle, but Mom had added her own signature to it. She had painted it like something out of an LSD trip. One side was fluorescent orange, the other canary yellow. There were giant hippie flowers, rainbows and peace signs all over it, as well as slogans from the sixties: "Make Love, Not War;" "Give Peace a Chance." In tiny letters on the door over the gas cap it said "ass, gas or grass, nobody rides for free." That last was a contribution from Jedediah, who had a surprising and seldom seen silly streak in him. Mom walked when she could, but she really needed the big van as she always seemed to be hauling things or people here and there.

This particular morning we delivered Meals on Wheels to a half dozen senior citizens around Buchanan. That was a lot more entertaining than it sounded, if a bit sad. Most of them had little or no contact with their families, and often Meals on Wheels was the only human contact they got on a typical day. My mom had crocheted each of her regulars an afghan, and we delivered those along with the meals.

Mom liked to stop and chat for a few minutes with each of them, and so by the time we left the last house it was almost 2:00. After that we drove over to Niles so she could pick up some cleansing supplies from Moonbeads and Earthwear, a little shop that carried everything from tarot cards to incense to hemp clothing to smoking paraphernalia. Not surprisingly, my mom knew the owner really well, and by the time we were done she drove me straight to Bob's house.

Bob was still more or less ignoring me. At least he came out of his room for dinner, but afterward he settled back into his bed with a thick book.

I passed the evening watching the news (nothing but accidents and shootings and wars, oh my!) and then Jeopardy.

About half way through the first round of questions Bob wandered out of his bedroom and sat in a chair on the far side of the room. At first he just stared at the TV, but after a few minutes he started muttering the answers.

By the time Double Jeopardy started we were racing to answer first, and lo and behold, Bob actually smiled at me.

When Jeopardy ended he finally spoke directly to me.

"I'm sorry I've been such a butthead, Rainie. I know this isn't your fault."

"I can't believe you think that all I care about is the money you pay me." That still stung. A lot.

Bob winced.

"I'm sorry, I shouldn't have said that. I know it isn't true, I was just being an asshole."

"Yeah, you really were."

He laughed. "No Rainie, tell me how you really feel! I mean, aren't you supposed to be all sweet and forgiving, telling me how you understand and all that?"

"That's how I am when someone says something they can't help. You knew exactly what you were saying and it was just mean."

Bob sighed.

"I know, that's what's pissing me off. I swear I always know what I'm saying or doing. I don't feel like I'm losing my marbles."

"I know you don't, but what else could it be? Since Daryl has been staying here the car hasn't moved once and the freezer has remained fully stocked."

"Which still doesn't make any sense. Why would I quit sneaking out if dementia's causing me to do it?"

"I don't know Bob. Dementia is..."

"I know, it's unpredictable." He blew out a rough breath. "Anyway, want to play some Scrabble?"

"Sure, sounds good."

Bob went off to bed at eleven, and I stretched out on the couch. I hadn't brought pajamas since I didn't expect to sleep much. I turned off all the lights and settled back with a battery operated book-light illuminating "Animal Farm." I hadn't read it since junior high, and I'd picked it up at the library on a whim.

Apparently I was more exhausted than I realized. Before I read two pages I was fast asleep.

I blinked against a bright light, disoriented, still half asleep. For a moment I thought I was being interrogated in some old movie, but then I realized it was just my book light pointing at my face.

I turned it aside and sat up, groggy and out of sorts, wondering what time it was.

Then it occurred to me that something had woken me. There it was again: the soft but unmistakable sound of footsteps on the front porch.

I heard the faint creak of Bob's bedroom door and I went in that direction, moving slowly in the dark. I met him in the hallway. He hadn't turned on any lights either, but he was carrying a small flashlight, pointing it at his feet.

"Shh, I think I hear someone outside." I whispered close to his ear.

"So did I. I heard a car door close, and it had to be in the driveway, right outside my bedroom window!" Bob started forward eagerly, but I restrained him gently.

"Hold on, let's think about this a minute." I couldn't believe it; Bob had been right all along, someone was breaking into his house! Suddenly my mouth was dry, my bladder overfull.

"Nothing to think about! There's a baseball bat by the front door. If you'll just let me go I'll get it, and then let that bastard come after my frozen food!"

I heard noises at the front door. Someone was trying to get in.

"Hey, lighten up there, girl." Bob pushed at my hand, and I let go of his shoulder, which I had been clutching painfully tight. My palms were sweaty and there were tiny little sparkles at the edges of my vision; one of these days I was actually going to pass out.

I was thinking about the guy who'd shot Missy and the cop. What if this guy had a gun? What if he were a rapist or a sadist? Hell, I wasn't even prepared to fight off a zealous Jehovah's Witness at this point.

Bob moved across the living room easily, familiar with the layout of the furniture, and I stayed on his heels. He stood next to the door and reached for the baseball bat.

"Wait," I whispered. "Maybe I should take that."

He frowned. "A man should defend his own house."

"Then why am I here? Besides, you just finished physical therapy for that torn rotator cuff. Do you really want to reinjure your shoulder?"

"I guess not."

He reluctantly handed me the bat and I scurried over to the other side of the door. Someone was definitely fumbling with the doorknob. Picking the lock? I wasn't sure how easy that would be; there was a deadbolt, and in spite of what you see in the movies I'm fairly certain those are pretty tough to pick.

I stood so I would be behind the door if it opened, and prayed that whoever was there would get frustrated and go away. Then again, if it was the same someone Bob had been complaining about, he'd been inside before, getting into the freezer.

The deadbolt latch suddenly turned, and as if it flipped a switch somewhere in my nervous system my legs dissolved into barely set Jell-o and I had to grab the wall with one hand to keep from falling down.

I took a deep breath as the door slowly swung open and got a two-handed grip on the bat. One good swing ought to do it: a crushing blow to the skull and whoever it was would go down.

I raised the bat, ready to aim for the cheap seats, when the reality of what I was about to do formed a gruesome image in my overactive imagination.

Crushed skull. In a flash I remembered a long-ago school project when we made maracas. We used a mix of flour and water to paste strips of newspaper over light bulbs. It dried hard, and then we whacked them against a hard surface and the light bulb would crunch up inside, and the glass shards would make noise when you shook it.

Is that how this would be? When I hit him on the head, would the bones of his skull shatter and rattle inside his skin like a paper-Mache maraca?

Or would there be blood, and spatters of brain matter and chips of bone...

Then it was too late to think anymore. I saw the head and shoulders of the burglar, and it was all or nothing. He hadn't hurt anyone before, but then Bob had always slept through his midnight forays. He might have a gun, or a knife. Who knew what he would do when confronted?

So I swung the bat.

But at the last minute the caregiver side of me, the one that was all about nurturing and empathy, contrived to change my aim and the force of my swing.

The bat came down on the guy's shoulder. There was still an ominous crunch, followed by a yowl of pain that might have come from my darkest nightmares. The guy dropped to the floor and rolled onto his back, clutching his shoulder and sobbing.

"Hey, hey! What was that? Hey, don't hurt me...I'm sorry...hey hey!"

"What the hell?" I heard Bob's voice, and then a lamp turned on.

The burglar was revealed: a kid, really, maybe 19 years old, his hair on the longish side, his face still marked with the agony of that adolescent scourge, acne.

"You broke my shoulder!" The kid was sobbing, in serious pain. I remembered that sickening crunch, and figured he was probably right about the broken part.

"Jeremy?" Bob stepped closer and stared down at the boy, incredulous.

"You know him?"

"Sure, that's Jeremy Baldwin, he shovels my walk in the winter, rakes the leaves in the fall. What the hell are you doing breaking into my house?'

Jeremy took a couple of gulping breaths, reminding me of a four year old who'd just fallen out of a swing.

"I-I wasn't breaking in. Not really. I have a key."

"A key? Oh well, that's all right then!" Bob's sarcasm was lost on the boy, who looked momentarily relieved.

"I'd never just break in," he looked earnest, despite the pain. "Can you call me an ambulance or something?"

"Hold on there. Where'd you get a key?"

"You gave it to me. Last year, when you went to Alabama with your son. You asked me to keep an eye on the place."

"So you just kept the key?"

"I'm sorry..." tears were flowing down his cheeks. "Please...it really hurts!"

"You're lucky you hurt!" Bob was showing no sympathy. "If Rainie hadn't missed, you'd be lying there with brains leaking all over my rug!"

My stomach turned at the new images his words evoked in my head, and once again I felt that weakness in my knees. I couldn't believe how close I'd come to killing this stupid kid.

"M-missed? I'd say she got me pretty good!" Jeremy dissolved into tears again, and Bob rolled his eyes.

"Come on, you sissy. Get up off the floor and take it like a man."

"Wha...?" Jeremy blinked up at him, apparently saw the cold steel in the old man's eyes, and staggered to his feet. He stood there swaying, still holding his shoulder.

"Have you been taking my car, too?"

"Well yeah, but you know...you don't use it at night, and I put gas in it..."

"That's still stealing!" I finally interjected a comment.

"It's more like borrowing. I mean, I didn't hurt it or anything..."

"Didn't hurt it? How about what you did to me? I've been going crazy trying to figure out who's been driving the damned thing. My son wants to put me in a nursing home, thinks I'm a danger to myself! And I was beginning to believe it!"

Jeremy looked stricken. "Aw geez, Mr. Davis. I'm really sorry, I never thought...I mean, I always got it back before morning. I didn't think anyone even noticed."

"Well we did." I tried to sound firm, but I could still hear the adrenalin shake in my voice. "Where the hell do you go in the middle of the night?"

"To see my girl." Jeremy dropped his head, embarrassed, and stared at the rug, which was thankfully clear of leaking brains. "She lives down in South Bend, and I can't afford a car. Her dad doesn't much like me anyhow, so I sneak down late to see her." He looked up suddenly, his eyes wide. They were bloodshot, and I suspected it wasn't just from crying. I could detect the faintest odor, not unlike the herbs my mother grew in the back of her greenhouse. "But we don't do nothing! We just go to the park, sit by the river and talk! Honest!"

"How old is she?"

"Eighteen. Well...she will be, in a couple of months."

"Uh huh. And what about the food?"

"Oh..well, I get hungry. But I replaced that, too!"

Hungry. More like munchies, but I didn't bother to correct him.

"And you think that makes it all right? You sneak into my house, you steal my car..."

"Borrow it! It's not stealing if you bring it back!"

The thing was, Jeremy obviously really meant it. He didn't think he'd done anything wrong.

"You dumb twit! I ought to tan your hide! You put me through all this, and then you stand there like you're an innocent kid, doing nothing wrong..."

"But I didn't hurt anyone!" Jeremy suddenly thought better of that statement. "Well, except for kind of driving you crazy. That wasn't so good, I suppose. I'm really sorry about that part."

"Oh for Christ's sake." Bob threw up his hands. "I knew you weren't the sharpest knife in the drawer, Jeremy, but come on!"

"Are you gonna call the cops?" He was wide-eyed again, as if that thought had just occurred to him.

"Well what do you think I'm going to do?"

"Oh please, don't do that, Mr. Davis. I just started college, and if I go to jail I'll miss classes and flunk out and they'll take away my grant..."

"*You're* going to college?" Bob was skeptical.

"Sure, at LMC. I'm going to be a teacher."

"A teacher?" Bob looked like he might be in danger of a stroke.

"Yeah, they need good teachers. There's a big demand. I'll have to transfer to a four year college to get my degree, but I can do all my general classes right here in town."

"A teacher." Bob shook his head. "Don't they test you people before they let you into college?"

"Sure. I had to take a basic test to prove I could read and write good enough and do math, like division and things. I did okay on those."

"Okay?" Bob looked at me, outrage in his eyes. I think he was more angered by the idea that this idiot might someday be allowed to teach children than by the fact he'd broken into his house.

"It's four years, Bob. Either he'll learn something, or they'll figure out he's better off in retail."

"Or politics." Bob snorted, but looked somewhat mollified.

"So? You gonna an ambulance?" Jeremy whined. "This really hurts!"

"What do you think?" I looked at Bob, who in turn looked at Jeremy.

"First things first. I'm going to call my son over so you can tell him what's been going on."

"But Bob, it's..." I glanced at the clock. "It's 3 am!"

"So? You think after all this I'm waiting until morning to clear it up?" Bob already had the phone in his hand and he hit the speed-dial button for Daryl.

"Daryl? I need you over here right now...damned right it's important! Yeah, Rainie's here...you want to talk to her, get your ass over here!"

He disconnected and returned his glare to Jeremy.

"I don't feel so good Mr. Davis. Can I sit down?" The kid did look a bit pale, and I wondered if he were going into shock.

149

"Go ahead. Sit right there." Bob pointed at the couch and Jeremy gratefully sank down on it, crying out when it jarred his shoulder.

"Oh shut up, you sissy. Wait until you get to physical therapy- then you'll know what pain is!"

Jeremy sniffed and bowed his head.

"Shouldn't we call the cops?"

"I suppose so, but not until Daryl gets here. I want to be sure he hears this kid's story before they cart him off."

He turned back to Jeremy. "And I want my keys back!"

"They're right there, on the rug. I dropped them when she hit me."

I picked them up and handed them to Bob.

"Hey," Jeremy wiped his nose on his sleeve. "Uum...do you think I could borrow the car..."

"What the hell is the matter with you!" Bob roared, and I jumped. I couldn't believe that much volume could be produced by such a skinny chest cavity.

Jeremy flinched and went back to looking at the floor. It was amazing, but he really didn't get how much trouble he was in.

"Jeremy, have you ever heard of breaking and entering? Grand theft auto?"

"You mean like the game, right?" His eyes lit up and he looked at me. "I play that with my friend Gary."

"Not the game, the crime! You could go to jail for twenty years for stealing cars and breaking into people's houses!"

"But... even if I used a key?"

I rolled my eyes and looked at Bob, who was shaking his head in wonder. The kid didn't seem exactly mentally deficient, more... naïve, like he didn't understand the workings of the real world. I wondered just how much time he spent playing video games.

Daryl showed up moments later, wearing a windbreaker over a pair of pajama pants, his hair in disarray, his eyes a little wild with worry.

150

"What the hell is going on? Dad?"

"He's what's going on!" Bob pointed at Jeremy, his tone brimming over with righteous indignation. "You think I'm nuts, huh? Well just look here what we caught sneaking into the house tonight!"

"What?" Daryl stared at Jeremy, trying hard to catch up with the program.

"He's been coming over and 'borrowing' the car," I informed Daryl. "He had a key to the house. He's been creeping in on a regular basis, chowing down on Bob's food after his little outings."

"Oh my god..." At first Daryl just looked amazed, but then his face clouded over into outright rage. "You little shit!" He snatched Jeremy up by the shirt and pulled him off the couch, heedless of the kid's new cries of pain. "I thought my father was losing his mind! I was going to have him locked up! And all so you could take a fucking joyride?"

He was shaking Jeremy, who was screaming in pain, and I was pulling at his arm, trying to get him to let go before Jeremy was permanently crippled, but Daryl wasn't paying any attention to me.

"That's enough!" Bob's voice roared out again and everyone froze. "Let him go, Daryl, he's already hurt."

Daryl looked like he didn't much care; looked, in fact, like he still planned to put a good hurt on Jeremy himself before it was all over, but he shoved Jeremy back onto the couch.

"Have you called the cops yet?"

"No, I wanted you to hear this, first." Bob clapped a hand on his son's shoulder. "I guess I owe you an apology. I thought you were happy to have an excuse to lock me up in that place."

"What, are you kidding? I love you, Dad, I just want you safe."

He put his arms around Bob, who awkwardly hugged him back. It was clear he wasn't used to demonstrations of affection.

I picked up the phone. "I'll call the cops."

"And don't forget an ambulance!" Jeremy whined.

"Shut up!" The order came from me, Bob and Daryl all at the same time.

He shut up.

Chapter Fourteen

Dawn was breaking by the time the cops finished their questioning and reports. They'd spent an inordinate amount of time questioning me, I thought; they made it sound as if my assault on Jeremy had not been justified. I think if Bob and Daryl hadn't been there to defend me they might have tried to haul me off to jail. They brought up the shooting I had witnessed downtown, and I had to go over it all again, with Daryl and Bob listening with wide-eyed amazement. To them I was just a mild-mannered caregiver, but now they were seeing a side of me they'd never suspected.

To be fair, I guess the cops had a right to be a little suspicious. Here I was involved in a second violent episode in the same week. I suspected the cops had also seen the TV coverage of my wild ride last weekend, but instead of being amused like most of the citizens in town they were just pissed I was getting away with something.

They finally left, Jeremy long gone in an ambulance. Bob was leaning back in his chair, exhausted but happy.

"I think I'll go back to bed."

"Me too, Dad. How about you Rainie? You taking off now?"

"Yeah..." Then I remembered I didn't have my car. "Oh wait, I can't. My car is in the shop."

"Of course!" Bob suddenly sat forward, a big grin on his face. "For a smart family, we were pretty stupid, Daryl! No wonder Jeremy never came while you were here. Your car was always in the driveway, blocking mine in!"

Daryl gave himself a light slap on the forehead. "How the hell did we not think of that?"

"Maybe because it was easier to think I was nuts." A brief flash of anger passed over Bob's features.

"Anyway, if it's all right I'll just wait for my mom to get here so she can take me to Alf's for my car."

"I could give you a ride home."

"That's okay, Alf's doesn't open until eight anyway."

"Damn, that Myrna lady is coming at eight o'clock. I'd better call her off."

"I'll do it if you have the number."

"Thanks, Rainie. The number is on the fridge." Daryl yawned. "Well, I'm off to home and bed."

"Me too." Bob heaved himself out of his chair. "My home, my bed. And I hope to die in it when the time comes."

"Yeah, well no hurry, Dad," Daryl laughed and impulsively hugged Bob again.

"I'll call you later."

"Yeah, yeah," Bob waved him off, but I could tell he was pleased by the show of affection. He went off to bed, a little spring in his step I hadn't seen for a while.

I always tried to reserve Saturdays for myself, no matter how busy my life got. Even though I kept things as simple as possible around the house, I needed one day to work on it, to keep it clean and organized so I didn't have to mess with it the rest of the week. I decided to put off Angela Perez until Sunday and spend the day doing my own thing.

I started with George's cage. I gave it a thorough cleaning and changed the water in his little swimming pool. A couple of the plants were dying off; I'd have to run down the road to Buchanan Floral and see what Chuck had in stock to replace them.

I did my laundry while I cleaned the rest of the house, even wiping out the fridge, although I didn't have much in there to make a mess. I would have to grocery shop when I went for plants. I was planning to buy more than cereal and peanut butter for a change; Jack was right, I was slipping into some poor eating habits.

I got out a ladder and cleaned the gutters over the front door where newly fallen leaves had gathered. The nights were cooling off finally, although the days were still unseasonably hot. I supposed that by next month all the leaves would be off the trees, most of them in my gutters, and I'd have to climb up again.

I did my shopping and found some new tropical plants for George's cage. By the time I finished planting them it was late afternoon and I realized I hadn't had lunch. My tummy was rumbling and I was feeling a little woozy, which reminded me that I hadn't had breakfast, either!

Now I was too hungry to waste time cooking, so I hurriedly threw together a peanut butter sandwich and grabbed an apple to go with it. That was one nice thing about Michigan in the fall; the stores were well stocked with delicious apples picked locally, and so fresh you could practically still taste the dew on them.

Once my tummy was full and happy I decided I'd earned a break, so I settled on the couch with Animal Farm. I had a little time before I needed to shower and get ready to go over to Mason's party. Everyone was expected early, at 5:00, for ribs off the grill before the drinking started. Mmm, ribs. Woman does not live by Cheerios alone!

Of course, I should have realized what would happen, since I'd been up since 3 a.m. when Bob's "burglar" came in.

I fell asleep.

I woke up when my cell phone started ringing. I answered it groggily.

"Sweetheart, where are you?"

"Hi Dan. What time is it?"

"6:00, and the ribs are flyin' off the grill. You're still coming, aren't you?"

"Yeah, of course." I yawned. "I had a busy day, just fell asleep. I'll jump in the shower and be right over."

"Well hurry on up, sweetheart. I'm waiting."

I hung up and practically staggered to the shower. I was normally a power nap type; give me 15 minutes to snooze in the middle of the day and I'm up and at 'em as if I'd had a full night's sleep. But let me sleep for an hour and a half, like I just had, and my brain slides into neutral and wants to stay there for the rest of the day.

I stood under the hot water long after I was done washing, enjoying the sensation of the pounding water while I just pretty much spaced out. Once I finally got out and dressed I was feeling pretty normal again, although part of me just wanted to climb back into bed.

I put on a skirt and a tank top, dried my hair, grabbed my purse and a sweater and headed out the door.

It was nearly seven o'clock by the time I pulled into Mason's driveway, and the party was in full swing. I found a place to park in the grass, a long way back from the house. Mason had fifty prime acres right about midway between Buchanan and Niles. A lot of it was wooded, the rest leased to farmers for corn and soy beans. The best part of the property, according to Mason, was that he had no close neighbors, and no one to complain if his parties got loud.

This one was certainly going to be. I could already hear music cranking from the direction of the barn, and there were knots of people all over the place, most of them drinking from red plastic cups, the staple of keggers everywhere.

I didn't drink very often. I was afraid I'd like it too much, and make a habit of it. It had been a long, stressful week, though, so I thought I might have a cup or two after I chowed a couple of ribs.

That wasn't how things happened, though.

You know how sometimes you look back at a situation and say "well hey, anyone could have seen that coming!" And yet at the time you just seem to be swept along, making one bad decision after another until you find yourself if the midst of a total mess?

Well, that's what happened to me.

First of all, the food was gone. Clearly Mason hadn't been expecting such a big turnout. There wasn't a rib to be seen, not a spoonful of potato salad. Not even a slice of what looked like (from the smeared remains on the serving plate) a chocolate sheet cake.

Secondly, Dan thrust an ice-cold beer into my hand as soon as he saw me, and like a fool I took a big swallow right off the bat.

Dan and I moved around a lot at first, chatting with everyone. I was smoking too much and drinking too fast in order to quiet my hunger pangs. I spoke briefly to Jack, who looked quizzically at my beer and asked if I was okay.

"'Course. Why wouldn't I be?"

"I've just never seen you drink much." He leaned in close to me. "And right now, I think maybe you're pretty drunk."

I laughed. "Who, me?"

Dan took me by the arm and pulled me away, maybe a little spark of jealousy in his eyes. Silly man. Didn't he know who Jack was?

I should have known Jack was right about that pretty drunk part when someone talked me into singing karaoke. I was not normally much for public displays but I belted out "Blowin' in the Wind" without a care in the world. Without the alcohol the mere suggestion of getting up on a stage would have caused me to nearly pass out from embarrassment.

Afterwards Dan and I wandered out back where there was a big bonfire burning. He stood behind me, one arm around my waist, and I leaned into him. He was comfortable to lean on; he was big and solid, with just a little padding over his muscles. He was one of those naturally strong guys, the type who never worked out but could still lift their own weight in a pinch. The softness was likely the result of pushing forty without subjecting himself to any real physical labor.

Didn't matter to me. It felt pretty nice. So did his hand, which was rubbing gently up and down my arm, the fingertips just brushing the edge of my breast. Huh, seemed Dan was hoping to take our relationship to the next level.

I wasn't sure how I felt about that. I'm not a prude, but I'm not easy, either. I thought it was important to have a relationship with a man before you went to bed with him.

A lot of people went by the three date rule: apparently that was how long you had to wait to not be considered a slut. Well, I'd been out to dinner with Dan once, and I'd had drinks with him twice in between sets when he was playing gigs down in South Bend. Now we were at a party together; did that count as four?

"Hey, it's starting to rain."

I put my hand out, and sure enough, I could feel a very light drizzle.

"We'd better move under one of the tents."

That was okay with me. Mason had several big tents set up just in case; the weather report had said a 20% chance. We stepped under the shelter of one along with a dozen other people, all laughing and talking at once.

I finished the last of my beer, ready for another one. I knew I was good and buzzed, but I kind of liked it.

"How about I get you another one?" Dan grinned when he saw me looking around for the keg. "If you think you're up to it."

"I'm fine." I rocked backwards when I said it, and almost fell over. He reached out a hand to steady me and laughed.

"You sure are!" He slid an arm around my shoulder. "You know, you didn't get anything to eat tonight. Maybe we should go back to my place. I can fix a late supper for you."

I looked up at him out of narrowed eyes. Late supper, then bed I supposed.

"I kind of want another beer."

"No problem, I've got a fully stocked bar, including two pony kegs on tap."

"Really?" I was hungry, and kind of curious to see his house; he had hinted that he was pretty well-to-do, and talked a lot about his "spread." Most of the time you'd think Dan was straight out of Texas instead of a local Michigan boy.

"So what do you think, should we blow this popsicle stand?"

"Sure, why not?" I handed him my empty cup. "But first I need to pee."

"Okay." Dan walked with me up to the house, which suddenly seemed a long, long distance. I found myself stumbling on the smooth grass, and now and then I saw two back doors where I was sure there should only be one.

We were almost there when we ran into friends of Dan's. He stopped to talk to them, back slapping and shaking hands, doing the good old boy thing. I endured for a few minutes, but I hadn't been kidding when I said I needed to pee, and even though the rain was still light I didn't particularly want to stand around in it.

"Hey, I'm goin' on in," I pulled away from Dan. "Be right back."

"All right sweetheart. I'll be here."

Mason had two bathrooms, and I suspected that most of the men were just peeing in the woods, so there wasn't much of a wait to get into one. I had a little trouble with my

159

skirt: it was a really full one, and I couldn't seem to gather it all together and get my underpants down at the same time. I finally had to lean one shoulder against the wall to keep my balance while I performed the complicated maneuver.

At long last I managed to sit on the toilet without trailing my skirt in the bowl. Sitting felt good. I was feeling a little strange.

Drunk, I mean. I was feeling a little drunk.

I laughed, but I cut it off quick. There was something a bit bizarre about sitting on the toilet and laughing at yourself.

Damn. I was really, really drunk. Going home with Dan was a good idea. Something to eat would be good, and as for his bed, why not? He was good looking in a rough sort of way, and he was talented, funny and rich. What more could a girl ask for?

I managed to get myself back together, double checking to be sure the back of my skirt wasn't stuck in my underpants. I stepped out of the bathroom, and there was Jack again.

"Hey, Rainie."

"Hey."

"You still okay?"

"Yep. Getting ready to take off."

"Wait a minute, you can't drive."

"You don't think?" I tried to stand straight and steady, but I was pretty sure I was listing heavily to the right. Or maybe the left. Or maybe I was swaying back and forth. Or Jack was.

"Let me give you a ride."

"That's okay. I'm gonna ride with Dan." And then, not knowing why, I told him, "It's our third date. Or maybe fourth. You know what *that* means!"

"Not really."

"Means we're gonna *sleep* together."

"Oh." There was a look on his face I couldn't quite read. Anger? Disappointment? I leaned closer to him, curious.

"Are *you* all right?" I asked him.

He smiled, but he didn't look all that amused. "Of course. I'm not drinking."

"You never do."

"Well, not often."

"That's 'cuz you got *control* issues," I informed him, poking a finger lightly into his chest.

"You're probably right. So where's Dan?"

"Outside. I better go."

I headed for the door, but the floor kept tilting and swaying. Jack took my arm.

"Let me help."

We stepped outside onto a wide front porch, and I realized I'd gone to the front door instead of the back.

"Oops, wrong way. Dan's out back."

"We can walk around the house."

"'K." There were four steps leading down off the porch. I grabbed the side railing and shook off Jack's hand. "I'm good."

And I was, for the first step, and the second. On the third my foot somehow got tangled up in my skirt, and the next thing I knew I was face down in the soggy grass. I was lucky I mostly missed the sidewalk.

"I'm all right," I assured myself and any onlookers as I struggled to get back up. My feet were still tangled in my skirt, and I couldn't seem to get them loose. I was rolling around in the wet grass, feeling like a fish caught in a net. Jack grabbed me under the arms and lifted me up.

"Thanks. Guess I better let Dan drive." I giggled. I suddenly wondered if I was making a fool of myself, and realized I probably was.

That's the last thing I remember about the party.

Chapter Fifteen

My first thought when I woke up was that my head hurt. Not that crushing, nauseating migraine pain that required dark glasses and quiet, but nonetheless a headache, and I decided not to open my eyes. Maybe not until the day had passed.

My second thought was that I was incredibly thirsty. It felt like I'd gone to sleep with a cotton sock in my mouth.

I reached for the glass of water I always kept on the nightstand, knowing it would be warm and stale but better than nothing.

The glass wasn't there. I couldn't feel my clock or box of tissues, either.

Reluctantly I opened my eyes.

I wasn't in my room.

I sat up abruptly. "Uh oh," I muttered. What the hell had I done now?

I was definitely in someone else's bed. The room was dim, but I could make it out well enough from light shining through a small opening in the curtains. The dresser, bed and nightstand were all of some dark, well-polished wood that gleamed even in the diffused light from the covered window. The drapes were hunter green, the walls some dark paint or wallpaper that I couldn't quite discern. I was covered in black sheets and a thin feather quilt that matched the drapes.

Holy crap! This was definitely a man's room.

I got up and stood by the bed. Maybe if I let some blood flow out of my alcohol-swollen brain I could have a coherent thought about the night before.

I'd never had a blackout from drinking, and if this was my first it would definitely be my last. There was a history of such things in my family, which was a big reason my mother stuck to smoking pot. My brother went on drinking binges more often than was healthy, although lately he seemed to be settling down. My father, although everyone who knew him (especially my mother) insisted he was the kindest, most thoughtful man they'd ever known, had gone on one too many binges. He'd gotten drunk, fallen off a bridge into the St. Joe River and drowned when I was only three.

Because of that I seldom drank and had never shown signs of abusing alcohol, but I was always on the lookout for the possibility.

I remembered the party. I remembered drinking beer and singing karaoke.

Then I remembered the porch, and falling down the steps. I looked down at my bare legs. My right knee was scraped where I'd hit the sidewalk.

Jack had helped me up, and we were going to find Dan. The thing was, I didn't remember riding home with Dan. In fact, the last time I remembered seeing him was when I went into the house to pee.

I had a vague recollection of stumbling across the yard, someone hanging onto my arm, and then I got into...a truck. Dan drove a big red truck.

That's right, I had decided to go home with him; he promised me a late supper. I flushed, remembering that I had also planned to sleep with him. Just how far had that gone? I took inventory of myself. I was wearing my tank top and panties. That was good; if I'd had sex I'd be naked. I wasn't the type to get up and dress after the festivities.

I rubbed my stomach. Hm, I don't think I ate either; I was ravenous. Had I passed out before he could cook food for me?

Damn, how stupid could I be? How could I have gotten so drunk that I had left myself at the mercy of a man I didn't really know very well? And had I really planned to sleep with him?

I had to get out of here. I snapped on the bedside lamp and looked around frantically for my skirt. The room was pretty neat except for the unmade bed and a small pile of discarded clothes in front of the closet; there weren't many places that my skirt could be, but I didn't see it. Great, how the hell was I supposed to get out of here?

Wait, I told myself. Calm down. Dan obviously hadn't hurt me last night; I wasn't in danger of much more than humiliation, and I'd certainly survived that before.

"Hey."

I froze like a deer in headlights. Jack was in the doorway, holding a steaming mug of coffee.

"Jack?" I hadn't considered this scenario at all! Why the hell wasn't I at Dan's? I glanced back at the bed, both sides equally mussed. Jack had slept beside me, probably listening to me snort and snore in my drunkenness. Had I been drooling, too? This went way beyond humiliation.

Jack was shirtless, wearing only a low-slung pair of pajama pants, his hair tousled as if he'd used his fingers for a comb.

As yummy as he looked, that made me think of my own hair, uncombed and probably sticking out in sixteen different directions from tossing on the pillow. I put a hand up to smooth it down and my tank top rode up over the top of my underpants, exposing the little roll of fat I could never seem to shed.

I immediately grabbed the hem of my shirt with both hands and tugged it down, hunching a little for more coverage.

Jack shook his head slightly and came across the room, passing me to go to the dresser. He set the mug of coffee on top and rummaged through the drawers. He pulled out a pair of sweat pants.

"Here, you can wear these. Your skirt was soaked and muddy, so I washed it. It's in the dryer now."

He stepped closer to me, and suddenly his hand was on my hip and he pulled me tight against him. He nuzzled my neck and I shivered. He spoke, his voice a bare whisper, his lips brushing that sensitive spot just under my ear.

"You shouldn't worry about covering yourself. You're beautiful, every inch of you."

He abruptly released me and headed for the door. Over his shoulder he announced: "The coffee is for you. I left a new toothbrush on the sink, and feel free to have a shower. I'll have breakfast ready in about fifteen minutes."

A toothbrush. Oh yuk, he'd nuzzled me, and here I was with hangover breath.

And here I was, so embarrassed by the whole situation that I wasn't enjoying the moment.

He said I was beautiful.

Maybe he was still drunk. Only I'd never seen him drink before, and that included last night.

I drank the coffee. It was strong and black and hot, damned near perfect. Geez, was there anything Jack couldn't do well? I mean, a man who can brew good coffee: now *there's* a catch!

I went in to brush my teeth, figuring to throw on the sweats and get the hell out of there. Forget hanging around for breakfast.

Jack's bathroom was the size of my kitchen. There was a tub big enough for two, complete with Jacuzzi jets. There was a shower stall - a huge affair with a clear but water-spotted glass enclosure. A shower would feel good, but it would mean being naked in Jack's house, and that simply wasn't going to happen.

166

There was a double sink with brass fixtures and a hunter green marble counter top holding the usual bathroom clutter: toothbrush, toothpaste, shaving cream, soap. At least there weren't any little beard hairs in the sink. Jack wasn't exactly a neat freak, but he knew how to clean up after himself.

Not that I really cared. I never expected to be in his house again.

As promised there was a toothbrush still in its package and a clean glass.

First I used the toilet and slipped into the sweatpants. They were a little baggy, but not by much, a reminder that I was no petite little thing that would look cute wearing a man's clothes.

I opened the toothbrush, and that brought another thought. Just how many women did Jack bring home in a week that he had a stash of spare toothbrushes on hand? No wonder his bullshit line was so good. He had a lot of practice.

That thought pissed me off. I'd almost fallen for it, his crap about me being beautiful. I was beginning to think Jack already knew I had a crush on him and he was just playing with me, a cruel little game more suited to junior high. Well, I'd never give him the satisfaction of thinking I was falling for it.

And once again I asked myself what the hell was I doing *here*, anyway? I'd been planning to go home with Dan, and I was pretty sure I'd told Jack that. Where did he get off bringing me here?

I ran Jack's comb through my hair, but it was pretty hopeless. My hair was matted from the rain, and nothing short of a shower would fix it. Oh well, so what? I didn't care what Jack thought of me.

Knowing it was a lie even when I thought it, I nonetheless was in a fit of pique by the time I left the bedroom and ventured into the hall.

There were two doors off the hallway that were closed, and then it opened up into a cozy living room with overstuffed furniture, floor to ceiling bookshelves on one wall and a complex looking stereo system. No sign of a TV. Polished hardwood floors, dark maroon walls, dark wood end tables. There was a matching coffee table that held a glass of water on a coaster, next to a thick, open book. I wondered what Jack was reading, but to see it I would have to divert around the big couch to my right. I didn't want him to catch me at it and think I was curious about anything he did, so I went to the left, following the heavenly scent of bacon frying.

I passed through a dining room full of the same gleaming hardwoods. There was a china hutch on one wall, empty except for a set of wine glasses. The whole room looked unused, even unfinished compared to the rest of the place.

I stepped into the kitchen. It was big and bright in contrast to the rest of the house, cheery without giving way to feminine. Marble counters, glass-fronted cherry wood cabinets, dark-brown enameled appliances with a brushed surface that nearly matched the wood finishes. No doubt, Jack got paid a lot more than I did.

Jack stood at the stove, tending to a griddle. He turned and grinned at me, spatula in hand.

"Bacon and eggs, toast, and a couple of pancakes for a quick sugar rush. Surest cure for a hangover I know." He pointed with the spatula. "There's plenty of coffee."

I wanted to tell him 'No'. I wanted to tell him I was pissed off and didn't need him interfering in my life, and I certainly never wanted to wake up in his bed again!

I wanted to, but there was bacon frying, and the smell was making my knees weak. And there was more of that great coffee! What was a girl to do, I ask you?

So instead of dramatically putting my empty coffee cup in the sink and demanding to be taken home I meekly poured myself a refill.

"Have a seat." He indicated a table under a large window. The surface was cherry, like the rest of the kitchen, but this piece of furniture looked well used; there were a few surface scratches, and a ring where something hot had scalded the finish. There was salt and pepper in worn wooden shakers, a small glass bottle of pure maple syrup, a tall pitcher of orange juice and two glasses.

I sat down and sipped my coffee. I looked out the window at his backyard. It was gorgeous out there, obviously professionally landscaped. There were paths leading through flower beds, most of them fading from the cooling weather. There was a waterfall bubbling into a rock-lined pond, and I thought I saw flashes of color in the water, probably koi. Overall, it was a very pretty backyard. Huh. How un-Jack-like.

I was startled out of my reverie when Jack spoke. "Bet you're thinking that doesn't look like it belongs to me."

I nodded. "But it's pretty."

"It's also soothing. I have a gardener, but I like to putter around out there, planting a little, deadheading the flowers."

"You like to garden?" I couldn't hide my astonishment, although on second thought, I could see him getting pleasure from cutting the dead heads off of things.

He must have read my skepticism; he shrugged, looking a little hurt.

I didn't know what to say. I'm no good at conversation in awkward situations, and as far as I was concerned situations didn't get any more awkward than waking up unexpectedly in a hot man's bed in your underpants.

"Why didn't you just take me home last night?"

"My house was closer."

I considered that. The party had been right between Niles and Buchanan; it was probably the same distance either way.

"Not really." I sounded churlish even to my own ears, but hey, good coffee or not, I was still pissed off.

"Is my hospitality so awful?"

"I didn't ask for hospitality, and I prefer waking up in my own bed."

"I thought you'd planned to wake up in Dan's."

"Which is another thing! Why didn't he take me home?"

"Because he asked me to take you."

"What? Why?"

"Maybe because he isn't into necrophilia, and you weren't going to be much use to him in the condition you were in."

"That's just nasty!" But maybe true, I had to admit. And now I was pissed off at Dan. So, if he wasn't getting anything he wouldn't take care of me? I was really glad I'd passed out and hadn't slept with the loser.

"I'm sorry, you're right," Jack admitted. "That was nasty. But hey, he was happy enough to turn responsibility for you over to me."

"No one needs to be responsible for me but me!"

"You were in no shape to take care of yourself. I was worried you might puke again and not wake up. You would have choked to death in your sleep."

I snorted. "Oh come on! That couldn't happen."

"Yeah, it can." Jack's voice was flat.

"Oh, I suppose you've seen it." I could really lay on the sarcasm when I wanted to.

"As a matter of fact, I have." He turned to me, a spatula clenched tight in his hand. His jaw was set and he looked like he'd just bitten into something bitter that he didn't dare spit out. "In Columbia a few years back. A young kid, a good soldier but still trying to prove his manliness to the rest of us. He was drinking the local moonshine, crap more

170

suited as a pesticide than a drink, and he passed out in the backroom. We went looking for him the next morning and found him. He'd passed out on his back, so out of it he couldn't even roll over on his side. He was 22 years old. So yeah, it can happen."

He abruptly turned back to the stove.

I didn't really need to hear that story; I was thinking of all the times I'd dropped my brother off at home and carefully propped him on his side for just that reason. Of course, Jason had always been blotto, blind drunk, three sheets to the wind...surely I hadn't been that bad.

"I was only drinking beer," I muttered.

"Beer vomit is no more breathable than moonshine vomit." He put a plate of food in front of me and sat down with his own. "Anyway, eat up before it gets cold." He reached for the syrup.

Ug, really? How could he eat after talking about vomit? And this was the breakfast of champions, or at least of Sumo wrestlers. Two eggs, three strips of bacon, hash brown potatoes, two pieces of toast (at least they looked like whole grain) and two pancakes. If I ate it all I'd have to do three hours of penance riding on my stationary bike to recover. Then again, it looked pretty damned good, in spite of the vomit comment. I was really hungry.

I compromised and ate half of everything, (except the bacon; I ate all of that) then pushed my plate away, feeling virtuous. Never mind that I'd just consumed about a thousand calories; at least I hadn't eaten two thousand.

I scraped my plate into the garbage disposal on Jack's direction and put it in the dishwasher.

"Could you give me a ride back to my car now?"

"I don't think your skirt is dry."

"I'll get it later. I just want to go home."

"Okay." Jack shrugged and put his own plate in the dishwasher, no scraping necessary: he'd finished every bite. That pissed me off, too. Why could he eat whatever the hell he wanted and still walk around without an ounce of fat on him and his abs defined like they were sketched on? I glared at him, but he didn't notice. He went down the hall without a word, presumably to get dressed.

Once again I knew I was being bitchy, but I couldn't help it. My headache was a little better thanks to the food, but I was still uncomfortable and out of sorts about the whole situation, and I wanted a smoke. I had no idea where they were; I'd had them in the pocket of my skirt, so for all I knew Jack had washed them.

Five minutes later Jack emerged, dressed in jeans and t shirt. He held out my keys and, wonder of wonders, my cigarettes.

"Let's go."

The drive back to my car was mostly silent. I was in a crummy mood, and Jack was just Jack, listening to the stereo. I still couldn't smoke; who would dare in Jack's precious truck?

He pulled up next to my car, one of three still left parked in the yard. I guess I wasn't the only one not fit to drive last night, which was some small comfort.

I popped the door and started to slide out.

"Hey." I turned to look back at him. "I'll bring your skirt over later on today."

"I'd rather you didn't. Why don't you just bring it to the office tomorrow?" I almost winced at my harsh tone.

Whoa. Now he looked hurt, making me wonder if I'd misjudged him. Now I not only felt crummy I felt like a true bitch, but I was in no mood to make nice with him.

I closed the door and he drove off without a wave.

So he was mad. Who cared? I lit a cigarette and got into my car, which couldn't possibly be harmed by a little smoke.

I found myself staring off at the back of his retreating truck, feeling a little teary eyed.

I guess *I* cared.

I took a couple over-the-counter pain killers and a shower and considered taking a nap, but I had work to do. I had already put off the search for James Bolin for most of the week, and although there was no actual time limit on finding a dead-beat dad, I assumed B&E would prefer I did it sooner rather than later.

My phone rang while I was on the bypass and I answered it. Now I know all about not talking on the phone while driving, but unless I'm in heavy traffic I'm afraid I'm guilty of it. I don't text while driving, though, and I don't read maps or put on my makeup, either. I mean really, when you look around at all the stuff people are doing when they're supposed to be driving, a little conversation on the phone doesn't seem so bad, does it?

"Hi sweetheart, how ya feeling?"

It was Dan, as bold and cheerful as if he hadn't dumped me last night.

"What do you care?" I didn't even try to sound happy to hear from him.

"Huh?" Dan sounded genuinely surprised. "You know I care about you, honey!"

"Look, would you knock off the honey and the sweetheart? My name is Rainie."

"Whew, do you have a hangover or what?"

"Hangover? You think that's why I'm pissed off?"

"Well honey..."

"No! Not honey! You ditched me!"

"Ditched you? Hell no, I did not!" Dan was indignant. "That Jack fella, he's a friend of yours, right? I mean, you seemed friendly enough last night, didn't seem to mind him dragging you around."

"So?"

"So, after you finished puking..."

"I was puking?" I didn't remember that, but it would sure explain the way my mouth tasted this morning.

173

"Hell yeah, all over the place. Right down the side of Jack's pretty little truck!" Dan gave a little snort of laughter, and it was maybe just a bit vindictive. "Anyways, I was going to take you home but Jack said you asked him to take you. He got you home all right, didn't he?"

For a long moment I didn't answer. I was so furious I wondered if there was steam coming out of my ears. I almost looked into the rear view mirror to check. I didn't know what was worse: Dan letting me leave in that condition with someone he *thought* was my friend, the fact that Jack lied to Dan so he could take me home (why the heck did he do that, anyway?) or the fact that I'd gotten myself into that situation in the first place.

"Are you still there?"

I took a deep breath. I didn't know what motivated either Dan or Jack to behave the way they had, but in the long run I was mostly angry with myself. Never mind that I hadn't intended to get that drunk; no one had poured the beer down my throat. I'd made a complete fool of myself and I just wanted to nurse my wounded pride in private.

"I'm driving, Dan. I've got to go." That was one nice thing about all the media coverage on the dangers of driving and cell phones: it made it hard for people to argue about you needing to hang up. Never mind that I'd been talking to him for the last six minutes with no mention of being on the road.

"Okay. Can I call you later?"

"Sure, I guess so."

"I'm sorry you thought I ditched you. I really thought Jack was a friend of yours."

"Yeah, me too." I ended the call.

Chapter Sixteen

Angela Perez was home, baking cookies. I could smell them baking, and my mouth watered. She didn't offer me any, though. She didn't even invite me in, just stood in the doorway and left me on the porch.

She was thirty-something, short, a little plump, darkly pretty. Her smile showed off well-maintained teeth that indicated Juan's company must provide good dental insurance. In the living room behind her I saw two small boys kneeling at a coffee table, coloring diligently.

I introduced myself, and her smile faded.

"Private investigation firm? What do you want?"

"I'm looking for James Bolin. I understand you were a friend of his."

"Who told you that?"

"A neighbor. She thought you might have some insight into where James moved to."

"Why would I? We just knew each other in passing. You should ask that Cailee girl that was living with him."

"Cailee? That was his girlfriend's name?"

"Yeah. I never talked to him much after she moved in."

"I didn't know she was actually living with him. No one mentioned that."

"I don't think most people knew. She always parked around back; kept kind of a low profile, you know?"

"I've spoken to his ex-wife and his kids. They didn't mention a live-in girlfriend."

"I noticed she always made herself scarce on the weekends he had the kids. I figured that was his choice, though. He was pretty protective of his kids, didn't want them to know he was dating or anything. He'd hardly even wave at me over the back fence when they were around."

"Do you think their relationship was serious? I mean, serious enough he might run off with her?"

"How the hell should I know? Maybe you should ask someone at that church he was going to."

"Which church is that?"

"The Newly Unified Church of Renewal." I felt my heart rate step up a pace. I was pretty sure that was the same church Jack had mentioned in connection with Brisby Financial. I tried to keep my expression neutral while Angela went on.

"It's just a little place, over there off of Russel Street, kind of behind the old Lincoln School. Jim took me there one Sunday, wanted me to send my kids to Sunday school there, but I didn't really like it." She frowned and shook her head. "Kind of weird vibe, you know? Like I was being recruited or something."

"Recruited?"

Angela shrugged. "I don't know, that's not quite right. They were just a little too fanatical for me. I'm a Catholic, but I don't get all freaked out if I miss a Mass, you know? These people seemed a little... intense."

One of the small boys came up behind Angela and tapped her softly on the hip. I'd never seen kids so quiet and apparently well-mannered.

"What is it, Joey?"

"Manny has to pee."

"Okay baby, I'll be right there." Angela turned to me, already pushing the door shut. "I've got to go. Good luck finding Jim; he's a nice guy. I hope nothing bad happened to him."

I was abruptly left staring at the closed door.

That was okay, I thought I had some pretty good information. I pulled out my cell phone to check the time: 1:15. I'd never been a churchgoer. My mother didn't actually believe in God; she believed we were Earth's children, bound to treat each other with love and respect just by virtue of having been born into humanity. Of course, she also believed in auras and fairies and a lot of other stuff that had never made a lot of sense to me.

In any case, I was pretty sure church services were usually held on Sunday mornings, so people could go home and have a big Sunday dinner afterward. I wondered if anyone hung around the church after services. I mean, where did the preacher or priest or whatever go? It seemed to me that some actually lived on premises, or at least right next door. Was that only Catholics?

Only one way to find out. I headed back to my car and drove over to Russel street.

Russel wasn't a very long street. It ran maybe 13 or 14 blocks parallel to the railroad tracks. The neighborhoods along the way were mostly shabby, some downright blighted. I drove along it slowly, looking for a church.

Surprisingly, I saw two churches before I found the right one. The first church, complete with a little steeple but no bell, had been converted into a house. The second one had once been a storefront, maybe a neighborhood grocery, with drapes covering the plate-glass windows. Hand-painted letters on the glass proclaimed it to be the "Bible Way Church of God."

Three blocks further on I ran across yet another little church, this one a little square box with a peaked roof, one stained glass window and a tiny steeple. A small sign to the right of the door identified it as "The Newly Unified Church of Renewal." It occupied a corner lot, not taking up any more room than a single dwelling home. There was a small parking lot where a back lawn would otherwise be, filled almost to capacity; apparently their services ran late. I

177

squeezed my little car into a spot on the far end and approached the church.

There was an unlocked door right off the parking lot. I walked down four steps and found myself in a tiny foyer that accessed three doors. I poked my head through an open door on the left and found a room that was obviously used for Sunday school classes. There were cartoon pictures of Jesus walking on water and baskets of hand puppets and craft items, all aimed at indoctrinating children into the faith. One wall was dominated by a painting of a gorgeous man in a brown tunic and loose fitting pants. He was standing barefoot in a sunny field of wildflowers with his hands held out palm up in a gesture of welcome. The artist had done a good job of capturing his piercing eyes, and they seemed to be gazing at me in benediction.

I backed away and peeked through the door to the right. It was a storeroom filled with shelves of office supplies, folding chairs and miscellaneous stuff.

That left only one door. I opened it to find myself looking at a rather large room filled with people sitting around cheap folding card tables. On the far end there was a small kitchen separated by a counter, and on the counter were stacks of paper plates and foam cups. There was the delightful smell of freshly percolated coffee.

I paused in the doorway, immediately the sole object of interest to the nearly forty people gathered there. Everyone froze for just a moment, as if posing for a picture.

The silence was broken when a pretty young woman approached me with a huge smile. "Welcome! Have you come for fellowship?"

"Uh..." there I went again with the quick rejoinders. I put on my best smile. "Maybe I am. I heard about your church, and I just had to come see for myself." There, that wasn't a lie.

"Oh?" The huge smile was reduced to something with a bit less wattage. "What did you hear?"

"Only good things," I assured her, which was mostly true. But now the time for truth, which wouldn't get me anywhere, was past. I took a deep breath and plunged into the murky lake of lies. "I've been looking for a new spiritual home, and I thought maybe this could be it."

"Wonderful!" the full smile was back. "I'm Cailee, the social director for our little church."

"Social director?" I'd never heard of such a thing, but as I said, I don't know a lot about the structure of church organizations. Besides, I had to say something to hide my delight at running into Cailee right off the bat. I mean, how many women named Cailee could belong to one small church?

Cailee laughed. "The job title sounds grander than it is. I mostly just make sure the kitchen is stocked for our Sunday afternoon fellowship. Would you like to join us?"

"Sure!"

"All are welcome here." She held out her hand. "What is your name?"

"Oh, it's R-Rhonda. Rhonda Kindig." I don't know if she noticed the little stutter, but it occurred to me at the last minute that I probably shouldn't give my real name. Rainie was unusual enough for people to remember, and I wasn't sure yet what I was up against.

She led me to the counter and filled a Styrofoam cup with coffee, then indicated an empty chair at a table where two other people were already sitting. Other conversation had resumed, and it seemed like a nice gathering. Maybe there wasn't anything to be suspicious of here. Maybe their connection to Brisby Financial was an innocent coincidence. These people sure didn't seem sinister.

"I'm Pat," a forty-something woman, maybe a few pounds heavier than her doctor recommended, introduced herself and then indicated the man across the table. "This is Larry." Larry was about the same age, well muscled, with a crooked nose but an otherwise quite attractive face.

I glanced around. "You have a pretty large congregation for such a small church."

"Oh, this isn't all of us," Cailee assured me. "There are about 50 other members in Retreat."

"In retreat?" I pictured them running through a large field pursued by soldiers, the losers of a holy battle. But no, that isn't what she meant.

"We have a campground where our members can withdraw for a renewal of their souls." Cailee looked rather dreamy-eyed when she said this, and I thought maybe she wanted to be in Retreat herself.

"Sounds terrific," I enthused, hoping she would tell me more.

"Oh, it is! Father Mika is there now, personally guiding the members on their spiritual journey. After a month of Retreat you feel like a brand new human being."

"They say it's like being reborn!" Pat hugged herself. "I get to go in November. I can hardly wait!"

"Wow! A month!" I shook my head, genuinely surprised. "I can't imagine being able to take a whole month off work like that."

Cailee patted my hand sympathetically. "Most people can't when they first join us. The cares of the secular world seem almost insurmountable, don't they? But once you've heard Father Mika speak, and you understand The Way, you'll see how easy it is to step away from the darkness of your mundane existence and into the light of His love."

"Oh." I wasn't sure what else to say to that. I didn't think my existence was all that mundane. Besides, who could afford to just walk away from their job for a month at a time?

Then I remembered James Bolin, his house sold by Brisby Financial. I wondered if he'd Retreated for good.

"Actually, that sounds like Heaven, not having to worry about the day to day routine." I tried to put on regretful expression. "Sometimes it seems I live only to pay my bills. It's more a matter of existing than living."

"Exactly!" Cailee looked almost triumphant, as if I'd just come around to her way of thinking after a long debate.

"So Father Mika can remove those cares?"

"Well, in a manner of speaking." Cailee visibly toned down her enthusiasm. "It's more that when you feel the warmth of the Light you'll find that those daily cares don't seem as important anymore."

"I feel liberated already," Pat assured me with shining eyes, "And I haven't actually attended Retreat yet."

"You feel the warmth of the light?" I hoped I sounded sincere. Inside I was practically gagging on the cloying nonsense. It's not that I don't believe people can find happiness in their church, but you had to see the look in these people's eyes. On closer inspection their happiness looked a bit more like fanaticism.

"You should come to services tonight," Cailee suggested. "Father Mika will be here."

"Doesn't he always conduct services?"

"He usually does both Sunday services, but Brother Thomas has been covering while Father Mika was in Retreat. Brother Thomas is wonderful too, but we miss Father Mika." She got that rapturous look again at the mention of the great man's name. "His month of Retreat ended today, so now he'll commute back and forth."

"Commute?"

"The camp is in Michigan, not far over the state line." Pat told me. Ah, that put it in my neck of the woods.

I heard muffled singing, and I cocked my head, trying to place it. Children's voices, singing in a minor key.

"Oh, you're hearing the children's choir." Cailee smiled. "They practice every Sunday between services. They're really quite good. If you come tonight you can hear them perform."

"That sounds good." It didn't really. Maybe because I didn't have any children or any prospects in the near future I just didn't find their amateurish, usually off-key attempts at song to be all that charming.

Still, here I was, invited to services, welcomed into their afternoon fellowship with no reservations. In spite of the hint of fanaticism they seemed quite open and friendly. Whatever the connection between the church and Brisby Financial, I doubted that these people had anything to do with it.

"So who did you say told you about us?" Cailee asked. Her question took me by surprise. Maybe I wasn't being welcomed as unquestioningly as I'd first thought.

"Um, well, no one really." I blushed at being caught in a lie, but the sneaky part of my brain, the part I hadn't really been aware of until a few months ago, hurriedly caught up with the program. "The truth is, I've been going from church to church for a couple of months now, trying to find one that suited me. I've been to all the big ones and quite a few of the mid-sized ones. None of them seemed to be what I was looking for, so I thought I'd check out a couple of small churches. I was driving by and saw all the cars and thought I'd stop by."

"Well, that certainly sounds like you've been led by His hand," Larry offered heartily. He looked up at the ceiling, his expression rapt. I couldn't help a little glance myself, wondering if there were someone up there looking down at us. But no, all I saw were stained ceiling tiles and worn but serviceable light fixtures.

"It does indeed!" Cailee was once again touching my hand and I resisted the urge to jerk it away. I wasn't much of a touchy-feely person, but I suppose those of us searching for spiritual enlightenment must learn to be more open. "It wouldn't surprise me if you heard the call of Father Mika and followed it here."

Uh oh. The call of Father Mika? Not God?

"Maybe I did," I said in my best sincere voice. "I certainly feel more welcome here than anywhere else I've tried."

"I used to belong to the mega church in Granger," Pat informed me. "Now *that* was a soul-destroying experience."

"Amen!" Larry agreed fervently. "Two thousand members, four pastors on alternating schedules for services, giant projection TVs so everyone got a good view."

"Sometimes it was hard to tell if I was at church or a sports bar!" Pat added. "And it was all about politics and business connections. Everyone was just trying to get your vote or your patronage. I'm not sure there was one true Christian among them!"

"Now Pat, don't be so judgmental," Larry admonished her. "I mean, we were there for almost three months, and I consider us both good Christians."

"I suppose you're right. I didn't mean to be so cynical."

"It's all right." Cailee patted her hand. "You're still troubled by the cares of the world. After November you'll see things in a much clearer light."

Really? I wondered how they would accomplish that. Maybe a month chewing funny mushrooms around the campfire while this Father Mika guy indoctrinated them?

"So what time do services start tonight?" I asked.

"Six o'clock. So we can expect to see you here?"

"Definitely!" I didn't have to fake my enthusiasm. I was very eager to meet Father Mika. "But I'd better get going. I have some errands to run, and I don't want to be late."

Cailee looked at my sympathetically. "I hope you'll soon find that no errands are as important as fellowship in the

Light, but I understand you're still bound by your cares. We'll look forward to seeing you tonight."

"I can hardly wait." I must have sounded sincere, because that earned me a little hand squeeze. I got up and left before I got sucked into some sort of enlightened group hug.

Chapter Seventeen

I only had four hours before services, but I was hung over and needed a nap so I drove the forty-five minutes home, shut off my cell phone and collapsed on the couch for a nap.

I should have set an alarm. Once again I failed to power nap, and instead slept for nearly an hour and a half. I woke up groggy and cranky and blinked at the clock on the wall: 4:15! I had a headache and my stomach was rumbling.

I stumbled to the kitchen and swallowed a couple ibuprofens with a glass of water before opening the fridge in search of food.

There was some slightly wilted salad and a cooked piece of chicken breast as well as a couple of apples and a loaf of bread.

Nope, not good enough. I needed carbs. Lots of them.

I shut the fridge, ran a brush through my hair and waved goodbye to George, who blinked his eyes at me and went on basking under his heat lamp. I probably should have put him in his cage but I was in a rush, and he rarely got off his perch anyway.

I made a beeline for McDonald's, my mind set on a Quarter Pounder with cheese, a big order of fries and a large, sugar filled coke.

I came to my senses at the last minute and turned into the Subway lot across the street instead. I needed carbs, not 300 grams of fat. I went into Subway for a six inch BMT, but not without a regretful glance back at the golden arches. There's a reason McDonald's is the number one fast food joint in the country; the food might not be healthy, but now and then it sure tasted damned good!

I drove to McCoy Creek Park and ate sitting in my car in the parking lot. I had still gotten myself a Coke. I really needed the sugar and caffeine. By the time I was done my headache was gone and I was feeling a lot better.

I started my car and headed for church.

I got to the church early enough to find a space in the lot, but even as I was crossing to the door a line of cars was pulling in. It looked like there would be a full house tonight.

Two couples were heading for the church ahead of me, and I saw that they were walking around to the front so I followed along.

The front door was accessed by a set of concrete steps, and I realized that we were actually entering one floor above the fellowship hall I'd been in earlier.

There was a small foyer with rows of hooks for coats - all full. I kept my coat on and stepped through an open set of doors into the worship hall, or whatever it was called.

It looked very traditional: rows of well-worn pews and a raised dais in the front. On the dais there was a polished wooden lectern and a couple of folding chairs. There was a huge but unadorned wooden cross on the wall behind the dais. On one side of the cross there was a five foot painting of Jesus walking on water; on the other side was the same size painting of the good looking man I'd seen pictured in the classroom downstairs. In this painting he was standing barefoot next to an old fashioned well, his eyes cast up at the sky.

Cailee was standing near the last pew, greeting people as they arrived. She saw me and clasped both my hands in welcome.

"I'm so glad you came back, Rhonda! I just know you'll find the service life-changing!"

Life-changing! Wow! That was a lot to promise.

"I hope so," I gushed. "I've been looking forward to it all afternoon."

"Have a seat anywhere. We'll talk again after the service."

I moved up the aisle as she turned to greet the next person, choosing a pew a little less than halfway to the front so I could surreptitiously watch the congregation without them knowing.

Others greeted me as I took my seat, including Pat and Larry from the fellowship, who sat to my right. Pat was carrying a slim book, which I first thought might be a bible. On closer inspection I saw that it was a paperback with a dark cover titled *The Way, The Truth, The Light*. When Pat put her copy down on the bench I saw that on the back was a photo of the man in the paintings; not Jesus, the other guy. It had to be Father Mika. What an ego!

At six 'o clock everyone settled in their seats and all chatting stopped. An expectant hush fell over the crowd, and I found my own attention focused on the empty dais.

A door to the left of the dais opened and about a dozen children, varying in age from about six to sixteen and dressed in light brown choir robes, filed in. They lined up in two rows, little kids in the front, tall ones in back, and a woman stepped forward from the front pew.

She held up her hands and all of the children's eyes locked on her. After a short, expectant pause she brought her hands down, and as one the children began to sing.

I have to admit, I was impressed from the first note. This wasn't the off key, overly cutesy stuff I expected to hear at a school recital. These kids were *good*. They opened with Amazing Grace, a hymn that even pagans like me were familiar with, and their harmony was spot on. An angelic looking girl of about fourteen sang solo on the second verse, her voice filling the room with a rich soprano that actually put chills down my spine. Amazing for sure.

I almost applauded when they finished, but fortunately I caught myself in time. Apparently you didn't applaud in church. Instead there were appreciative murmurs and a few louder "amens."

I listened with rapt attention through two more songs, neither of which I recognized. Both of which were heavy on the "His love" and "my devotion." The children sang with enough heartfelt sincerity to almost make me wish I was a believer.

The children filed back through the door, as perfectly disciplined as soldiers right out of boot camp. I wondered how the choir director, a tiny woman with big hair and even bigger glasses, managed that. She didn't look like a retired drill sergeant; maybe she had once been a nun. From what I've heard their teaching methods are similar.

Once the children were gone an even deeper hush fell over the room, a stillness, as if everyone was holding their breath at the same time. All eyes were fastened on the dais, and the feeling of anticipation was so thick I found myself barely breathing, wondering what amazing event was about to unfold.

A door to the right of the dais opened and a man emerged. He moved to the podium, almost seeming to glide as if he were riding one of those airport conveyor belts. I recognized him from all the paintings. This must be Father Mika.

The portrait had not done him justice. He was far more beautiful than mere paint on canvas could capture. His features were perfectly symmetrical, his eyebrows were delicately arched - perfect frames for his large, dark brown eyes framed by thick lashes. His hair was dark and thick, a little curly; the type that invited fingers to run through it.

This is not to say he was effeminate. His jaw was just square enough, his nose just bold enough, to make him all man. He could easily have graced the cover of GQ Magazine, or a bodice-ripper romance novel.

I tore my eyes away from his nearly perfect face to look at the rest of him. He was dressed just like in the painting: all in brown, in a simple, soft-looking tunic with no buttons or zippers, which was wrapped around a slim, strong-looking torso and tied with a cloth belt. His pants were of the same material, loose-fitting and hanging in casual folds to what looked like soft moccasins covering his feet.

Then he smiled, and a sigh went over the room as everyone expelled their held breath at the same time.

And oh, that smile! It was as beautiful as the rest of him: a welcoming, open smile that revealed perfect teeth.

"Welcome." He raised both long-fingered, strong looking hands to the expectant crowd.

"We feel welcome, Father Mika." The whole congregation spoke as one, making me feel a little left out.

Then Father Mika started his speech, or sermon, or whatever it was, and I listened along with everyone else.

"I see we have a few new faces tonight," he cast his glance over the room, and he met my eyes for a brief instant before moving on and catching the eye of a man far to my left. That momentary contact was almost like an electrical shock, a mild one such as you get from dragging your feet across carpet and then touching a doorknob. I found myself wishing he'd look at me again, and I literally shook myself. What the hell? I was not the type to fall for a pretty face.

"All are welcome, all are wanted here." And when he spoke the words they sounded sincere, and as if they were directed right at me.

I hardened myself against his charm and ordered myself to listen objectively.

That worked for a while. He spoke of God and the universe and our place in creation, all stuff that I guessed most preachers talked about. I kept scanning the room, trying not to be drawn in, but the man had charisma, and a way of projecting his voice at just the right volume so you found yourself leaning forward to be sure you caught every word. He was constantly scanning the crowd, much as I was, but he was making sure to catch an individual's eyes every few moments, and when he did that person would stare back with something akin to joy.

Then something he was saying really caught my attention, and I found myself listening harder.

"And so we work a little harder to buy ourselves a piece of that new technology that everyone seems to be talking about. A new cell phone, a bigger, clearer flat screen TV. But there is less and less time to enjoy those toys as we put in more and more hours at the office or the factory to buy the newest upgrade. But the neighbor has a 46 inch screen, and your brother just downloaded a computer program to remote start his car. So you work some overtime to get that for yourself.

"You get home from your 12 hour work day and enter your home, filled with every convenience man's prolific mind can conceive, and drop in front of that big new TV. And on the news or on a sitcom you see yet another new gadget, and so you go to your bed, weary, dispirited, because what you want seems out of reach.

"But is it? What you must ask yourself, my friend, is: *what is it you really want*. Under all the hype and groping for goodies, what is that one thing you're looking for?"

He paused, and everyone, including me, leaned forward in anticipation of this revelation.

"Happiness. That's all." Father Mika shook his head and smiled at the simplicity of it all. I *should* have been thinking that it was not only simple, but kind of stupid. But I wasn't. I found myself nodding my head with the rest of the congregation. What he was saying not only made perfect sense, it struck me almost as an epiphany.

"But friends, we don't really derive happiness from things.

"Every human, since Creation, has first needed the basics: food, shelter, clothing. After those needs are met we can seek our pleasure. But back in the beginning, some of that pleasure was derived from the satisfaction of accomplishment. The knowledge that we had built ourselves walls and a roof, and made it warm, that we hunted or found food to fill our bellies. A man could sit back as the sun went down and smile at the comforts he'd wrought.

"We're missing that today. Most of us have never had to struggle that hard to put a roof over our heads. Oh, of course we've worked, maybe even a few have been threatened with homelessness, but which of you has ever felt the pure joy of pounding a nail into a roof you built yourself, a product of your sweat that didn't rely on a landlord or a mortgage company?

"Let me tell you friends, there is nothing quite as pleasing as sitting at the table you assembled with your own hands and eating a meal that you grew for yourself. Suddenly you wonder at what you'd been pushing yourself for all that time. For a little electronic entertainment that gives only the briefest, shallowest moment of pleasure? Now you find yourself surrounded by people who love you, sitting near the fire on a chilly evening singing songs of praise or exchanging stories - really connecting with the people that matter to you.

"You find that elusive dream: happiness. And you didn't have to work under another man's thumb for 12 hours, being belittled and ordered about like a servant, to get it."

He stopped to let us absorb his words, and around me I could sense the acceptance, the almost mystical calm that had settled over the crowd.

"We don't need all that 'stuff'. In fact, by giving it up, by letting go of the junk we've accumulated in our lives, we find ourselves unfettered, free to feel the pure joy of being alive."

He went on about the Retreat, and the joy of moving there permanently, leaving the stressful and dog-eat-dog existence we'd all been roped into. He spoke of the excitement of hunting and killing your own meal for the first time, of the satisfaction we would feel the first night we went to sleep in a home we had literally built with our own hands. Now I was beginning to understand: give everything you own to Father Mika and in exchange he would give you a spot in the woods where you could struggle to survive. I wondered what sort of home Father Mika lived in; I doubted it was a rugged log cabin in the woods.

It seemed the whole congregation was hanging on his every word, but for me the spell, if that's what you want to call it- and it certainly felt as if I'd been truly mesmerized- was broken. Give up my stuff? I didn't think so. I didn't have a lot, but I'd worked hard for what I had and I intended to keep it.

But at the same time I suddenly understood what had happened to James Bolin. For a few moments there I had been completely taken in by Father Mika's charismatic delivery of what seemed like perfect common sense. For that very brief time I had almost been ready to sell my own house and join him in the simple life, free from the stress and unhappiness of modern society.

Except for one thing: I liked my life. I didn't feel a need to scrape for the latest gadget. My cell phone was three years old, a simple device that made calls and texts and nothing else. My television had a 25 inch screen and I had to have the little box on it just to run digital signals because I didn't even have cablevision. My car - well, everyone knows about my car. I was already practically living the simple life, just with flushing toilets and central heat. Why would I want to move to a primitive camp where I had to skin my own dinner and chop wood to get warm?

But I suppose for some people the relief of no longer struggling to maintain a lifestyle that was only practical for actors in a soap opera was very appealing.

Look at Jim Bolin. No more sitting in an office, working overtime to pay child support.

Of course, no children to support, either. He'd effectively cut himself off from his own family. Did Father Mika's congregation fill that need?

My mind came back to Father Mika, who seemed to be drawing the service to a close.

"Now I'd like to bring our lovely children's chorus out again to lead us in a hymn." He held a hand out toward the left hand door and the children once again filed out, as if created by him at that very moment with his simple gesture. It was odd, watching the guy. On one level I thought every move he made, right down to the speed of his breathing, was calculated, yet at the same time he did it all so fluidly that I couldn't really put my finger on why I thought that. He was a pleasure to see and listen to, yet under the surface there was something that made my skin crawl. Like watching a horror movie that was showing a scene of a beautiful, sunlit lake, but then there was a tiny ripple, nothing really, but the music playing let you know there was something sinister and horrific lurking under the water.

"Please, join hands," Father Mika invited the crowd. Cailee grasped my hand on the left, and Larry took my hand on the right, his face cast in an expression of rapture. I wanted to snatch my hands back; I hated casual touching. But this was undercover work; I had to pretend I was a part of it all. So I smiled back and tried to pretend my hands were not part of my body, that there wasn't the sweat of a stranger's palm against my skin.

The choir took their places, the little lady with the big hair raised her hands, and once again the children started singing Amazing Grace, only this time the whole congregation joined in.

Strangely, even though many people in the congregation were perhaps singing a bit off key, the addition just added a slight atonal counterpoint to the music that enhanced rather than detracted from it. Although I didn't believe He'd saved a wretch like me I still found myself transported by the beauty of the sound, and I was sorry for it to end.

When it did, everyone turned to a person next to them and shook the hand they were holding. "So happy to know you," they all said as one. Clearly it was a practiced ritual, but Larry sounded so sincere. Whatever else was going on here, some of these people were true believers.

The people were breaking up into little knots, talking softly among themselves, but even so the noise level was moving up the scale. Father Mika had come down from the dais and was circulating among them, stopping at each group and offering his hands to be held. I was reminded of watching the Pope on TV when he had come to the United States for a visit. Everywhere people were trying to touch him, even if it were only to brush the hem of his sleeve, as if he had some magical power that would transfer to them. Now I saw people touch Father Mika on the shoulder, or the elbow, as if just that brief contact would change their lives.

"So what did you think?" Cailee asked me.

"It was amazing," I answered, not really lying. I *was* pretty amazed by this whole thing: Father Mika's charisma, the wonderful choir, and the congregation's obvious devotion to a man who seemed to be presenting himself as a messiah.

"And Father Mika's message, what did you think of that?"

"I felt..." I hesitated, realizing I was too calm. I didn't want to sound analytical; if I wanted more information I was going to have to be rapturous. "I felt almost... an epiphany, I think that's the word. As if Father Mika was describing my own dreary life!"

"Yes, that is the word," Father Mika's perfectly modulated voice came from my left, and he laid a hand briefly on my arm. I turned to him and his eyes met mine with a force akin to two freight cars locking in place. I almost gasped, but instead I placed my own hand on top of his, as if reluctant to break contact. "Most people feel that way when they first consider The Way. But you my dear," he smiled and for just a moment I was the only person in the room with him. "You were so rapt during the service, so intent on my words, that I knew you understood."

Huh. I'd been intent? I did remember being drawn in a couple of times, but it seemed I'd spent much of the service travelling around my own head as I was inclined to do. Apparently he had mistaken my expression of dreaminess for devotion. That was good; I was willing to go with it.

"Oh, I did understand. I've been seeking something, and I thought I just needed a new church, but I see now that I was looking for a new life."

"It was His hand that led you here to our humble assembly. Those who sincerely seek enlightenment are always guided by His loving hand." He withdrew his hand and spoke to Cailee. "Take good care of our new little sister." They exchanged a look I couldn't quite interpret and Cailee nodded.

"I will, Father Mika."

He moved on to the next group.

"He's a great man," Larry murmured.

"Yes, he is!" I turned to Cailee, wanting to keep the momentum going. I needed to look transported with the joy of my new revelation if I was going to get into that camp to look for James Bolin. I'm not sure I'd ever been

195

rapturous myself, but my sister has been, many times. When she finds a new hobby or cause she jumps in with both feet, often so carried away I think she's floating a couple of feet above reality, but the important thing is her enthusiasm is always sincere, and that's what I needed to project. So I imagined my sister's face the day she and Thelma had decided to open their store and I tried to copy it: eyes wide and shining (I had no idea how to get my eyes to shine; it's not like I could grab a paper towel and polish them up. I would just have to hope the light was right), mouth not exactly smiling but turned up slightly at the corners, lips slightly parted as if to draw in extra oxygen. I tensed my shoulders, raised my chin and grasped Cailee's arm for emphasis, hoping I looked joyful and not as if I was having a heart attack.

"Please, Cailee, I want to go to Retreat. I want to spend that month in spiritual renewal!"

Cailee patted my hand in understanding but looked regretful. "I know, you want this feeling to go on, and it will! But Retreat is not something a person goes into lightly. Normally a new member spends at least a month coming to services, getting to know us, getting their thoughts and spirits in line with The Way."

"A month?" I wailed the word as if she'd just told me that was all the time I had left to live. The truth was I couldn't imagine having to come here three nights a week for a whole month. There had to be a shortcut.

"Please Rhonda, listen to me," Cailee spoke as if she were trying to talk me down from a hysterical fit. "I know it seems like forever, but it's important to have your spiritual life in order before you enter Retreat."

"What?" I was genuinely confused. "But I thought that was what Retreat was all about."

"Not exactly." Cailee looked around at the crowd, which showed no sign of dispersing. "Come with me, we'll find some place quiet to talk." I followed her out of the main room to the foyer and down the stairs to the fellowship hall. She led me through a door next to the little kitchen into a small, simply furnished office.

Behind the desk there was another portrait of Father Mika, this one just from the shoulders up. His eyes were focused up, as if gazing at Heaven, and although there was no halo, the artist had managed with a trick of light and delicate brushstrokes to give the impression that there was a glowing aura around his head. I had seen similar paintings before, but they were depictions of Jesus. I assumed the similarity was deliberate.

As soon as she shut the door behind us I continued my plea.

"Cailee, I know there are probably good reasons to wait so long, but try to understand!" I tried to bring up real tears, but uh uh, not today. If I was going to make a regular thing of this undercover stuff I'd have to work on that trick. "I've been searching so long! I told you, I've been all over the area, visiting every church I could think of, looking for that special something. I believe Father Mika is right, that I was led here by the hand of God. I don't see how waiting a month could make me any more ready than I am now."

"But Rhonda, Retreat is a big commitment, and not something you enter into lightly. Besides, you'll need to make arrangements. You'll be away from your job for a month. What about paying your rent? And you should talk to your family..."

"I work for myself, and I don't rent, I own my house outright." I wanted to make my financial situation sound appealing. "As for my family," I rolled my eyes. "All I have is my mother, and she's off in Florida somewhere with her new boy toy. She'll never even know I'm gone." I lowered my head. "Maybe that's why I've been searching for something, and why this church just... calls to me."

197

"It still seems you're rushing this. You've only attended one service."

"But what a service!" I widened my eyes - with rapture, I hoped. "I don't see how anyone could listen to Father Mika and not be instantly transported! I want what you all have!"

Cailee stared at me for a moment, and I could see the calculation in her eyes. Any thought I had that maybe I shouldn't be so suspicious of this place, that maybe Father Mika really believed he was doing good, was erased by that look. This was a con, and Cailee was clearly debating whether I was really on the hook or not. Like any good fisherman, she knew that if she jerked the line taut too soon I might slip away.

Apparently she decided I'd really swallowed the hook deep, because she nodded and touched my arm again. Sheesh, I was going to have to start wearing long sleeves around these people; they couldn't seem to go three minutes without touching me.

"Maybe you're right. Sometimes a person is ready from the first time they hear Father Mika. He speaks to that place deep in your soul where you truly know what you need."

"Yes! That's it exactly! As soon as I heard him I realized that everything about my life is off-kilter somehow. I want to start fresh and find that inner peace the rest of you have."

"Very well, I'll see what I can do to move you up on the list." Cailee moved around behind the desk and opened a file drawer. In a moment she came up with a thin sheaf of papers and handed them to me. "First we need to officially admit you to the congregation."

"That's wonderful!" I gushed, and then looked down at the papers in my hand. It looked like a job application, except there had to be five or six pages. "What's this?"

198

"Just a little survey, a way for us to get to know you better."

I scanned the first page: name, address, phone, basic stuff. I flipped to the next page. It asked for a brief employment history, including salary. I tried to keep the frown off my face and instead project an aura of innocent curiosity.

"This looks almost like a job application."

"I know," Cailee smiled and touched my arm again. "It may seem a bit strange, but Father Mika has found that before we give up our old lives it's important to confront and analyze them. You have to take a long, critical look at how you've been living before you can make the choice to walk away from it. With this information in hand it will be easier for me to counsel you."

"You'll counsel me? Not Father Mika?"

"I know, everyone would prefer to speak to him directly, and you will get that opportunity at Retreat. But understand everyone wants his time. He has designated me to be his representative for this initial stage - the tedious part. Believe me, you'll prefer to spend your time with him speaking of much loftier spiritual matters."

"I guess I can understand that." I made sure she could hear the disappointment in my tone. "So I fill this out and bring it back on Thursday so we can discuss it?"

"Yes, but you don't want to be in a rush when you fill it out. There are questions in there that require a bit of soul searching, and I want you to be sure you've answered them as honestly as possible."

"I wouldn't lie to you!" I lied, looking stunned at such a horrible suggestion.

"Of course you wouldn't," Cailee patted my arm in a calming gesture. "The thing is, I don't want you to lie to yourself. It's important that you really think about the questions and don't just give the first answer that pops into your head. Most people tell themselves little untruths every day; it's one way we cope with a reality that is almost too harsh to bear."

"I suppose that's true."

"So, take it with you, find a quiet place to contemplate, and fill it out the best you can."

"Okay." I was more than ready to take my leave, but I knew what was required of me here. It wasn't as abhorrent to me as say, sticking my hand into a bucket full of crushed worms, but it was pretty close. Nonetheless, in the spirit of maintaining my carefully cultivated new-found enlightenment I pulled Cailee into a hug.

She hugged me back, obviously not suffering my aversion to strangers man-handling her. We broke the embrace and I stepped back, hoping the expression on my face reflected gratitude instead of mild disgust.

"Thank you so much, Cailee. I already feel like a new person."

"Of course. That's why Father Mika calls this the Church of Renewal. Just wait until you get to Retreat!" Her eyes were shining with what looked like genuine fervor, and I envied her ability.

"Well, I'll see you Thursday." I turned to go, acting reluctant to be away from her comforting presence.

As soon as I drove out of the lot I lit a cigarette. This was getting a lot more complicated than I'd expected, but then, didn't that always seem to happen when I was on a job for B&E?

It occurred to me that the membership application would also provide most - if not all - of the information Cailee would need to perform a background check on me. As soon as she did, it was all over. I'd given my name as Rhonda Kindig, never expecting anyone to check.

Was it possible to fake a background check? How complicated would that be? I didn't know, and the truth was right now I didn't want to think about it anymore. My head was pounding and I just wanted sleep. I would deal with this tomorrow.

Chapter Eighteen

Bob was in an excellent mood the next morning. I guess there was something liberating about discovering you weren't crazy. His mood was infectious, and by the time I got to B&E to run some computer checks I was pretty happy myself.

That is, I was until Jack sauntered into the computer room, carrying my neatly folded skirt. The last thing I needed was a reminder of Saturday night's fiasco.

"Here's your skirt." He was smiling cheerfully, as if nothing had ever happened. I snatched the skirt from him and tossed it on the desk.

"Thanks." I was deliberately curt. I went back to my computer work.

"Hey, what's the matter with you?"

"I'm busy."

"No, you're pissed. What the hell did I do?"

"What did you do?" Now I stood up. I *was* pissed. "You *lied* to me! You told me Dan didn't want to take me home."

"I never said that, I just said he was quick to let me take you."

"All right, then you led me to believe it."

Now Jack looked pissed. He glanced over at Mike Forsey, who was sitting at another computer, doing the same thing I was supposed to be doing. Jack jerked his head toward the door, and without a word Mike got up and scurried out, closing the door behind him. Maybe I should have been worried; Jack looked pretty scary when he was mad, but instead that just made me angrier.

"What are you bullying Mike for?"

"I didn't bully him. I just didn't think you'd want your dirty laundry aired in public."

"*My* dirty laundry?"

"Yes yours, Rainie! You're the one that got so drunk you couldn't take care of yourself, so quit taking your embarrassment out on me. I didn't pour that beer down your throat. I didn't do anything but keep you safe, so quit blaming me for your stupidity."

That hurt, mostly because it was true. Hadn't I thought the same thing, in almost those same words? I felt tears threatening but no way was I going to cry in front of Jack, so I worked on getting madder.

"Oh yeah, big hero. What the hell did you save me from? I was never in any danger."

"Maybe not, but even if Dan didn't force you to drink he was sure in a hurry to keep your cup filled. You don't think maybe he had an ulterior motive for helping you get drunk? I thought you'd be safer with me."

Now I was staring at the floor because I was too humiliated to meet Jack's eyes. He was right. I had been a total idiot, and I needed to own up to it. I needed to swallow my pride, but it was like a big chunk of something awful, like maybe a frog in a blender, and I couldn't seem to make it go down.

Jack had fallen silent, waiting for my response.

Come on Rainie! I tried to encourage myself. *Just say it!*

"You're right," I mumbled grudgingly, still staring at the floor. "I'm sorry." That last was so quiet even I could barely hear it, but apparently Jack's special forces training also gave him super hearing.

"That's all right, no big deal." He gave me a light fist bump on the arm. "So we're good?"

"Yeah, we're good." But I still couldn't bring myself to look at him. I wanted to crawl into a closet somewhere and hide my stupid head.

"Great. I've got to hit the road." His tone was cheerful again, his anger switched off like a lamp. "Give me a call if you need anything."

I knocked off at five o'clock and went home. I still hadn't figured out what to do about the application for the Church of Renewal. Should I just let the whole thing drop?

I hated the thought of just letting Father Mika get away with his con. I hated people who took advantage of those who were lonely and vulnerable. It happened all the time: elderly people who answered calls for sweepstakes, younger people searching for romance. And always there were bad guys out there, waiting to swoop down like hawks on mice caught out in the open. Now that I knew about it, I couldn't just ignore it.

So, I needed to find out if it was possible to fake a background check. I called Eddie, but his phone went straight to voicemail. I couldn't think of any message to leave that wouldn't make him worry so I disconnected.

That left Jack.

Did I really want to call him? He had seemed so willing to just forget the whole weekend, but I was still pretty embarrassed. The problem was I would likely feel that way for a long time; my self-esteem had always been a fragile thing, fluctuating up and down more frequently than my weight. Well, as my mom would say, just go with the flow, honey. Do your own thing and don't worry what anyone else thought about you. That was their problem, after all, not yours.

Even so I sat with my phone in my hand for several minutes, Jack's number called up on the contacts list. I took a deep breath and hit send.

He answered on the first ring. I could hear music in the background. Sounded like Styx, one of my mom's favorite bands. The lead singer was originally from Niles, and I think maybe she'd partied with him back in the day.

"What's up?" Jack asked.

"I'm just wondering: how hard is it to make up a fake background on someone?"

"You mean like one you want to tell someone, or one that will actually pass inspection?"

"Pass inspection."

Jack was silent for a few seconds. "You at home?"

"Yeah."

"I'll be there in twenty minutes."

I sighed and closed my phone. I should have known he wouldn't let the question go without an explanation.

Jack arrived twenty minutes later, as promised, looking as delicious as ever. His jeans were tight in all the right places, his t-shirt dark blue and taut enough to bounce quarters off of the chest, his hair...

"Hey, you shaved your head!"

"Yeah." Jack grinned and ran a hand over his now shiny scalp. He hadn't just buzzed it; there wasn't a shadow of hair to be seen. It looked like he'd polished it. Did they make scalp wax or had he used Lemon Pledge? "I figured there was no sense waiting around for the inevitable, I might as well get right to it."

"You aren't that bald yet."

"Yet." Jack grinned again. "What, you don't like it?"

I shook my head. "Not particularly. Too shiny."

"Really?" Jack ran his hand over his head again, looking a bit nonplussed. "You like the buzz cut better?"

"Well yeah. It looked more natural. This makes you look like you lost a bet."

"Huh." Jack pulled a baseball cap out of his jacket pocket and slapped it on his head. "Better?"

I laughed. "You can wear it however you want. It's your head."

"Yeah, but I don't want to look like a loser."

"That's not..." I broke off and laughed. "Never mind."

"So what are you up to?" He finally asked. "You aren't investigating another serial killer client, are you?"

"Nope. Actually it's B&E business. I'm still looking for James Bolin."

"The dead-beat dad?"

"That's the one."

"Hell Rainie, he only skipped out on child support. It's not like he stole secret government documents to sell to Iran."

"I know, but I think I'm on to something here. Have you learned anything new about the connection between Brisby Financial and the Church of Renewal?"

"From what we've found it seems it's just a normal business arrangement. Brisby handles some of the church's finances, that's all."

"Including selling member's donated assets? I can't see how that's a legitimate practice for a church."

"I told you before, it's not that strange. People leave entire estates to their churches every day."

"Sure, when they're *dead*! But Jim Bolin is still alive and kicking. He turned everything over to the church to go live in a campground!"

"Are you saying you know where he is?"

"I'm pretty sure he's at the retreat the church has built for itself somewhere here in Michigan. If I can get the address I can go check it out for sure, but I don't think they'll just tell me unless I get them to trust me."

"Rainie, are you forgetting that your only job is to find the guy? If you've got this good a lead you're supposed to turn it over to the P.I. in charge. He'll find the address and confirm Bolin's whereabouts."

"But I've put so much in to this!" I protested.

Jack laughed.

"What's so funny?"

"You are. Sometimes you're the overly-cautious caregiver who barely wants to leave the house, and other times you're like a pit bull with a hambone, clamping down and hanging on to an idea for dear life. You really want to pursue this so bad? So what if a couple of people signed over their houses. Maybe they're really happier."

"And maybe Father Mika is filling his off-shore bank account before getting them all to drink the Kool-Aid."

"You don't really have any proof of that."

"I've got my intuition, and let me tell you, there's something not right about the place. I've been to a few churches, and the vibe at this one isn't natural."

"So what's your plan?"

"I've got an in. They're about to let me join the church, and shortly after that I'll get to go see the campground for myself."

"Yeah?"

"Yeah. Only I told them my name was Rhonda Kindig, and now they want me to fill out these forms with all my information and I'm pretty sure they'll do a background check. When they do it's all over; I'll never get near the place, and worse, they'll know someone is on to them."

"That's a good point." Jack considered for a minute, staring at the floor. I stared with him, wondering if he was noticing the irregularly shaped coffee stain to the left of his foot or the unidentified but nearly perfectly circle-shaped one to the right.

"Here's the thing," he finally said. "I don't think Harry is going to sanction the expense of putting together a false background for such a petty case, even if it might involve two clients. What we need is a computer hacker. Did you try Mason?"

"Mason? He's good with computers, but I don't think he's at that level."

"Hah! You need to listen between the lines when your friends speak. He knows about a hell of a lot more than that software he does support for. Trust me. Call him."

So I called Mason, my computer guru. I've always said that the next been thing to educating yourself about everything you need to know in this world is making friends with people who already knew it. Mason had a knack with computers and spent a lot of time online, researching the latest technology and keeping up with all that stuff that fascinated me in passing but which I didn't take time to fully understand. Still, I found it hard to believe he could do what Jack claimed.

Pam answered Mason's cell and we exchanged pleasantries before I asked to speak to Mason. "I'll get him. He's in the basement, reorganizing his album collection." That was another oddity: in spite of his vast knowledge of all things 21st century, Mason still avidly collected - and regularly listened to - vinyl records. It was as if he straddled some invisible timeline, refusing to step fully into the future, but equally reluctant to remain hunkered down in the past.

"Hey Rainie! What's up?" Mason sounded really cheerful. He must have been listening to some upbeat tunes while he sorted. In fact, I thought I could hear the strains of a Monkees song in the background. Never mind that Mason claimed that the Monkees were just a pre-packaged band created to compete with the Beatles; he still owned every record they ever made and even had his kids listening to them. I guess that was a lot better than his kids learning too early the harsh tunes of Tupak or whatever the most recent rapper's name was.

"I have a question. Is it possible to make up a fake background check?"

"I'm not sure what you mean." Mason didn't sound all that surprised by my question. Maybe he was used to the odd little tangents I often went off on.

"Like say someone was going to do a background check on me and I was going to give them a false name and information. Is it possible to set it up to pass a background check or is that just in the movies?"

"What, are you trying to defraud someone?" Masson laughed, and I was glad to know he didn't really think I'd do such a thing. Yet of course, that's exactly what I was trying to do.

"Kind of," I admitted. "But it's for a good cause."

"This something to do with B&E?"

"Yeah."

"Why don't you ask Jack?"

"I did. In fact he's right here, but he suggested I talk to you."

There was a moment of silence while Mason digested that.

"I'd say it's mostly movie possible, but I suppose with the right access it could be done. Of course it's way beyond the scope of my computer skills. You'd have to hack into a lot of places to put your false information there: companies you'd supposedly worked for, credit card companies, hell, maybe even utility companies. Not really possible for all practical purposes."

"That's what I thought, but Jack was pretty sure you'd know how."

"Why doesn't B&E do it?"

"Because the case isn't big enough to justify the expense."

"But it's big enough for you to want to go to all this trouble?"

"I think some decent people are being scammed by a guy hiding behind the façade of a church, screwing people in the name of God. I think I'd like to put a stop to it if I can."

Mason sighed, and I could almost feel a subtle shift in his thought pattern. Mason wasn't exactly a do-gooder, but he was a good guy and always willing to help out if he could. And I think the reference to hiding behind a false church helped; Mason really believed all that Catholic stuff and took his churching seriously. We've had plenty of arguments on the merits or lack of them in organized religion, and I don't think he appreciated someone using religion for fraud. It tended to give all religions a bad name.

"Let me think about this. How soon do you need it done?"

"By Thursday night."

"Thursday!" Mason was shocked. "That's only a few days!"

"I know it's short notice, but I didn't expect this to come up."

Mason sighed again. "Let me talk to Jack."

I held the phone out. "He wants to talk to you."

Jack took the phone. "Yeah?" he listened for a minute, then grinned. "Just a lucky guess."

Since I couldn't hear Mason, I tried to glean what I could from Jack's side of the conversation. He listened for a few minutes, then said, "Sure, I can do that. State of the art, fastest out there." Listening, then: "60 gigs? Easy. Hang on a minute." He looked at me.

"I need paper and pen."

I got him the pad and pen I always kept close by in case the poetry muse smacked me upside the head, and he told Mason to go ahead. For a few minutes it was just a matter of Jack scribbling and saying "Uh huh," and "What was that?"

Finally Jack ended the call, saying "See you then," and handed to phone back to me.

"So?" I was impatient.

"Mason can do it if I provide an untraceable laptop and some other equipment." Jack held up the list he'd written.

"He'll be over tomorrow night at seven o'clock, so I'd better get on it."

"You're going to go buy him a computer?"

"Hell no!" Jack laughed. "I don't have to buy this kind of stuff. You want to come along and I'll show you how it's done?"

"Absolutely not!" I backed a step away, as if proximity would get me drawn into his scheme against my will. "Besides, I have to fill out this application." I picked it up off the coffee table and Jack took it from me, quickly scanning through the pages.

"Odd thing for a church to ask for. And what's with these questions?" he read one aloud. "I cherish my house because…" he looked up at me.

"I'm not sure, but I think the idea is to discover your reasons for hanging on to things, so they can convince you to give them up."

"Ah." Jack shook his head. "Are people really that gullible?"

"Some people are really that lonely," I corrected. "They'll do almost anything to feel accepted and loved. Besides, you should hear Father Mika talk. He's incredibly charismatic."

"Yeah? Are you thinking about joining him for real?"

"What? Of course not! I find the whole thing kind of creepy. But I can see how a needy person could get drawn into it."

"You don't have anything to worry about then. You sure aren't needy."

I looked at him, not sure what he meant by that. He almost sounded disappointed. I decided I didn't particularly want to delve into Jack's mind, though, so I changed the subject.

"I'd better get to work on this."

"You should answer the weird questions, but wait on the basic information until you talk to Mason. He might have an easier time of it if he can make the stuff up himself. He knows better what he can hack into."

"Good point. Okay, I'll do that."

"Good. Well, I'm off on a shopping trip." He grinned his mischievous grin - one of my favorites. "Sure you don't want to come along?"

Grin or not, I refused to be sucked in.

"No thanks. I'll see you tomorrow."

He shrugged and headed for the door. I wondered just how he'd go about finding an untraceable state of the art laptop and that other stuff. I was pretty sure he wasn't going to borrow it from anyone.

Just as he was about to close the door I called out, "Be careful!"

He poked his head back in. "Aw, what's the fun in that?"

Chapter Nineteen

Tuesday with Thelma was blessedly uneventful. I helped her putter around the store, which was already getting some foot traffic. She was doing what she called a "soft opening." Basically that meant she was letting word get around but hadn't actually started any advertising. She was waiting until the end of October for a grand opening - an event that would be advertised on radio, TV and the newspapers. I shuddered inwardly at the cost of such a blitz, but hey, it was her money.

My mother stopped by around three o'clock with my niece Sierra in tow. Sierra was ten, a blond haired, blue eyed little genius always on the hunt for something new to do.

"Sierra has a business proposition for you," my mom told Thelma. Then she stepped back and let Sierra make her pitch.

Sierra had been indulging her creative side, and she'd come up with a gimmicky little creature that she believed would be the next pet rock. It was a tiny little puffball with big feet and big googly eyes and little antennae sticking out the top of the head.

Sierra had affixed a tiny strip of Velcro to the bottoms of the little critter's feet, and she demonstrated how you could stick it on your shoulder so it could be with you all the time.

"They're called Pompets," she explained proudly. "And see? They come with accessories." She started lifting tiny items out of a box: a little tiny cage for the Pompet to sleep in, miniature food dishes, tiny leashes. They were so cute I couldn't help but smile.

"I'm trying to design costumes for Halloween. I've already made these for Christmas," she held out a little white Pompet wearing a red Santa hat, "And these for Valentine's Day." This one was pink, it's feet cut into the shape of a heart.

"Those are pretty cute," Thelma agreed, taking a closer look at the Santa Pompet. "So why are you showing me?"

"I'm going to sell them, and I want to put them in your store on a commission basis. I'm also going to make a website and sell them that way."

"I see," Thelma nodded, her expression serious. "Can you make enough of them to keep me well stocked? I don't want to have just one or two to sell. No one would even look at them. If you can give me maybe fifty of them, I'll let you display them right in the front window."

"Really?"

"Sure, I think people will stop in just to look at them."

"How much will I have to pay you?"

"Hmm, let me think about that." Thelma looked up at the ceiling, pretending to mull it over. "I'll tell you what, seeing as how you're practically family, and your mother owns half this store, I'm thinking maybe we can let you display for free."

"Really?"

"Sure. I'm surprised you didn't just ask your mother in the first place."

"Gramma didn't think that would be es...I mean, ethical. It would be nepo..." she frowned and looked at my mom, who smiled.

"Nepotism, honey."

"Right."

"Well, nepotism is only a bad thing when the 'nepotee' is a worthless sack of... never mind. This isn't politics or a big corporation, and you seem worth taking a chance on. You come back with your little critters and we'll set up a nice display, okay?"

"Thanks Mrs. Thelma! You rock!"

"You bet I do!" Thelma laughed and gave Sierra a fist bump.

I went home and took care of George, who looked pretty happy about getting out of his cage. I mean, it's not like he smiled or anything, but there was just something satisfied about his otherwise deadpan reptilian expression. Maybe you just had to get to know him to understand.

Jack showed up at 6:45 with a pizza from Luigi's down in South Bend. It was excellent pizza, with a thin, crispy crust, flavorful sauce and thick, gooey cheese. The owner would sell them half-baked so you could take them home and finish cooking them; otherwise by the time you drove the half hour back to Michigan it was cold.

"Half sausage and pepperoni, half green peppers and black olives, all of it extra cheese."

"Sounds great," I said over my rumbling stomach as Jack heated my oven and unwrapped the pizza. "But I already had dinner."

"What, an apple? Maybe a raisin for desert? Forget it, Rainie. You'll eat pizza and like it."

"When did you appoint yourself my dietician?"

"It's part of the job description when you have a friend. You know, counselor, taxi service, drinking buddy, dietician. It's all in the rule book." He popped the pizza in the oven. "I'll be right back."

He went out to his truck and brought in a rather oversized laptop computer and a canvas bag full of smaller electronics. "Should I set up in your office or at the dining room table?"

"Dining room. There's more space."

I watched in silence while he set everything up. Mason came in the back door just as Jack was booting up the computer. "Got everything?" He sounded serious and all business, nothing like his usual jovial self.

Mason fiddled with the array of gadgets Jack had set up around the laptop, most of which I couldn't identify. I did recognize the wireless router.

"Hey, won't they be able to trace you back to my internet service? I mean, hacking *is* illegal."

"Yet you asked me to do it for you, anyway." Mason smiled for the first time. "Besides, I can get around that. I'll send the signal from here to hell and over to Siberia first. It would take a month to trace it back, and I won't be at it that long."

I nodded doubtfully. I could use a computer, and I understood the basics of hacking; you had to get through passwords and firewalls to change data on other computers. I had also heard of that bouncing the signals stuff, but only in the movies. I was a little awed that Mason knew how to do it.

I brought the church application and explained Jack's idea that Mason might want to decide what information to provide. He nodded and looked it over.

"By the way, if Pam asks I was here to fix your computer, okay? I told her your hard drive crashed and I needed to do a full wipe and recovery." He looked unhappy about lying to his wife, and I felt a twinge of guilt.

"Sure, Mason. Look, I really appreciate this."

"Yeah, well." Suddenly he grinned and cracked his knuckles. "To tell you the truth I've been looking forward to this. I mean, I do a little here and there just to keep my skills sharp, but I haven't done any serious hacking for a while." He looked at me over his glasses. "Pam doesn't really approve."

"Might have something to do with that whole husband-going-to-jail thing."

"Maybe." Mason went back to studying the application, dead serious again.

"Okay, this is good. So fill it out with your own address. I'll just change the name in the tax rolls to Rhonda Kindig."

"Wait a minute, isn't that like giving my house away?"

"Only for a while. When you're done with this I'll change it back. Unless you've changed your mind? Is this case really that important to you?"

I took a moment to consider it. This did seem pretty drastic just to track down a dead-beat dad. But of course, that wasn't what this was all about. It was about a man taking advantage of vulnerable people.

"Yeah, it's that important. Go ahead."

"See? Pit bull." Jack smiled and went to get the pizza.

I stood and watched Mason as he flashed through screens on the computer, typing and clicking at a phenomenal rate. Jack brought the pizza and Mason stopped to wolf down a slice and look over the application.

I grabbed a piece, burning my fingers in the process. I took a bite anyway, and of course burned my tongue. Mmm, it was worth a little pain!

"Okay," Mason said, wiping grease off his fingers with a paper towel. "For work history I'm going to say you worked for Caring Hands for three years before going off on your own. It's a home care business out of Mishawaka, and they aren't likely to have great security on their server. Write that down."

I did, and he glanced at the next page. "It's kind of strange that they want to know the balances on any credit cards or loans you have. They aren't asking for account numbers or your social security number, though, so this shouldn't be enough to run a real credit check." Mason smiled up at me. "Unless, of course, they have a hacker working for them."

"They might, for all I know. This is no ordinary church."

"Do you have any credit cards?"

"Nope. My mom raised me too paranoid for that."

"Okay, that'll make it easier." Mason went back to typing and clicking and I ate a second slice of pizza, ignoring Jack's approving look. I still thought watching someone's diet was far overstepping the boundaries of friendship. The pizza sure was good, though.

At eleven o'clock Mason shut down the computer with a sigh of satisfaction.

"All done, Rainie. Or should I say, Rhonda?"

"That's great!"

"I even inserted a few things in case they take the easy way out and just Google you. Did you know you were caregiver of the month three times the last year you worked for Caring Hands?"

"Wow, I must be good."

"Yeah, and you also spear-headed a food drive for the elderly last Christmas and the year before you were Secret Santa for fifty people confined to nursing homes."

"Geez Mason, did you have to make Rhonda better than me?"

"I'm sure it's all stuff you've been planning to do." Mason shut the lid on the laptop and ran a loving had over it. "This is one sweet machine."

"You like it?" Jack waved a hand at it. "It's all yours."

"What? No way, man, that thing must be worth close to five thousand."

"I didn't pay for it, and there are plenty more where that came from. Don't worry, it won't be missed."

"Where did you get it?"

"I can promise you that the cost is just a drop in the bucket for the people I got it from, and you'll put it to much better use. Do you really need to know more?"

Mason stared at the computer, conflicted. He really wanted it, but...

"It's not like I can take it back," Jack added. "If I keep it I'll just use it to play solitaire and maybe send a few emails."

Mason looked aghast at that thought. It was just the right thing to say.

"All right, I'll take it. You sure no one can trace it?"

"It's never been used, and it's already been through so many sets of hands figuring out the original owner would be tantamount to solving a Rubik's cube in the dark."

"All right." Mason scooped it up and tucked it under his arm. I handed him the power cord.

"I don't know how to thank you."

"That's okay, Jack did." Mason hefted the laptop. "I'd better get home or Pam will have me sleeping on the couch for a week. See you at poker."

Chapter Twenty

I gave Cailee my application on Thursday night, when I dutifully attended services. Father Mika wasn't there. A short balding man they introduced as Brother Thomas gave the sermon. He wasn't of the same caliber as Father Mika, but he was still a pretty skilled orator, and the children's choir was as amazing as before.

I got through Friday and Saturday, worrying about how my fake background check would pass but trying not to obsess.

Sunday rolled around again, and I went for Sunday morning services. Cailee was there and welcomed me with open arms.

"It's so good to have you, Sister Rhonda!"

Sister Rhonda. Well well, I guess I had passed the test!

"I spoke to Father Mika and he's agreed to let you come to Retreat early! I'll have to find a place for you, but it might be as early as next week."

"That's great!" I hugged Cailee, and I don't think she had any idea how much I hated it. I was in!

I begged off afternoon fellowship, claiming I had some business to take care of if I was going to be away for a month. I was crossing the parking lot to my car when a man's voice called "Hey Rainie!"

I turned expectantly, belatedly remembering that I was supposed to be Rhonda.

Two men were coming toward me; one was big, the other was bigger. They didn't look friendly.

"Oh, I thought you called me." I was doing my best to act casual but I probably wasn't pulling it off very well. They knew my real name; I was busted.

"I did." The biggest guy smiled, and it was all mean - no friendly welcome here. They rushed me and I barely managed a squeal before they had me. The biggest one wrapped an arm around my neck and clamped a hand over my mouth to shut me up and the other one grabbed my legs. I twisted and kicked frantically but to no avail. I tried to bite the hand over my mouth but the guy's palm was thick with callous and I couldn't get a grip. They moved fast toward a dark, non-descript Buick and the smaller one let go of my legs long enough to open the back door.

"Hold still and keep quiet or I'll break your neck." The guy was exerting enough pressure that I was afraid he almost had, so I went limp and let him drag me into the car.

"Hold still."

The second guy tied a blindfold on me and stuffed a rag in my mouth. With practiced movements he pulled my hands behind me and fastened them together with a plastic zip tie. I panicked and started struggling again, and immediately the arm clamped tighter on my throat.

"I swear I'll kill you." He said it calmly, which was far more frightening than if he'd shouted. I forced myself to hold still. The car door slammed and a moment later I heard the other guy get in the front and start the engine.

It seemed like we rode for hours, but that was probably just because my panic had me in a weird time warp.

I'd never had my hands tied behind my back before, and let me tell you, it was terrifying! This was far worse than claustrophobia. I felt completely vulnerable, totally helpless. This guy could do anything to me and I literally couldn't raise a hand to stop him.

I was breathing hard, but with the rag in my mouth I was restricted to the meager air coming in through my nostrils, and it wasn't enough. I was going to suffocate. Little sparkly lights were exploding behind my eyes.

I squirmed and immediately the arm around my throat tightened. Now I was gagging. If I threw up with the gag in my mouth I would choke to death!

"Calm the hell down!" the big guy growled at me. "You're making this worse than it has to be!"

Easy for him to say. He wasn't bound and gagged and blindfolded and in danger of suffocating!

But for all that, he was right. He relieved the pressure on my throat and I took a long, slow breath in through my nose. I felt my lungs expanding. In spite of everything, I was getting plenty of air.

Calm down. Slow breath. Calm down. Slow breath. I repeated it like a mantra in my head, and slowly but surely I came to the conclusion that I wasn't going to die. Yet.

Eventually the car stopped and I heard the driver get out. After a minute or two the car pulled forward and he got out again. I guessed we were going through a gate and he was getting out to open and close it.

"We're supposed to take her to his office."

His office. Well, that didn't sound so bad. Maybe he was just planning to question me and let me go.

And maybe I was Elvis.

The car moved forward slowly over a rough surface and finally stopped again.

"Behave and we won't hurt you," the bigger guy promised as the other one pulled me out of the car. They led me across a smooth surface and through a door. I almost tripped on thick carpeting; it was so deep it was like standing in soft mud.

The marched me across the room and shoved me down in a deeply cushioned chair.

I heard someone tap softly and then the bigger guy said, "She's here, Father Mika."

A moment later I heard a door open.

"What is this? What have you done?" It was Father Mika's voice, but it wasn't using the controlled, dulcet tones I'd heard at the church. This was Father Mika pissed off.

Suddenly the blindfold was snatched off my head and I blinked in the sudden light.

"Why is she bound and gagged?" Father Mika was snarling in barely controlled rage. He pulled the rag out of my mouth and tossed it in a wastebasket with a little grimace of distaste.

"Uh... you said... I mean, she's a troublemaker..." The big guy was stammering like a six year old caught playing with matches. The smaller one never said a word, hadn't said anything since they'd grabbed me. Maybe Mika had his tongue cut out for saying something stupid.

"I told you to bring her, not kidnap her!"

"Well you was mad, and I thought..."

"You weren't hired to think! I have cabbages in my garden with more capacity to think..."

The tirade went on, but I was busy scoping out the room, hoping to find some means of escape.

The office was big and very well appointed. The deep chair I was sitting in was upholstered in a rich looking plaid featuring deep blue and burgundy stripes. There was an equally plush looking couch in solid navy blue to my right. Across the room there was a large cherry wood desk polished to a high sheen, a blotter and a set of what looked like gold pens the only adornment.

The walls were paneled and hung with oil paintings, and off to one side I could see a panel that wasn't quite closed that partially concealed a very large plasma TV.

223

All in all, this one room probably cost as much to decorate and furnish as I'd spent on my whole house. At least I knew where some of the congregation's money was going.

"You two wait outside!" Father Mika finished his tirade and I hadn't thought of a single escape plan. He strode over to the desk and pulled an oversized folding knife out of the top drawer. He popped it open and came at me.

I freaked and threw myself out of the chair. I had planned to run, but let me tell you, getting out of a deep chair without use of your hands, especially in a big hurry, isn't as easy as it sounds. I landed on my knees and started for the door like a penitent late for confession.

Of course Father Mika caught up in just a few steps. He grabbed my arm and I jerked away, but all I managed to do was fall on my unprotected face. Good thing the carpet was so thick or I probably would have broken my nose.

"I'm just cutting you loose!" Father Mika explained and once again he grabbed me, but this time with one powerful stroke cut the plastic tie. I immediately rolled onto my back, my hands in front of me.

"Get back in the chair. Sit." He commanded. I did as I was told. He was still holding the knife, and anything that cut through that tough plastic so easily would have no trouble rending my flesh.

He folded the knife and slipped it into a pocket in his baggy pants.

"I'm sorry for the rough treatment, Miss Lovingston. Are you all right?"

"No! I'm not all right!" My wrists were abraded and bleeding from the zip tie, my mouth was bleeding from the rag being shoved into it, my throat was bruised and I was scared nearly to death. Nope, I wasn't all right by half.

"Again, I'm sorry. This wasn't what I had in mind. Can I get you something? Tea? Maybe a cocktail?"

"A *cocktail*?" I glared at him, furious. "Are you kidding me?"

"I'm a civilized man, for all that my men acted like barbarians." He moved to the other side of the room, never quite taking his eyes off of me, and opened another panel in the wall to reveal a well-stocked bar. He selected a bottle of water and brought it to me, removing the cap.

I hated to accept his belated hospitality. I wanted to spit on him, but my mouth was dry and my throat hurt and I really wanted that water, so I accepted it wordlessly. I forced myself to take a small sip, trying for nonchalance.

"Got a cigarette?" I asked it casually, but the truth was I would have given a lot for one right now. Not my right arm, but maybe the tip of my little finger.

"That's a bad habit. It will kill you someday."

"Someday isn't really my concern right now."

Mika smiled thinly.

"Give me your cell phone."

"I don't..."

"Miss Lovingston, do you want me to have my men search for it?"

Hell no, I did not! I pulled the phone out of my pocket and handed it to him. He pulled the back off, removed the battery and tossed it on his desk before coming back to me.

"So Miss Lovingston," he perched on the arm of the sofa. "Tell me what interest a private investigator has in my church."

"I'm not a P.I."

"No? But you do work for B&E Security in Niles?"

I took another swallow of water. I guess there was no more sense lying; he obviously knew all about me.

"How did you figure it out?"

"Ah. Have you ever heard the expression 'small world?' Of course you have. Well, here's more proof. Do you remember meeting Verna at Fellowship? No? Well, she remembered you. She's Bob Peck's aunt. You do remember him, right?"

I swallowed. Yep, I remembered him. I had gotten him arrested, right after his buddy shot me.

"Verna remembered you from the trial." Father Mika glanced piously at the ceiling. "The Lord surely watches over me."

"Oh please! Do you really still claim to do God's work?"

Mika just smiled.

"So I ask again, what is it you want here?"

"I'm looking for James Bolin. He's behind on his child support."

Mika stared at me for a good ten seconds, processing that information. He frowned and shook his head.

"A dead-beat dad? That's all this is about? You came up with this elaborate ruse, a false ID... just to track down a man for a few hundred dollars in support payments?"

"It's a lot more than a few hundred, and it's his responsibility to support them!"

"I agree. So why didn't you just ask to see him?"

"Ask?" Now it was my turn to process information. "Do you mean to say if I had just asked you would have let me talk to him?"

"Of course. He isn't a prisoner."

"So let me see him now."

"Why, so you can tell him I had you kidnapped? I don't think so."

"No, so I can tell him his kids miss him. Unless you really do have something to hide and you're just bullshitting me."

Mika smiled thinly. "Don't try psychology on me, Miss Lovingston. I know all the tricks, and I've probably used most of them."

"All right, then let me see him for my own curiosity."

"Now there's an honest answer. Nonetheless, I don't want him needlessly upset by our little... situation."

"I won't say anything, I swear!"

"Oh, and your word has certainly proven reliable so far." Mika gave me that thin smile again. "But I will think about it. After all, if you did say anything... well, we're a long way from anywhere, aren't we?"

"I don't know. Where exactly are we?"

"At Retreat, of course. Isn't that where you wanted to go?"

I just glared at him, and he sighed.

"Drink your water, Miss Lovingston. I have a bit of business to tend to, and then I'll decide what to do with you." He went to the door and called his muscle men in. "Keep an eye on her. I have to make a phone call."

I sipped my water and ignored the two bruisers, debating if I had any prayer on making it to the door. I didn't see how. One of them was standing right in my path. I sat and stewed instead, wondering if this was my last day on earth. I blinked back tears. I was going to miss living.

Finally Mika came back, and I glimpsed the room behind the door. It looked like a very nicely furnished living room.

"It's hard to achieve genius when you're surrounded by incompetents," he said by way of greeting. I didn't answer, since I had no idea what he was referring to. "So now the question is, what do I do with you?"

"I don't know, how about let me go? Forgive and forget? Isn't that what the Bible suggests? Or haven't you ever read it?"

Mika sighed. "Miss Lovingston, you clearly have the wrong idea about me. I'm not a monster! I have provided a very good lifestyle for many people. I've saved them!"

"And took all their money for yourself."

"I admit, I have carved out a nice little niche for myself here," Mika glanced around the room. "I do like nice things. But I haven't hurt anyone to get them."

"How can you say that? You're cheating them out of everything they own!"

"Cheating? No, no I'm not. That would mean that I am getting something of more value than they are, and I can assure you that isn't the case. My people are very happy with their situation." He cocked his head and looked at me, obviously trying to decide something. Finally he nodded, his decision made.

"I think I'll take you on a tour, Miss Lovingston. You should see for yourself what I've accomplished here."

We stepped out into bright sunlight reflecting off leaves that had finally changed into their autumn splendor. We were surrounded by forest, and the view was glorious. How had I not noticed that the color change had come? Had I been so involved with this case that I hadn't taken time to look around? That wasn't like me. The poet in me was usually on constant lookout for beauty. Once again I wondered if this job might be changing me in ways I didn't like.

I glanced back at the building that housed Mika's elegant quarters. On the outside it looked rather crude - a good sized log cabin, chinked with the red clay so common here in southern Michigan. The door was rough hewn planks, although I knew on the inside it was paneled in that rich cherry wood. This guy was no dummy, and he obviously didn't want his flock to know he was living in luxury.

Mika (I could no longer, even in my mind, think of him as "Father Mika") gestured for me to accompany him along a single lane dirt road. His two goons fell in behind us. So much for any plans to just dart off into the woods and disappear. Besides, if Mika was taking the time to give me a tour, maybe he was having second thoughts about killing me.

We walked for quite a distance, all the while Mika telling me about the Retreat.

"We have 264 acres here, much of it wooded. There's a 10 acre spring-fed lake well stocked with fish, and so far 50 acres planted for corn and wheat. We plow with mules, and everyone takes a hand in the farming in exchange for a fair portion of the crop."

"Everyone?"

"The labor is assigned according to ability. Even with the mules the plow runs hard through this clay soil, so it takes a certain physical strength to manage it. But there are other chores: removing the large stones, which we use for building, planting the seed, which is done by hand. And then there is the harvest, which is quite labor intensive as well. In fact, we're in the midst of harvest right now, although no one is working this afternoon. This is the day of rest, as our Lord commanded."

We came out of the trees and the little road cut through a tall crop of corn that had been partially harvested. A little breeze rattled the drying tops with a whispering sigh. Above us the sky was intensely blue, the few clouds just enough to accentuate the vibrant color. I felt tears prick the backs of my eyes again. I didn't want this to be my last beautiful day on earth. I clearly hadn't taken enough time to appreciate life.

Ahead there was a sizable barn built of solid but rough planks, whitewashed and brilliant in the sunshine. There were big double doors, and overhead the smaller access door to a hayloft, a beam and pulley system rigged above it.

"This was built with everyone's cooperation just last spring. There are two smaller barns, but this is our pride and joy."

"It's quite an accomplishment. How did you know how to do it?"

"I hired consultants," Mika smiled. "Actually I hired an Amish man and his sons from Indiana to supervise the work. Wonderful people, the Amish, they understand the idea of living without technology. Sadly, they often have to work for English money, if only to pay their taxes."

"English money?"

"That's what the Amish call you modern Americans."

Right. As if he didn't have a plasma TV and a fully stocked bar of his own. I didn't bother to correct him.

We moved on past a field of wheat and a couple of fields already harvested before the road led us back into the woods. We didn't go far before we came to a large clearing, maybe 3 acres, that appeared to be an isolated village.

There were four solid looking log cabins, each with a stone chimney running up one side. Shutters covered most of the windows, but a few were open, revealing quite modern glass nestled in crude wooden frames. Apparently Mika still allowed his people some amenities from the commercial world.

Each cabin had its own garden; all but one was surrounded by a low stone wall, obviously some of the field stones that the laborers had removed from the plowed acreage. The fourth one had a large pile of rocks beside it; they must be getting ready to fence theirs in. I saw several large groups of chickens pecking around here and there, what my mother would call "free range."

Mika stopped on the road, not venturing any closer to the cabins.

"This is one of our settlements. We scatter them around to prevent any feeling of overcrowding, but humans are social creatures and we've found that most are more comfortable with at least a few other families around."

He pointed at an outbuilding on the far side of the clearing. "That's the blacksmith shop. He takes care of plow blades and whatever other metal work needs doing, and in exchange others tend his farming chores. We have others that tend to our weaving and a few other things that require special equipment that it isn't practical for everyone to have. We have quite a micro-economy here, all based on trade."

Behind one of the cabins two little girls were jumping rope. By the front door of another a small boy was doing something in the dirt, but I couldn't tell what. Nearby a woman, presumably his mother, was sitting in a wooden chair, reading a book.

"Let's go on," Mika gestured toward the road. "We'll walk past the lake."

It was a long hike, but finally I saw the glint of sunlight off water. The lake was smooth and clear, just a fringe of lily pads at the edges. There were several row boats out on the water, the occupants dangling lines in search of fish. It was beautiful and peaceful and I couldn't think of one negative thing to say about it.

"What's that?" I pointed to a long, low building about a quarter of the way around the lake.

"That's the public area. I don't believe there are any outside visitors today, but many of my people choose to gather there for fellowship on the Lord's day."

There were picnic tables set here and there under the trees, and all of them seemed to be occupied. I saw other people coming and going from the building, all wearing the same simple clothes Mika wore, but in varying shades of brown and off-white. Children were playing on crude swings hung from low branches, jumping rope and playing marbles in the grass. It looked like a scene right out of *Little House on the Prairie*. I had to admit, they all looked happy enough.

"So if someone's family wants to come see what's going on, they're allowed?"

"Of course, I told you, no one is a prisoner here."

"Yet no one has any visitors today."

"There's nothing sinister about that, it's just a coincidence." Mika seemed to consider for a minute, then added. "It is true that most of my people don't have any close family other than those they bring with them. But is it so surprising that those that are the most lonely would chose to live with an extended church family?"

I shrugged, not willing to concede anything.

Mika sighed. "I really want you to understand the nature of Retreat."

"Why? If you plan to kill me anyway what difference does it make what I think of the place?"

"I haven't decided what to do with you yet." But Mika's eyes slid away from mine, and I knew he was lying. I shifted my own eyes slightly to the left and right; the goons were still there, just a few feet behind us. Could I outrun them? Just take off into the woods…

"There's nowhere to run, Miss Lovingston." Mika seemed to have read my mind. "Don't make this more difficult than it already is."

"You want me to make it easy for you to kill me?"

"I never said anything about killing you."

"Then why haven't you let me go yet?"

"You know, I've rarely had to resort to violence."

"Rarely? But you're going to make an exception with me?"

"Miss Lovingston, please!" Strangely, Mika did look regretful. Gee, wasn't it nice that he wasn't happy about killing me.

"If I let you speak to Jim Bolin and he tells you he's here of his own free will, do you think that will convince you that I'm not evil?"

I just couldn't figure this guy out. Why did he care what I thought if he was just going to kill me? Was it ego? Or was he really considering letting me go? I decided my best bet was to play along.

"It might."

"All right then, I'll take you to him." Mika started off down the road again and I fell in step with him. "Just remember Miss Lovingston, Jim is a loyal follower, and he isn't likely to believe your accusations against me. I can easily convince him you are just trying to undermine his happiness." His voice hardened. "Remember also that no one knows where you are. If you disappear you'll never be traced back to me. Am I clear?"

I swallowed and nodded, made speechless by the threat. I was thinking of some future archeologist finding my bleached bones in an unmarked grave. Would he be able to tell I'd been murdered? Would he care?

I would bide my time, and hope for a better chance of escape.

Chapter Twenty-one

Jim Bolin's cabin was one of three in a small clearing. None of these gardens had rock walls around them yet, and the forest showed signs of still being cleared. There were freshly cut trees at the perimeter in varying stages of dismemberment, some stacked in long, straight logs and some chopped for firewood. There were fewer chickens wandering here, but still a nice-sized flock.

"Jim, are you here?" Mika called in a clear, friendly voice. A moment later a man came from behind one of the cabins, smiling broadly.

"Father Mika! Welcome!"

Mika stepped up to meet him and they clasped hands, getting all four limbs involved. Jim was staring at the preacher with a look of utter devotion, like the kind a puppy gives its master during a good belly rub.

Jim was a good looking guy in the picture I'd seen, but I didn't really go for his new mountain man look. His hair was long and tied back with a strip of rawhide, his beard full and in need of trimming and combing. He was wearing the now familiar tunic and baggy pants but his were a bit splotchy, as if improperly dyed. He was wearing moccasins held by big, crude looking stitches; whoever made them had apparently not gotten the hang of it yet.

"Jim, I have someone here who would like to meet you." Mika stepped back and gestured at me. "This is Rainie Lovingston."

"Please to meet you," Jim offered his hand and offered me a shy smile. I could see a hint of the charm that his ex-wife had spoken of; there was something in his eyes and the quirk of his lips that made you want to cuddle him.

"I haven't had any visitors since I came here. Should I know you?"

"Not really." I glanced around his little homestead. "This is quite a place you have here."

"Well, be it ever so humble..." he smiled. "I'm still getting settled, but I'll have all the essentials done before the first snowfall."

"It looks like a lot of hard work."

"It is, but I love every minute of it. For the first time I'm working only for myself, not to pay taxes to the government or to support some huge retail corporation. Every drop of my sweat goes to something I will use directly or trade for something else I will use. No one else is getting rich off my labor."

Except for Mika, I thought but wisely didn't say. "So you're happy here?"

He offered me a full wattage smile. "Happier than I've ever been in my life."

"So you don't have any regrets about giving up your house? You really don't want to leave here?"

"Of course not. Why do you ask?"

"You have to admit it's unusual, selling everything you own and donating the proceeds to a church, then coming to live in... well, primitive conditions."

"You should do some research, Miss Lovingston. More and more people are going back to the basics, learning to live off the land and off the grid. Here my food is fresh and completely organic. I don't have to wonder what my chickens were fed before they laid their eggs, or what was sprayed on my tomatoes. I've never had so much as a minor headache since I've come here, but for a year before that I was plagued with migraines. I sleep well, have more

235

energy, and I haven't needed a cup of coffee to get me going since after the first week. Why wouldn't I want to do this?"

Why not indeed? He made it sound like Utopia. This is the kind of place my mother and Jedediah would love if not for the overt religious references.

"But Jim, what about your kids? They miss you."

"Nah, they don't." For the first time Jim lost his smile. "For the past year they've hardly come on my weekends to have them. There was always a dance or a basketball game, something more important than seeing their old man. And when they did come we fought the whole time. Nothing I said was right."

"But Jim, they're *teenagers*! It's practically their job to argue with their parents. We all did. Testing your boundaries is part of growing up. As for having things to do, don't you remember how important your social life was when you were 14?"

Jim shrugged and looked at his shoes. "I don't know." Suddenly he looked up at me. "Hey, how do you know about my kids, anyway? Did my ex-wife send you?"

"Sort of. I work for a private investigator's firm, and she hired us to find you when you quit paying support."

"Quit paying?" Jim looked at Mika, wide-eyed. "But that can't be right! You said part of the money from my house would be put away for that. You said you'd see that it was paid every month!"

"Yes, I'm sorry, Jim. It was an oversight, and I didn't know anything about it until Miss Lovingston told me this afternoon. I've already spoken to the accountant, and a check will be taken to the court first thing tomorrow."

"You pay his support?" I was stunned.

"Of course. We aren't in the practice of abandoning a man's family."

I couldn't believe it. No wonder Mika had looked so surprised when I'd revealed my purpose here. If the support had been paid there wouldn't have been any reason for me to investigate the church, and Mika could have gone on collecting his nest egg. And what about me? I couldn't believe I was going to die because of a clerical error!

"Satisfied, Miss Lovingston?" Mika asked.

I looked back at Jim. He certainly seemed happy. He was tanned and fit, lean but well-fed. Clearly he had come here, and was staying here, of his own free will.

"I guess I am," I answered reluctantly. "But Jim, you should contact your kids."

"I'll think about it, Miss Lovingston. Maybe in a few weeks. I'm not sure I'm ready yet."

"Well, I'll see you at services." Mika and Jim did that four handed clasp again and Mika led me away, the two goons silently bringing up the rear. If Jim thought it odd that we were accompanied by the two bruisers he never gave any sign. Maybe Big and Bigger always followed Mika around at Retreat.

"So now what?" My voice came out a little softer and a lot more scared than I wanted it too. Mika shrugged.

"I'm not sure, I'm still considering that question."

"Are you considering if you'll kill me or just how you'll do it?"

"I told you, I'm not normally a violent man. I must consider my options; I don't want you to suffer unnecessarily."

"I'd rather not suffer at all. I'd rather just go home." I felt tears threatening again, but I didn't want to cry in front of him.

We didn't talk again, just walked in silence down the narrow dirt road. The sun was down past the tops of the trees by the time we got back to Mika's cabin. He led me around to the back and stopped in front of a very small but sturdy looking shed. Several shovels, rakes and other viable looking weapons were leaning against the outside.

"I had this emptied out for you. I have to conduct services in an hour and then welcome the newcomers to Retreat, so you'll have to wait until morning in here."

"In *that* little place?" I could already feel my heart rate increasing. The shed had a low roof and no windows, and wasn't more than six feet by eight. If he locked me in there overnight he wouldn't have to have me killed; I would die of fright.

"I'm sorry, but it isn't as if we have jail facilities here."

"Why not just let me go?" my voice sounded weak and whining to my own ears, but I couldn't help it.

"I'm sorry, Miss Lovingston, but I've built something wonderful for these people, and yes, provided a nice bank account for myself along the way. I don't care for violence, but sometimes I have to protect myself." He shook his head regretfully. "If you had only approached me directly." He flashed a murderous look at his henchmen. "Or if these idiots hadn't *kidnapped* you!" He sighed and looked back at me. "But what's done is done, and I can't spend the rest of my life in jail."

"I'll forget about the kidnapping." I was desperate now. "It was just a misunderstanding, after all!"

He regarded me silently for a moment. "I wish I could believe you."

"You can! I'm really a very honest person!"

"Really Miss Kindig? Oh, I mean Miss Lovingston."

He smiled, as calm as if we were having tea, discussing a baseball game. For all his manners and reasoning tone, I was fairly certain he was nuts.

"You two take turns guarding her, four hours on, four hours off." He turned back to me.

"Again, I'm very sorry." He gestured at the goons and they stepped forward and grabbed my arms. "I'll see you in the morning, Miss Lovingston."

They shoved me through the door and slammed it behind me. I immediately rushed back at it and tried to push it open, but they were already fitting a padlock through the hasp and it was far too late.

After several minutes of futilely pounding on the door I finally collapsed with my back against it. I tried to slow my breathing; a place this small wasn't likely to have enough air for a whole night! My heart was racing, my chest felt like it was going to explode from the pressure. I knew it was just a panic attack, but knowing it wasn't the same as being able to control it.

But wait... I could see light passing between the imperfectly fitted planks. If light could get through, so could air!

That thought helped a little. It wasn't like being buried alive. It wasn't as if I could slip out through those cracks, but the lack of complete solidity gave me some hope. Maybe I could kick a board loose...

And instantly have Big or Bigger in here subduing me with a chokehold. Still, being in a chokehold probably wouldn't feel any more suffocating than being trapped in this tiny space.

I felt the panic rising again and got to my feet. I went over to one of the bigger chinks in the wall, barely a quarter-inch wide, and breathed deeply of the crisp, fresh air.

I could see Bigger sitting nearby under a brilliantly colored maple tree. He was whittling with what looked to me to be an oversized knife.

"Hey!" I yelled at him. "I need to pee!"

"So?"

"So let me out so I can pee!"

"It's a dirt floor, just pee in the corner."

"Ew! No!"

He went back to his carving, ignoring me.

I gave up, kicking at the floor in frustration. Wait. A dirt floor!

I dropped to my knees in the failing light and felt along the bottom of the wall. The planks were nailed into solid looking 2x4s, but the whole structure was built straight on the dirt, no floor.

"Aha!" Yes, I actually said that out loud. A bit of work and I could be out of here!

I went to the far side of the shed, away from Bigger, and dug my fingers into the dirt. Or at least, I tried to. I was instantly reminded of the harsh realities of clay soil: at this time of year it was dried hard, like crumbly concrete. If I was going to dig any kind of hole I would need a tool.

The shed was pretty empty, especially after they'd removed the shovels and other useful tools. I suppose Mika didn't do much actual farming. I went to investigate the shelves affixed to the wall.

There wasn't much there, just a bag of nails and a stack of old newspapers. I shoved the papers aside, and that's when I saw it: a screwdriver.

It was a pretty good sized tool, the handle about five inches long, the thick blade seven or eight inches. I hefted it, and it occurred to me it would make an excellent weapon. If I could get Bigger to come in here...

What? I was going to stab him? He was twice my weight and had a good foot of reach on me. I'd been held up against him long enough to know that he was covered in a solid slab of muscle. Could I even hit him hard enough to pierce that layer and get to something vulnerable?

I shuddered at the image that brought up. Just the thought made me want to gag.

Besides, more than likely I would just piss him off and he would return the favor by beating the crap out of me. No, it wasn't practical as a weapon. It would, however, help me break up the soil and dig a hole.

I dropped to my knees and got to work, chopping at the packed soil with the furious stabs I could never use on another human being. After a minute or so I heard Bigger right outside the door.

"Hey, what are you doing in there?"

I froze. What was I thinking? Why didn't it occur to me he might wonder what I was chopping at? I resorted to a repeat of my earlier complaint.

"I need to pee! Let me out of here!"

"Give it a rest already! What a whiney broad!"

He stomped away, and I stood in the middle of the shed for a few minutes before creeping back to the crack and peeking out. He was back under the tree again, back to whittling. I spent a moment trying to figure out what he was making, then shook myself and pulled away. What difference did it make what he was whittling? I certainly had more important things to worry about.

I went back to the corner and pulled away the dirt I'd loosened. Underneath, the ground was a little softer, and my spirits went up as I dug. I got down a good six inches before I had to stop and use the screwdriver again to widen the hole. This time I worked slower and quieter.

I chopped for a while and then dug for a while, back and forth. I was concentrating on my work, which was doing a good job of keeping the panic at bay. Now and then I wondered how long I'd been at it and how much time I had left, but I kept shoving that thought aside. Knowing how much time I had left wasn't going to make me work any faster.

It was full dark now, and I was working entirely by feel. Periodically I would find the 2x4 at the base of the wall and use my hands to measure the depth of the hole. I was making pretty good progress; I already had it about a foot deep and sloped out about two feet into the shed.

"She givin' you any trouble?" The unfamiliar voice was right outside the shed. I spun around and sat staring in the direction of the door. If they came in with a flashlight...

"Nah, she was kinda noisy for a while but I think maybe she went to sleep. Haven't heard a word for an hour or so."

"Think we should check on her?" This must be Big; so he could talk, after all.

"Father Mika said lock the door and leave her in there. You want to tell him you went against his orders?"

"Guess not," Big mumbled. "All right then, see you in four hours." He yawned loudly.

"You'd better stay awake!" Bigger warned. "If Father Mika comes by to check on you..."

"I'll be awake!" Big growled. "You just make sure you get back in time!"

"Yeah yeah," Bigger's answer was muffled by distance; he was already walking away.

I crawled over to the far wall and peered out the tiny crack. Big was sitting under the same tree, a blanket around his shoulders, a little battery operated lamp on the ground beside him. He had a magazine of some sort; it was too dark for me to see details, but it seemed to have a lot of color pictures. I had a pretty good guess what kind of reading material this genius would choose.

I waited until he was well settled, then crawled back over and got back to work on my hole.

My fingertips were sore and cut in places from pulling at the rough soil, and there was so much dirt packed up under my nails it was beginning to hurt as it bent the fingernails backward. I weighed the pain against the very real possibility of death and decided I could stand it a while longer.

I was lying on the floor now, partially in the hole, reaching under and past the wall, chop-chop with the screwdriver followed by frantic pawing at the loosened dirt.

Then I ran into a problem.

I had dug out as far as I could reach from where I was. The only way to make the hole big enough on the other side was to actually get down in the hole and stick my head out under the wall. I had seen dogs dig out under a fence that way. There was always a certain amount of time that they had to spend half in and half out of the yard, the bottom of the fence across their back. This was followed by a lot of squirming and wiggling while they struggled to work themselves free.

My mouth was suddenly dry, my heart pounding with what felt like the speed of a plucked guitar string. Squirming, struggling to break free. Stuck in a hole, half in and half out...

I sat back on my heels and stared at the slightly blacker outline of the hole in the darkened shed. I couldn't do it. No way, not even to save my life.

The tears really came then, hot tears of shame and terror: shame that I was actually going to let this phobia beat me, terror that if I didn't figure out a way to overcome it I was going to die.

"Come on!" I whispered to myself. "Get it together!" But the little pep talk just made it worse. I couldn't get it together. Although I knew it was an unreasonable fear, my claustrophobia was as real in my mind as my love for my mother. I couldn't just set it aside because it was inconvenient.

Thinking of my mother made me cry all the harder. Would she ever know what happened to me? Would she think I'd just run off, or would she know that I had met with a violent death?

I was sobbing for real now, rocking back and forth on my heels, thinking about my mother and my brother and sister and Thelma and Eddy and all the poker guys and even Jack. Would they have a funeral even without my body?

"Hey! Knock it off in there!" Big pounded on the door and shouted at me.

"Go to hell!" I shouted back. "I can c-cry if I w-want to!"

"I don't wanna listen to that crap. Shut up!"

I ignored him and kept on crying, wiping my streaming eyes and nose on my jacket sleeve, which was really gross and just made me cry harder.

What was the matter with me, anyway? Why had I assumed the worse about this stupid church in the first place? Why hadn't I just gone and talked to Father Mika? So he was taking people's savings. So what? Jim seemed happy enough. If he felt he was getting value for his money, was Father Mika even stealing from him?

"Stupid! Stupid! Stupid!" I yelled at myself, punctuating each repetition with a fist on my thigh.

"All right, that's enough!" I heard Big fumbling with the lock. "You got no right to call me stupid!"

The door slammed back and I jumped to my feet. The moon was half full in a cloudless sky, providing just enough light to outline Bigs frame in the doorway. He stepped in and stopped, his head swiveling back and forth in search of me. I realized he was night blind from sitting next to his little lantern, and for a few precious seconds I had the advantage.

What good was it going to do me? Even if I'd been willing to use the screwdriver I had left it back in the hole. Big was towering over me, a full head taller and an easy six inches wider. I didn't have a prayer.

But then I remembered my training sessions with Eddie. From the very first lesson he had emphasized to me that the size of an opponent, while certainly a factor, wasn't necessarily all that mattered. The trick to fighting someone bigger than you was to fight dirty.

Yep, that's what he told me. None of those silly rules like "not below the belt" or "no biting." Eddie had explained that when threatened I should use every single weapon in my arsenal: teeth, nails, feet, or anything I could pick up and swing.

I took a fast step forward before Big could figure out where I was and set my left foot. This was one time I was glad I wasn't petite; I had some weight to work with. I raised my right foot and brought it down as hard as I could right on the outside of Big's knee.

There was a sound like stepping on bubble wrap and his leg collapsed inward. His screech of pain seemed delayed, but I wasn't waiting for it anyway. I took advantage of his shock and followed Eddie's number one rule: I ran like hell.

Big didn't even try to stop me. He was on the ground, grabbing his ruined knee and keening in a strange high pitch more suited to a grieving widow than an injured tough guy.

I dashed out the door and ran straight ahead, so happy to be out of confinement that at first I didn't even think about where I should run.

Even with my dark-adapted eyes and the moon it was hard to make out details, but I could see the back of Mika's place coming up on my left. I didn't see any light, but that might just be because all of the shutters were closed. Either way it worked for me, because he wouldn't be able to see out, either.

The thing was, which way did I want to go?

I stopped, my heart pounding, Big's wails diminishing to sobbing behind me, and tried to think.

264 acres was a lot of ground, and I had no idea where in that space I was. I could be right in the middle or near an edge. Either way if I made the wrong choice in direction I would be running for a long time through the woods without really getting anywhere.

I heard Big in the background, and it occurred to me that now he was talking, loud and fast, no longer wailing. He was giving orders to someone...of course, his radio! I had no way of knowing where Bigger was; maybe right next to me in Mika's dark house.

I got my feet moving again, not even realizing I'd made a decision.

We'd come through a gate and driven a relatively short distant when they brought me here earlier. My guess was we'd come in a back way, and Mika's place was very near one edge of the property. Besides, if I ran along the road I wouldn't get lost in the woods. Of course, I would also be an easier target, but maybe I could get some distance before Bigger came after me.

I ran as hard as I could, letting my fear propel me past Mika's house and down the driveway. I saw the moonlight glinting off the Buick and I slowed; was it possible they had left the keys in it?

I angled over to it and pulled the door handle. Locked. What the hell? Who would bother to lock their car out here in nowhere land?

It didn't matter. The front door of Mika's place opened, spilling out a rectangle of yellow light, framing someone tall and broad. I could contemplate their unreasonable paranoia later.

I took off down the driveway as fast as I could move.

"Hey! You! Stop!"

Yeah, right. That was going to happen! I ignored Bigger's command and tried for a little more speed, but I wasn't a track star. I was a thirty-something caregiver who spent a lot more time sitting on my butt than I did toning it, and there was no doubt I hadn't been spending near enough time on my bike. And just how much had I been smoking lately? I didn't think it was all that much, but I was sure having a tough time getting enough air to sustain my run. Adrenalin can only take you so far.

I heard Bigger's feet pounding along behind me. I didn't think a guy that big would have much on me as far as speed and stamina went, but what did I know?

I found the road and kept running, but after a relatively short distance I realized that Bigger was catching up.

246

Already I could make out the sound of his harsh breathing only a few yards behind me.

All right then, new plan.

Without breaking stride I made for the edge of the road and plunged into the woods.

I'd done this before when trying to escape a couple of meth heads, and it wasn't any more pleasant this time than it had been then. Low hanging branches smacked me in the face and tangled in my hair, and thorny vines, always the first to green up in the spring and the last to die off in winter grasped at my jeans and tore right through to the skin.

I couldn't worry about the pain. I put an arm up in front of my face so no thorns would get me in the eyes and kept on running.

My move into the woods must have taken Bigger by surprise, because I soon realized I couldn't hear him behind me. I stopped for breath, bending over at the waist, my hands on my knees, taking in great whooping gasps of air.

I finally quieted down enough to really listen and almost moaned aloud in dismay. I hadn't gained much ground. I could hear Bigger crashing through the underbrush right behind me. I got running again.

I thought maybe I had finally found my stride, or maybe I was just making better use of the adrenalin. Maybe I could run all the way back to Buchanan... but that's when I found the fence.

It was only about three and a half feet high, an old rusty thing that had probably just been intended as a boundary marker a few decades before. I probably would have flipped over it with no problem at all if not for the strand of barbed wire that ran along the top.

I hit the fence full tilt and fell over it, the barbed wire digging deep, through my coat and into the soft flesh of my stomach. I felt it rake through the skin at the same time it shredded my jacket, and I couldn't help but cry out.

"Hah! Found the fence, didn't you bitch?" Bigger was nearly there, so I forced myself to my feet and started off down the road again at a staggering run. I was just about out of juice, but Bigger sounded energized and ready for another round.

Ahead of me I saw headlights, and I felt a new surge of hope. If I could get whoever it was to stop it might at least scare Bigger off. Unless of course Mika was driving the car, or maybe another of his henchmen.

That was a chance I would have to take. Bigger was already over the fence, having stepped over a lot more gracefully than I had, and he was running down the road after me.

As soon as the car got close enough I started waving my arms over my head, yelling "Hey! Help! Hey!" the activity slowed me down, but I needed to be noticed.

It was a pickup truck, not a car, and it was one of the big ones. Lights on top of the cab suddenly flashed on, bathing the country road in near daylight, and a moment later I heard the screech of brakes.

"Shit!" Bigger cursed, but I didn't turn to look at him. I was still waving at the guy in the truck, who had stopped and was reaching behind him for something. Seconds later a tall, lean guy in a baseball cap jumped out of the driver's seat with a rifle in his hand. He was wearing denim instead of shining armor, but right now he qualified as a knight riding to my rescue.

"What's going on, little lady?"

Oh thank goodness, a good old boy! They might not all be college graduates, or even high school graduates, but when it came to a rescue they were all guns and glory.

"He... he kidnapped me..." I gasped out, pointing back toward Bigger.

"Is that right?" the good old boy narrowed his eyes. Bigger had already read the situation and was back over the fence and into the woods. "Who did?"

"He went back into the woods. You scared him off."

The guy nodded, as if that was no surprise, and took a good look at me in the glare of his headlights.

I must have been a sight with my jacket and jeans half shredded from thorns and barbed wire, dried blood on my lips from the gag being stuffed in it, my hair in who knew what condition.

"You get in the truck. I'll go get that bastard." He was already moving in that direction.

"No! Wait!" I didn't want this guy's death on my conscience. I'd already made a big enough mess. "There's more than one, and I don't know how well they know the woods. They have a campground back there. Maybe we should just call the cops."

He stopped and looked back at me, sucking his teeth, undecided.

"Please, mister, I just want to get out of here!"

He stood for another long minute, gazing at the woods, his rifle cradled in his arms as if it spent a lot of time there and was quite comfortable. I had no doubt if he caught up to Bigger he would know what to do with it, but I really thought this was a job for the police.

"All right, little lady, you win. Get in."

He jumped back into the truck and was securing his rifle to the rack behind the seats by the time I climbed in.

"You should call the cops right away." I prompted him.

"Hell, you want me to stick my head out the window and holler? I ain't got a cell phone. No service out this way. We'll have to go to my house and call."

His house? Some country place a mile from any neighbor, most likely. What if he turned out to be a pervert instead of just a heroic gun-toting good old boy? I suppose I could just break his knee, too. The thought brought to mind that bubble-wrap-popping sound, and I shuddered. Nope, didn't want to do that again. Ever.

"Why don't you just take me to the nearest town and drop me off? I can call the cops from there."

"Just drop you off? Lady, you don't look to be in any condition to be wandering the streets by yourself at four o'clock in the morning."

"Please! I'll be fine, just take me back to civilization!"

"Hey, calm down!" Until he said it I didn't realize I was screaming. I took a deep breath, trying to still the panic that was rising up again.

"I'm sorry. Please, I just want to go home."

"You sure you ain't suffering from shock or something? Maybe you should go to a hospital, get yourself looked at..."

"No, really," I took another deep breath and when I spoke again my voice was still shaking but at least not traveling into high ranges only dogs could hear. "I know what I'm doing. I'll make a report to the police, but there's no need for you to get involved. I appreciate your help, but I'd rather go into town."

The guy nodded sagely. "Oh, I get it. Guess I was a bit slow on the uptake. 'Course you don't wanna go to my place, I'm just another scary stranger." He grinned and held out a lanky, calloused hand. "My name's Judd Waller, and you may have seen a road here-abouts that carries my family's name. Not that we're so well off as my great granddaddy was when they named it after him, but we still do all right."

"You mean Waller's Road? The one that runs between Buchanan and..."

"And no where!" Judd laughed, and I finally put out my own hand to shake his. Having a road named after your family didn't necessarily mean you weren't a pervert, but at least it meant you were a well-established one.

"So I'll take you into Buchanan if that's okay; it's the closest."

"It is?" I glanced around as if the ink-black road would suddenly look familiar, but of course it didn't.

"Sure, maybe six or seven miles east." He put the truck in gear. "Where are you from?"

"Buchanan! But I didn't know for sure where they brought me."

"That's the old Sedgewick place, been vacant for thirty years or more. I didn't know anyone had bought it."

I'd never heard of the Sedgewick place; the information didn't help me at all.

"So why did they kidnap you? You rich or something?"

"Hardly! It's kind of a long story. See, I'm a private investigator's assistant, and I was looking for a guy, and I... well, I guess I stepped in a little over my head."

"Huh. Well, I guess you did at that."

I hunched down with the collar of my jacket up, hoping he wouldn't pry anymore. After a couple of attempts to draw out more details he finally let it drop, and we rode on to Buchanan in silence.

Chapter Twenty-two

There was another brief argument when we got into town. Judd wanted to take me straight to the police station, but I just wanted to go home. I finally convinced him that I would be better off calling the county police, since the kidnapping had taken place outside city limits. I didn't bother to explain that I'd actually been kidnapped in Indiana. I wasn't really sure whose jurisdiction it was.

By the time he pulled up in my driveway the sky to the east was just beginning to lighten a little.

"I'm wondering should I hang around?" Judd suggested. "I mean, I'm a witness, even if I didn't get a look at that fellow that was chasing you."

"How about if I just tell the police about you, and they can follow up?" I popped the door and got out but stood in the opening to wait for his answer.

Judd looked at me for a good twenty seconds, and I felt myself beginning to squirm. "Are you really going to call the police, or is there something else going on here?"

"Why wouldn't I call them?"

"I don't know. I'm smart enough to figure out that something ain't right here, but I guess I'm just dense enough not to get what."

No doubt, for all his good old boy ways Judd Waller was no dummy. The truth was I *had* been thinking about not calling. The whole situation was just too embarrassing. I had gone off half-cocked and overplayed my hand. I had risked Mason going to jail and me getting killed because I didn't try the obvious route first.

He was watching me patiently, waiting for an answer, not seeming to mind that I had gone off on one of my little mental tangents, when headlights washed over the cab of the truck and someone pulled up in front of my house. Almost before the vehicle stopped the driver's door opened and someone jumped out.

"Rainie, is that you?"

"Jack?"

"Where the hell have you been?"

He was striding across the lawn and I was hurrying around the truck to meet him. Judd got out too, looking like he was ready for anything. I'm not sure what he thought; maybe that Jack was a jealous boyfriend spoiling for a fight.

"What are you doing here?" I countered.

"Looking for you! I texted you last night to see how things went at the service and you never answered. I tried calling but your cell was out of range, and then it started going straight to voice mail, so I knew you either turned it off or the battery went dead." He stopped and took a good look at me. "What the hell happened to you? You look like you went through a paper shredder."

"Thorns and barbed wire," I answered, and then, maybe because I was just so damned happy to be alive and back on my home turf, I laughed. "You know, just a typical Sunday night."

Jack laughed with me. Judd shook his head. "Maybe I should have been the one worrying about picking you up. I think maybe you're a bit crazy, lady."

I laughed a little harder, feeling a fit of hysterics coming on, and Judd backed up a step.

"Rainie, don't do this. Take a breath." Jack had a hand on my shoulder, and he was watching me intently. I bent over at the waist and forced myself to take a couple of deep breaths. Even so it was several minutes before I could get a hold of myself and talk coherently.

I told the whole scary story. Jack went all bad-assed steely-eyed when I told how Big and Bigger had snatched me up. By the time I got to the end his jaw was clenched so tight I thought I heard teeth cracking.

Judd was looking pretty steely-eyed himself. Maybe it was just my jangled nerves, but it seemed there was an ugly vibe in the air, as if their anger had taken on a life of its own. I could feel it thrumming between them, like invisible lines of force waiting to be unleashed. It felt so real I actually took a step back from them.

Jack looked at Judd.

"You say you know where this place is?"

"I can get us there in ten minutes."

"Let's go." They turned toward their respective trucks.

"Hey, wait a minute, what are you planning to do?"

"We're goin' hunting, little lady." Judd told me.

"Go on in, lock your doors, Rainie. We'll be back in a while."

"Now wait a minute! I told you, Mika might not even be doing anything wrong..."

"He had you *kidnapped*!" Jack snapped.

Well, there was that.

"Fine. Then I'm going with you."

"No way..."

"Don't be getting all macho on me, Jack. You've dragged me into enough of your crap. Don't be trying to tell me I can't see my own job through to the end!"

Jack looked at me for ten long seconds. I'm sure I was quite a sight with my shredded clothes and bloody lip, but I was far from crippled. Finally he nodded.

"Right. Get in the truck. We'll follow you, Judd."

Judd looked like he wanted to argue, but he just shook his head and jumped into his truck.

They drove fast, bouncing and swaying down the country roads in the half-light of the coming dawn.

By the time Judd pulled over on a piece of road that looked the same as every other piece we'd passed, the sun had just barely cleared the horizon.

"This is it." Judd said when we all got out of our vehicles. He was pulling on a camouflaged-patterned army jacket. His name was on the breast pocket: WALLER. So, ex-serviceman, probably Army or Marines. I suppose that practically made him Jack's spirit brother; that might explain the energy I felt flowing between them.

I forced my attention back to what he was saying.

"There's a gate about fifty yards up, used to lead to the back forty of the Sedgewick property. I'm guessing that's where they took her in."

"Good." Jack nodded. "Let's go."

Judd already had his rifle in his hands, but Jack shook his head. "We're on shaky ground here. We aren't law enforcement, so technically we're trespassing. My plan is to take them down without killing them." He held up a small black handgun. "Of course, just in case." He automatically checked the safety on the gun before sticking it into his belt in the small of his back.

"Right." Judd nodded and put his rifle back in the gun rack. He pulled down another handy tool that no redneck knight in camouflage-and-denim-armor should ever be without: a baseball bat. Then he reached under the driver's seat and pulled out a heavy steel box. He rapidly worked the digital combination and pulled out a sleek looking handgun, easily twice the size of Jacks.

"I'm all about 'just in case,'" he grinned.

"Here, Rainie." Jack held out a small revolver.

"I'm not going to shoot anyone."

"Even if they shoot at you first?"

I had to admit, that kind of thing did piss me off. I accepted the gun, checked the safety and shoved it into my pocket. I didn't know how Jack could stand that hard metal poking him in the back.

"All right, let's go." Jack said. "But remember, no shooting unless they start it."

"With any luck they'll come out guns blazing."Judd grinned. He looked at me. "You sure you don't want to wait out here?"

Jack answered before I could. "Don't worry about her, she's good at this stuff."

I didn't know about that good part, but it pleased me to hear Jack say it.

We moved up the road, staying toward the shoulder but not trying to be stealthy. I peered through the gloom, searching for the barbed wire fence, but I couldn't make it out.

Judd held up a hand and we stopped. He pointed at the gate in front of us. It was constructed of metal poles, the kind of heavy-duty gate farmers used to keep their livestock in, but it was no good for keeping people out. There was a good two feet between the top and middle post, easy to duck and step through.

Beyond the gate I could just make out the dirt road that wound through the woods. The sun wasn't high enough to penetrate back here, but we could see well enough to navigate.

We climbed through the fence and walked up the little road in a tight cluster. I was taking the time to wonder why the hell I was here. I had been home safe, after all. What in the world had possessed me to come back out here?

The answer was simple. I had found something besides adrenalin that overrode fear: anger. I was, to put it mildly, pissed off, and I wanted to get back at these guys for terrorizing me.

We went quite a way before we saw light through the trees. Jack held up a hand and we all slowed down.

We crept around a bend in the road and before us there was a clearing.

I recognized Mika's cottage. The light was coming from the open door. The Buick was parked close by, the trunk and one of the back doors open. The dome light was bright enough that I could make out a man sitting in the back seat. He was leaning with his back against the other door, facing us. I was pretty sure it was Big.

Jack motioned us to follow him back down the road a way so we could hold a brief, whispered conference.

"That the place?" Jack whispered in my ear.

"Yes. I think that's Big in the car."

"The one you hurt?"

I nodded.

"Good, he won't be much trouble. You get to him, hold your gun on him so he stays quiet."

"What good will the gun do if I don't plan to shoot him?"

"Just give him the look. He'll never believe you won't shoot."

"What look?" I glared at him, and he nodded.

"That's the one. All right, are we good?"

"Let's go." Judd urged.

Jack and Judd moved into the clearing and I followed. Part of me couldn't believe they hadn't taken the time to discuss a real plan, but the other part of me could still feel that strange vibe and wasn't surprised at all. It seemed that all that testosterone shut off the brain cells that made a man consider little things like pain and death and other dire consequences. Come to think of it, I wouldn't mind a big shot of it right now myself.

I was in this now though. No sense getting all squishy inside about it; I'd had my chance to stay behind.

Jack waved me off to the right while he and Judd crept around to the left, staying just inside the tree line. I moved as quickly through the trees as I could without giving myself away to Big.

I heard voices and I froze. Bigger came out of the cabin carrying a box. Big called out to him in a decidedly whiney tone.

"Hey, you guys about done? Those pills Mika gave me aren't helping much. This shit hurts!"

"Shut up already. What the hell use are you anyway, you get taken down by a *girl*?"

Big shut up and Bigger went back into the cabin, presumably for another load. I continued circling around the clearing.

I didn't think I was being all that quiet, but apparently whatever pain meds Big had taken were buzzing in his ears, because he didn't hear me until I was on him. I took the gun out of my pocket, stepped into the open door of the car and assumed what I hoped was a solid stance. I pointed the gun at him, glared, (hoping that Jack was right, and that it was an appropriately scary glare) and snarled softly at him.

"One word, one twitch, and I'll blow your balls off."

He stared at me, his mouth opening and closing like a fish thrown on the dock, making a little wheezy sound of distress.

"Y-you..."

I pointed the gun more directly at his crotch and tried to look meaner. "Not one word!"

He nodded submissively. This was going well. I wondered how Jack and Judd were doing, but I didn't want to look away from my captive to find out.

Someone had done some efficient but hurried first aid on his knee. The leg was being held straight by two flat pieces of wood held firmly in place with an ace bandage. His eyes were a little glassy, maybe from the pain, maybe from whatever drugs Mika had on hand to feed him.

Suddenly a tree limb crashed down on my arms!

I cried out as the gun hit the dirt, but that was the last sound I could make. A second later two tree limbs wrapped around me, pinning my arms to my sides and squeezing all the air from my lungs as they lifted me off the ground.

Holy crap! It wasn't a tree, this was a man! A giant of a man, at that. I instinctively threw my head back, hoping to connect with his chin, but all I got was chest. The ineffectual blow did nothing more than make him squeeze harder.

Damn. I should have known if there was a Big and a Bigger there was bound to be a Biggest!

I kicked at his legs, but it was clear my rubber-soled shoes were having no effect whatsoever.

Big chose this moment to get brave. He snarled at me. "Stupid bitch!"He kicked out with his good leg and got me in the stomach. I would have grunted if I had any air. Instead I endured the jolt of pain with a wheeze.

"Crush her, Joe!" Big cheered the giant on gleefully. "That's it! Pop her like a big ugly zit!"

Incredibly I felt his grip tighten even more. The pressure was unbearable. I feared something really *was* going to pop, like maybe my heart or lungs. Or maybe my eyeballs would be dislodged from their sockets and loll on my cheeks...

Okay, I had to stop the gruesome images and figure a way out of this. I was going to pass out from lack of air any minute.

Or maybe I should do that now.

I forced myself to go limp. It was maybe the hardest thing I'd ever convinced my brain to do. I imagined myself doing a "dead-man's float" in a swimming pool, the kind where you hung face down in the water, holding your breath and pretending to be drowned. Fun stuff when you're a kid, not so much when you think it might shortly be for real.

It was easier than I thought to bring up the image, probably because I was forcibly holding my breath already.

I let my head droop and my legs swing free. I stopped struggling.

It seemed he still held on for hours, but in reality I think it was only a few seconds.

"Aw, I think I broke her." He laughed and dropped me. He was like a dog with a squeaky toy; once it stops making noise it isn't fun anymore.

I couldn't keep up the charade on the way down. My arms moved of their own accord to protect my face from hitting the dirt, but either it was still too dark outside or it was too dim inside their little pea-brains for them to notice.

"Hell, I can't believe you let that wimpy chick break your knee." Biggest was bragging about being able to take me down. Yeah, real tough guy.

At the same time I was glad he was talking. I hoped it would mask the sound of me taking big, painful breaths in an effort to re-oxygenate my brain. I figured I didn't have much time before Biggest decided to haul me off somewhere, maybe to bury me.

I wanted to push myself to my feet and run like hell, always my favorite plan in these situations, but I wasn't sure how much cooperation I was going to get from my abused body. I was about to give it a try when I saw something practically right in front of my nose. The gun.

I snatched it up without much forethought. I flicked off the safety and rolled over onto my back.

That got the giant's attention, and he turned to me faster than I would have thought those thick limbs could move him. He was already reaching toward me and I could have easily put a bullet right into the center of his face, but my brain recoiled from the idea. Instead I aimed lower, and blasted him right in the knee.

It was a good shot, and almost simultaneously with the minor explosion of blood and gore came his yowl of pain.

He instinctively reached to grab the injured part, lost his balance and toppled onto me.

I tried to roll away but I wasn't fast enough; he landed on my legs. He was rolling back and forth and caterwauling like a coyote with its tail on fire, and every time he moved I swear I could feel the bones in my legs being ground to powder. The guy was heavy!

"You stupid bitch!" Big was shouting and struggling to get out of the car, but with his own knee immobilized by the crude field dressing he couldn't maneuver over Biggest, who was thrashing around right outside the car door. I suppose I should have been worrying about the gun, which I had dropped at some point, but all I could think about was getting my legs free before they were pulverized into useless sacks of boneless skin.

I finally managed to free one leg and I used it to push against him while I jerked frantically with the other one. At long last I pulled it loose, leaving my shoe behind. I wondered why I even bothered to wear shoes; I couldn't seem to keep them on in any case. It suddenly occurred to me that this was why Jack and Eddie always wore tightly laced boots.

Never mind the minutia! I scolded my meandering brain. *Get the hell out of here!*

I started to crawl away, unable, for the moment, to get to my feet. I had gone only a few feet before I encountered a familiar pair of black boots.

"Rainie! What the hell?"

"B-Biggest!" I gasped, trying to point behind me.

"You! Hold it right there!" Jack pulled his gun and trained it on the two men, who weren't really going anywhere. Biggest was still hollering, although now there were real words interspersed with the howling. Not very nice words, I might add, and most of them describing *me* in very unflattering terms.

"Are you all right?" Jack kept the gun pointed at Big and Biggest while he held out his free hand to help me up. I accepted the boost and climbed painfully to my feet. I hurt all over, but my legs, while shaky, seemed willing enough to support me, so I guessed nothing was broken.

"I'm fine," I managed to grunt.

Judd came strolling up almost casually, bringing Mika along with him. Mika's arms were secured behind his back. One eye was swollen shut and his nose was bleeding; he hadn't gone down easily.

"Where's Bigger?"

"In the house, secured." Jack answered shortly.

"Trussed up like a chicken ready for roasting," Judd elaborated almost cheerfully. "You know, I think maybe you were toying with him a bit. I swear you got in a couple of extra kicks after he was done fighting."

"Yeah?" Jack shot back at him with the tiniest hint of a smile. "And did you really need to punch Mika after he put his hands up in surrender?"

Judd grinned back. He'd obviously had a great time. "Well hey, I didn't shoot him!"

Jack looked back at the huge man on the ground.

"What is it with you and knees, Rainie?"

"I don't know, but it seems to work."

Jack laughed. "You did good. I think there's a land line in the cabin. It's time to call the cops."

Chapter Twenty-three

Once Big and Biggest were secured I wandered into the cabin to sit down, and wonder of wonders I found my cell phone, still lying on the desk where Mika had tossed it. I was grateful for two reasons. Number one, I had just replaced the phone last spring when I had left it under a car in a rain-soaked parking lot, and the things were expensive. Number two, it had the phone numbers of pretty much everyone I knew programmed into it. My mother knew every phone number of her family and friends by heart, but I was so used to having the phone remember them for me that I had never bothered to learn them.

I promised myself that I would at least write them down somewhere – didn't they make little books just for that purpose?

In the meantime it was almost seven o'clock, and I was due at Bob's in an hour. I told Jack I had to get moving.

"Are you serious? Have you looked in a mirror?"

"Bob is expecting me."

"Bob can do without you for one morning. Besides, the cops are definitely going to want to talk to you."

I rarely called off from a client. As a rule they were vulnerable and dependent on my appearance, and I took that very seriously. On the other hand, I wasn't kidnapped and threatened with death every day. I suppose it was a pretty good excuse to call off.

I finally called Bob, knowing he would be up and puttering around, waiting for me. I told him I'd run into some trouble and couldn't make it, but offered to send someone else. I knew several caregivers that would fill in for me in a pinch, just as I would cover shifts for them.

"Nah, don't send anyone," Bob said. "I'm all right. I still have some of that soup in the freezer that you made me last week, and I can have a bowl of cereal for breakfast."

"But how are you feeling?"

"Stop worrying. I'm fine. I promise I won't drop dead this morning, okay?"

He did sound good, so I told him I would see him Wednesday. I had just enough time to call his son and let him know the situation – leaving out the details of my little escapade – before the cops arrived.

The Michigan State Police arrived first. They were professional and competent,

but questioned me at some length before one of them suggested I should go to the hospital to get checked out.

"I really just want to go home and soak in a hot tub."

"That's going to be a while. We've called the FBI in on this since the kidnapping took place across state lines."

"How about you give them my address and tell them to talk to me there?"

"I think it's best if you wait here or at the hospital." The cop was polite but firm.

"Are we under arrest?" Jack demanded.

"No. Should you be?"

"Of course not. But if we're not, I see no reason why I can't take Rainie home to get cleaned up."

There was some argument, but in the end Jack won, and he took me home.

264

Jack insisted on staying while I went in to bathe and change.

"I'll need to talk to the feds when they get here, anyway. Go ahead, I'll fix us something to eat."

"Good luck with that," I told him, thinking of my bare cupboards, but I staggered into the bathroom and started the water in the tub.

I peeled off my clothes, every movement a reminder of the rough night I'd just survived. My shirt was stuck to the dried blood from the scratches on my belly, and every joint and muscle seemed to be aching.

I stripped and looked in the full-length mirror on the back of the bathroom door, something I rarely did when I was naked. This time I wasn't appalled by my body shape, though. All I could see were the numerous bruises and scrapes and scratches on nearly every part of me. There was a thick semi-circle of bruising around my ribs from the giant's arms, but gentle probing didn't make the pain much worse; I doubted if any ribs had been broken. The scratches were deep enough to bleed freely but I didn't think there would be much scarring. My lip was swollen and caked with dried blood and my hair looked like I'd styled it with a blender.

I was a wreck.

But oddly, I found myself grinning at my reflection. I might be a mess, but this time I really could say "you should see the other guys." At least both of my knees were intact.

I laid back in the hot water, wincing a little from the sting on the scrapes, but overwhelmingly grateful for the heat on my battered body.

"Rainie! Hey, are you in there?"

I jolted awake at the sound of Jack's voice calling me. I couldn't believe I'd actually fallen asleep in the tub! Then again, I had been up for more than twenty-four hours already, spurred on by not one but several bursts of adrenalin.

"I'm fine!" I shouted back before Jack decided to come busting in to check on me.

"The FBI agents are here. They'd like to talk to you."

"All right," I sighed. "Give me a minute."

The water had cooled off appreciably and wasn't much comfort anymore. I hurriedly washed my hair and got out, toweling off quickly but being careful not to get anything bleeding again. I needed to get some antibiotic cream on the deeper scratches, especially the ones from the rusty barbed wire, but it would have to wait. At least I'd had a tetanus booster a few months ago after being shot; I wouldn't likely end up with lockjaw.

I came out dressed in sweatpants and a t-shirt, my hair still wet and only finger-combed. The FBI agents looked just like the ones you see on TV. They both wore dark suits and conservative ties and well-polished shoes, and they fired questions at me in short, efficient sentences.

I repeated the whole story for them, and they did a lot of nodding and jotting of notes. I was careful not to mention the whole false identity thing. I hoped it would never come up, but if it did I wouldn't give them Mason's name even under threat of torture.

Or so I told myself. I'd sure like to think I'm that tough, but I really hope I never have to find out.

On the bright side, later that day one of the investigators informed me that while my escape hole was impressive for having been dug in the dark through hardened clay soil with bare hands, it wasn't nearly big enough to allow an average sized human being to pass through. I mentally thanked him, first of all for calling me average sized, and secondly for giving me an out for being such a gutless coward.

As for the camp itself, it was mortgaged to the hilt, and there wasn't enough in the church coffers to keep it running much more than a month or two; Mika must have siphoned most of the money off into private accounts, probably of the off-shore, untraceable variety. There was some hope that a forensic accountant could locate it and the assets would be seized, but even so the camp would be sold.

Mika was going to be spending a long time in jail. Maybe he could start a new Church of Renewal there, helping the inmates find happiness. He did preach about the simple life, after all, and it couldn't get much simpler than living in a six by eight cell, your whole life planned for you down to when you had access to the showers.

Then again, Mika was a very good-looking man. Maybe someone was going to show him a new road to bliss. Whenever I started to feel a little sympathy for his situation I just reminded myself of that tiny shed he'd locked me in to await my execution, and suddenly I didn't feel sorry for him anymore.

Another plus: Mika must have actually called his accountant as he claimed, because first thing Monday morning a woman had appeared at the courthouse with a check to pay all of Jim Bolin's back support. Mika might be crazy, but he wasn't stupid; if you wanted to steal a rich man's money don't leave a trail for his family to follow. It was just my luck his accountant had missed that one.

That, of course, made B&E happy, because they could close another account and call it successful. Harry Baker laughed at my mistakes, told me that he would rather be lucky than smart every time, and once again suggested I consider a job as a full time PI.

So I've learned a good lesson here, but I'm still not completely sure what it is. Jack says don't worry about it; I followed my instincts, and I wasn't really wrong. Mika *was* taking most of their money for himself.

But was he really stealing? It seemed to me he had given something of value to Jim. The guy had been happy and safe, and wasn't that really what we all want in the end?

A week went by. I was sitting on my front porch smoking a cigarette and thinking about my future with B&E when Tommy stopped by.

"How are you, Rainie?" It wasn't a rhetorical question. He was looking at me with more than a little concern.

"I'm fine. No permanent damage."

"This time," Tommy grimaced. "I know I said I wouldn't question your career choice anymore, but really, is this what you want to do?"

"Funny, I was just sitting here thinking the same thing."

"Yeah? And what did you decide?"

I didn't answer right away. Was this really what I wanted? Sure, it was fun part of the time, and I did like hanging around with Jack. But was the break from boredom really worth putting my life in danger?

I had to say no. And this time I'd endangered myself for no good reason, and could have taken Mason down with me. Worse, in the long run I think I had done more harm than good. James Bolin had been perfectly content in his little log cabin, but now he would have to leave it. And if I had handled things right his kids would have gotten their support anyway. I was a complete screw up in the P.I. world.

"I guess it's not worth it," I gave Tommy my delayed answer.

"I'm glad to hear that." Tommy leaned back in his chair, looking relieved. "I'm sure you can fill those hours with something a little less life threatening."

I nodded.

This was it, then. I would get my cards circulating again and find a new client and go back to full time caregiving. I would give my notice to B&E first thing in the morning and go back to my safe and happy life.

My cell phone rang and I checked the readout. It was Jack.

I wouldn't answer it. Jack was the one who got me started on this craziness in the first place, and I'm quite sure he wasn't calling now to invite me to tea. I was still bruised and sore, and I wanted no part of anything he had going on.

"Who is it?" Tommy was watching me stare at the phone.

"It's Jack. I'll let it go to voicemail. He can call Rachel and drag her along on his little adventure."

"Good idea."

Two rings. I wasn't going to answer. It was definitely best if he called Rachel.

Three rings. Well, this last time hadn't really been his fault, had it?

I sighed and hit the little green button, ignoring Tommy's glare of disapproval.

"Hey Jack."

"Hey Rainie, are you busy? I need someone to go with me on a little excursion...?"

Made in the USA
Charleston, SC
23 September 2011